Kentucky Folktales

KENTUCKY FOLKTALES

Revealing Stories, Truths, and Outright Lies

Mary Hamilton

UNIVERSITY PRESS OF KENTUCKY

Scholarly publisher for the Commonwealth,
serving Bellarmine University, Berea College, Centre
College of Kentucky, Eastern Kentucky University,
The Filson Historical Society, Georgetown College,
Kentucky Historical Society, Kentucky State University,
Morehead State University, Murray State University,
Northern Kentucky University, Transylvania University,
University of Kentucky, University of Louisville,
and Western Kentucky University.
All rights reserved.

Editorial and Sales Offices: The University Press of Kentucky
663 South Limestone Street, Lexington, Kentucky 40508–4008
www.kentuckypress.com

16 15 14 13 12   5 4 3 2 1

Cataloging-in-Publication data is available from the Library of Congress.

ISBN 978-0-8131-3600-4 (hardcover : alk. paper)
ISBN 978-0-8131-3601-1 (pdf)
ISBN 978-0-8131-4030-8 (epub)

This book is printed on acid-free paper meeting
the requirements of the American National Standard
for Permanence in Paper for Printed Library Materials.

Manufactured in the United States of America.

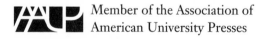
Member of the Association of
American University Presses

To the members of the National Storytelling Network,
especially to my storytelling colleagues,
Cynthia Changaris, Carrie Sue Ayvar, Yvonne Healy,
Jeannine Pasini Beekman, and Bobby Norfolk.
Without NSN's recognition of my work,
this book would not exist.

To my husband, Charles Wright,
for your love, your support,
and your incredible story listening.

To my family, for your years of storytelling.

CONTENTS

INTRODUCTION

Welcome to this collection of oral tales frozen in print. Frozen? Do I mean lifeless? Absolutely not! As you read these stories you will bring them to life in your imagination much as you would if I were standing before you telling them. And when you read them a second time, you might imagine them differently even though the text remains unchanged—frozen. Even if we were face to face and I told you these stories, the words I spoke would not be an exact match for the text you can read here. And if you heard me tell one of these stories a second time, those words would not be an exact match for the first telling.

Storytelling is an interactive and ephemeral art composed of three essential elements—story, teller, and audience. No two tellings of a story are alike, even if the same teller tells the same story to the same audience. Think about it. When someone tells you a tale for the second time and they know you've heard it before, much background information can be left out because the teller knows you already know. The wise teller will skip some sections because your nod (especially if your nod is an impatient nod) says, "Move along now. I know this already. I want to hear my favorite part again." And the way your expression turns to delight when your favorite part of the story is reached tells the teller, "Ah, linger here. I want to savor this." We—teller and audience—cannot influence one another on these pages the way we could in person.

The stories in this book are all stories I've told to audiences. Some of them I've told for well over twenty years; others I've told for just under one year. I'm a professional storyteller. I tell stories, usually to audiences of people who have gathered for the specific purpose of hearing stories. Sometimes there are people I know among the listeners. Most of the time the listeners are people I've not met before, but we come together through the shared pleasure of hearing stories. I also teach others about the art of storytelling and the related arts of reading aloud and writing.

In this book I've written stories down close to the way I currently tell them. You may be thinking: close to? The stories I tell are not memorized word-for-word, like a script. I learn the story, not the words. No two tellings are identical. The words change. The situation or context for the telling changes. The listeners change. I change. And all that changing, coupled with our influence on each other, makes storytelling an interactive and ephemeral art.

Most of the stories in this book are folktales—stories that did not originate in my imagination or in my memory. Most of them are also Kentucky folktales, stories told by other Kentuckians long before the stories reached me. I've included source notes for every story so you can learn how I found them, and because I want to acknowledge those folks who are responsible for making it possible for me to come across these tales. Those who told them before me shaped them for telling, usually to people they knew, which is the typical audience for traditional storytelling in Kentucky. Like tellers before me, I have also shaped the stories for telling. My story shaping has been influenced by my imagination, by research, by marketing ideas, by my colleagues in story coaching sessions, and by audience after audience. I've also included anecdotes on how those influences molded my retellings. I've even included some true Hamilton family stories to both acknowledge the type of storytelling common in my family and to encourage you to treasure those casual, everyday tales your family probably tells too.

So welcome. Enjoy! Read the stories to yourself. Imagine them. Then daydream them later, thawing out the print and giving the tales life. Read them aloud to others. Let the sound of your voice coupled with the reactions of your listeners enliven them even more.

Okay, so you made it this far, and you're probably wondering, "Where are the stories?" If you picked up this book primarily for the stories, just skip the rest of the introduction. If you are the sort of person who wants to know who is this Mary Hamilton who tells the stories in this book, and how did she come to call herself a storyteller? Stay here. This section is for you.

My relatives are not at all surprised that I became a storyteller. They look at each other and say, "Of course she's a storyteller. Look at her daddy." My daddy is one of those fabulous kitchen table storytellers.[1] He is the kind of storyteller that when he starts telling about an event you sit there, you listen, and you can't help but almost wish you *hadn't* been there yourself. That way your memory of it wouldn't be quite so at odds with what he's telling. Oh, it's sure enough the same event, and he is telling the truth, but now it's story.

You might read the above and say to yourself: Oh, the author is a traditional storyteller who learned how to tell stories from her father while she was growing up on a Kentucky farm, and now she is passing along her father's stories to her readers. Wrong! Well, the Kentucky farm part is correct, but the traditional storytelling part is not so true. If my storytelling repertoire consisted only of the stories I retell that I heard from my daddy, it would be a slim repertoire indeed. (Should you want to jump straight to those stories, skip ahead to the Family Tales and Personal Narratives section.) While I no doubt did absorb some storytelling technique from my father, my work is not that of a folk and traditional artist, as described by the National Endowment for the Arts.[2] Although there is a tradition of retelling events in my family, my repertoire is not bound by the stories I've heard within my family setting. Nor is the manner in which I tell stories a match for how my father tells them; however, I do suspect I began learning how to tell stories at a fairly early age.

I am a child of the 1950s, born in 1952. While I cannot recall exactly where a television was located in the house we lived in before I turned seven, I feel confident a television was there. I don't recall being read to by family members. My mother tells me my father read to me. My youngest aunts are just three and four years older than I am, so they may have read to me as well. The only person I recall reading aloud to me was Captain Kangaroo, who read to me from our television. I can clearly remember him reading Virginia Lee Burton's books *The Little House* and *Mike Mulligan and His Steam Shovel*, as well as Esphyr Slobodkina's *Caps for Sale*. I loved those stories and can easily picture them today.[3]

I do not remember learning to read, but I have vivid memory of the tension in first grade as I read ahead to find out what happened in stories, while simultaneously keeping track of exactly what portion of the text was being read aloud by various classmates. If called upon I knew I had to be prepared to read aloud from the proper place or face punishment.

I also have equally vivid memory of telling a story in the third grade. We were expected to take turns telling what we had done over the weekend. I remember standing in front of my classmates on the day it was my turn. I was sure I had not done anything worth telling. I had simply worked on our family farm on Saturday and gone to church on Sunday, just like most of my classmates. And yet, there they were, all my classmates seated before me waiting for me to speak.

So I told them, "This weekend I went horseback riding." (We did not own a horse; Daddy claimed horses "ate money" so we did not have one.) "When I went to the barn, I couldn't find my horse's saddle, so I rode my horse bareback. My horse started going really, really fast and I started sliding off." (I remember using my hands, making a downward curving motion to show them how I started sliding off.) "But I wasn't worried. I just grabbed the long hairs of my horse's tail" (I used my hands to show my classmates how I did this) "and pulled myself back onto my horse. Then I inched my way up to my horse's mane" (hands demonstrating again) "and held on" (hands again as I made fists to show them how firmly I held the mane) "and I finished my ride. That's what I did this weekend."

I still remember how my classmates enjoyed my adventure, and how my teacher tried in vain to make me admit what I had told was not what really happened. But I couldn't let my listeners down, and besides, I knew lying was a sin, and sins were punishable offenses. I also knew my teacher owned a paddle, and she used it. So, even though she asked repeatedly, I steadfastly replied, "Yes, Ma'am, that's what I did this weekend," while nodding and maintaining the most wide-eyed, innocent, and honest look I could muster. Finally, she gave up.

Not long after that, report cards went home. Mine had a note on it. I wish I could tell you it read, "Wow! Your little girl sure is a wonderful storyteller!" Instead I remember it reading, "Mary June seems to have difficulty understanding what is and is not true."[4] My parents were neither amused nor impressed. "You'd better not be telling stories at school," they warned.

For the longest time I tried to break my storytelling habit, dutifully reporting each transgression in the church confessional. Indeed, where I grew up "storytelling" was considered a moral failing a child needed to overcome, not an artistic skill ripe for development. I was a graduate school student before I ever encountered "storytelling" as an activity to be both practiced and encouraged in others.

After third grade I either succeeded in avoiding storytelling or succeeded in entirely blocking out memories of engaging in it. Instead of telling stories, I read and read and read story after story after story. I loved plot, including predictable plots. I devoured the folktale and fairy tale books in my school library, reading my favorites again and again. I read every school reader available on the shelves in the back of my various classrooms. When school was closed, I read the lives of the saints from our tiny church library. I became, and still am, an avid reader.

In sixth grade I was called upon to read aloud—every day. Yep, every day I stood in front of my class after lunch and read aloud. Sometimes I read stories, but more often I read from our social studies textbook or from *Junior Scholastic* magazine. Every day? I know—I'm willing to concede my memory could be exaggerating, because surely the same student did not read aloud every day, but that is how I recall sixth grade. And whether I really read aloud every day, or just many days, I developed the vocal skills of reading aloud effectively—projection, articulation, fluency, vocal expression in synch with meaning—all skills still serving me well in my storytelling.

In high school I remember that we all were expected to stand up front and talk in our English classes. I will never forget the time one of my classmates stood before us in Junior English and delivered a how-to speech on growing tobacco. He started with a cigarette and worked backward from there, step by careful step, ending up with the burning of the ground to prepare the plant bed. It was clever, daring, and I still remember how we laughed and applauded his creativity and speaking skill. I remain grateful to have been taught by teachers who expected us to learn to speak in front of others and to be a responsive audience.[5] In high school, I was a cheerleader at a time when cheerleading required primarily the skill of clearly leading pep club members and other fans chanting in unison, not gymnastics. I remember making up cheers, and to this day, when I give workshops on crafting and telling audience participation stories, I encourage participants to "embrace your inner cheerleader" as a means of smoothly facilitating audience participation.

After college I became a high school English teacher. I wish I could tell you I was one of those very smart teachers who understood how to incorporate storytelling into her classroom instruction and consciously utilized storytelling to great effect, but I wasn't. I did require my students to speak in front of the class, and have received a belated thank you or two because of that requirement. I also remember deriving much more pleasure from teaching literature than teaching grammar. Again, a love of story.

Finally, as an adult studying for a master's degree in library science at the University of Kentucky, I took a course taught by Anne McConnell titled Creative Library Programs for Children, and I encountered the activity called storytelling. Later I moved from Kentucky to Grand Rapids, Michigan, to accept a job as a public library children's librarian. My duties included presenting both book-based reading aloud programs and storytelling programs. (These are different skills—I mention both because I want to be clear that I am not using "reading aloud" and "storytelling" as synonyms.) In late 1979 or early 1980 I attended a conference for children's librarians where, for the first time, I heard professional storytellers, The Folktellers.[6] My reactions to their work included: (1) a realization that the quality of the storytelling I was offering in my library programs needed to improve, and (2) an intense desire to hear more storytelling.

I began seeking out opportunities to hear professional storytelling and take storytelling workshops. My storytelling abilities steadily improved, and my repertoire expanded rapidly. After all, when I heard professional storytellers say, "Go retell these stories," I took them at their word. I not only retold the stories I had heard them tell, but I did my darndest to retell them just like I heard them, too. I was also fortunate to be working in a library with an extensive 398.2 collection, so I had lots of folktales available. I began to search out easily retellable tales in various folktale collections, adding them to my repertoire. By 1982, I had become so enamored of storytelling I started saving my money, dreaming of the day I would start my own business by joining the ranks of professional storytellers I had so come to admire. I was pretty sure that as soon as I had a solid financial cushion saved, I was ready to make the transition. I had the needed storytelling skills—I could remember and retell stories I had heard, and I could retell stories from books. People even began to contact me wanting me to tell stories on my days off and evenings off from my job at the library. I was a storyteller, and I was quite sure I was a pretty good one too!

Then I heard Laura Simms tell stories in Grand Haven, Michigan. She told a folktale I had especially enjoyed, and she cited the source where she had found it. When I returned to the library and read the story in the book, I was astonished. While the plot was the same, the words were far different. In the book the story was not readily tellable. It was literary, very literary. The words did not flow off the tongue and sail into the ear creating images the way her telling of the story had. I knew I had a great deal to learn about this activity called storytelling. When I heard that Laura was offering a storytelling residency in late June 1983, I secured permission from my library director to attend.[7]

Then my job left me. Those were recession days, and I was laid off, effective July 1, 1983. But I already knew how I hoped to be able to earn a living someday, and lucky for me I had some savings to rely on. Equally fortunately, I did not understand how difficult building a business could be, nor did I really understand what it meant to embrace the profession of storyteller, or I might have been afraid to try.

Nevertheless, jobless days in sight, I forged ahead with plans to attend Laura's storytelling residency. As part of the preparation she asked each participant to write her a letter on the role of storytelling in our lives, and for the first time, in the act of writing that letter, I became consciously aware of having grown up with storytelling. My people, especially my father, talked in story all the time. I had been exposed to the art of storytelling all my life but had never really noticed.

Since then, I've been steadily learning about this activity and art called storytelling. I've paid more attention to the storytelling in my family, noticing both technique and content. I've studied with Laura Simms and with many other fine storytellers, and I've learned from them all. Yes, I have learned that "go retell these stories" is said to encourage parents and children to retell them at home, teachers to retell them in their classrooms, and librarians to retell them to their library patrons, not to encourage colleagues to add the stories they've just heard to their professional storytelling repertoires. Like I said, I had a lot to learn. But I knew I had found my calling.

My early years as a professional storyteller were spent in Michigan. Over and over again, I had conversations with folks who, when they learned I had grown up in Kentucky, said, "Well no wonder you're a storyteller. You're from Kentucky." Such comments mystified me since I had not grown up hearing folktales retold, and these were the sort of stories I was drawn to tell. By 1986 I was traveling more and more for my work. In the spring of 1986 my mother became seriously ill, and I realized that even when I was at home in my Grand Rapids apartment,

I was still over eight hours away from my home home. So, in the summer of 1987 I returned to Kentucky. For my storytelling business, it was starting over. In Michigan my reputation for storytelling had grown enough that people I had never told about my work had started calling me, wanting to hire me to come tell them stories. In Kentucky, no one called. Nevertheless, I was home.

Reactions to "I'm a professional storyteller" have surprised me. On two different occasions, at parties in Michigan, that statement was greeted with a look of wonder, followed by, "You mean, if I want to call in sick to work, I call you, and you'll call my boss . . . ?" Did I possess the necessary skill to pull that off? Probably, but that was not what professional storytelling meant. In Kentucky, on multiple occasions, I heard, "Professional storyteller? You mean people actually pay you to tell them stories?" Hmm, maybe this is what people in Michigan had meant when they had connected Kentucky with storytelling? Although I had not grown up hearing folktales, perhaps other Kentuckians had? Perhaps telling the sort of stories I felt drawn to tell was a common everyday activity, just not in my family?

Many years have passed, and I've learned a great deal more about storytelling in my home state of Kentucky. It was, and is, more prevalent than I had realized from my childhood experiences. It is not at all unusual for me to tell Kentucky folktales at a public library only to have someone in the audience come up afterward and tell me their father or mother used to tell a story they've just heard me tell. Unfortunately, when I ask if they've retold the stories to the next generation, their answer is usually no, and "they don't care about that sort of thing like we did." Fortunately, I can follow up by asking if the person noticed how well the next generation just listened when I was telling, and use that observation to encourage them to try telling those remembered stories again.

For over thirty years now I've been enjoying storytellers, telling stories, and marveling at how storytelling works. I can't imagine spending my life any other way. If you want to know more about how I explore storytelling, visit my website, www.maryhamilton.info. This book represents one more step in bringing told stories to audiences. It may be able to go places where I can't. It may serve to remind people of stories that were once told in their families. Or it may serve to encourage people to value the storytelling still happening in their families. After all, our society does tend to take more seriously what is in a book over what is on the tongue, even though the book version is frozen and the tongue version alive. So, go ahead, turn the page, read the stories frozen in print; then thaw them out and bring them to life again.

Haunts, Frights, and Creepy Tales

So who decides what stories are truly haunting, frightening, or creepy? The audience, of course!

Nevertheless, storytelling event producers frequently offer evenings of such stories to the public, and they count on storytellers to rate the intensity of each story they will tell. The event emcee uses the ratings to arrange a story sequence that creates an evening of ever more intense stories. In events with intermissions, stories are commonly divided into pre-intermission family friendly tales and post-intermission tales for teens and adults.

Here I've arranged the stories in the order I would present them if asked to create an evening of haunting tales. Because I like to send people home on a lighter note, I've placed "The Open Grave" last.

STORMWALKER

Several years ago, in that part of Kentucky where Russell and Adair counties meet,[1] a little girl named Roberta Simpson was growing up on her daddy's farm. When she grew old enough to go to school, she walked, for everyone walked to school in that time and in that place.

Now Roberta had a real smart teacher. If her teacher looked out the school window and saw a storm was on its way, she said, "Children, stop everything. A storm is coming. You need to go on home before this storm hits."

You may be wondering: That was a smart teacher? You see, back when Roberta was a little girl, people believed that if you got caught out in a rainstorm and got soaking wet, you would catch a cold. And if you caught a cold, it could go into pneumonia. And if you came down with pneumonia, who could say how long it would be before you'd be back in school? So, in her own way, Roberta's teacher made sure most of her students were in school most of the time.

There were children who smiled big whenever the teacher sent them home early, but not Roberta. Little Roberta Simpson was afraid of storms. Nothing scared her more than thunder and lightning.

In a rural area, everybody knows everybody, and most of the time everybody also knows all about everybody. So it's not surprising that a neighbor of the Simpsons, Jim Cravens, an older semi-retired farmer, soon learned that Roberta was afraid of storms. If he was out on his place and could tell a storm was coming, he'd start walking toward the schoolhouse. He would meet up with Roberta, offer her his hand, and walk her home through the storm. Roberta wasn't nearly as afraid while holding on to the hand of big Jim Cravens. In fact, she thought of him as her very own stormwalker.

On their way home Roberta and Jim had to cross a clearing. Roberta told me that sometimes the thunder would be so loud she would feel like she was right inside it. She told me that one time lightning struck the fence, and sparks just skittered along the barbed wire. At times like those Roberta would feel so scared, she would start to shake. Jim would say, "Now, Roberta, I feel you trembling. You're shaking 'cause you're scared, and it's reasonable to be scared in a storm like this. Why, if you were out here by yourself, you might get so scared you'd think the smart thing to do would be to run over to that one big tree over yonder and stand under it to hide from the storm. But don't ever go standing under a tree in a storm. Lightning will strike a tree faster than anything. No, you just keep walking like we do and that will be your best chance for reaching home safe."

Jim told Roberta many things about traveling safely in storms, and I suppose she heard what he said, but she didn't really try to take it in. She didn't figure she needed to. After all, he was there, and he was her stormwalker. Jim walked Roberta home through storms all through first grade. And he walked her home through storms all through the fall of second grade. But in the winter of Roberta's second year of school Jim Cravens took sick.

He had what folks back in those days called heart dropsy. That meant there was a lot of fluid around his heart, and it made him terribly weak. If he wanted to get up in the morning and eat breakfast, he would have to have someone help him sit up in his bed. Then he would need to rest before he could be helped over to his table, where he would need to rest again before someone could help him eat. Then he would need to rest again before he could be helped back over to his bed.

One day, in the spring of Roberta's second year of school, her teacher looked out the window. She saw the sky wasn't blue. It wasn't gray. It was that strange yellow-green sort of color that sky sometimes turns here in Kentucky when a horrible storm is on its way. Back beyond the yellow-green, the teacher could also see dark clouds tumbling and boiling over each other.

She looked at her students, "Children, stop everything. I know some of you play when I send you home on stormy days, but today do not play. There is a horrible storm coming and you need to run. Run! Get home before this storm hits."

Roberta went running from the schoolhouse. She had just reached the clearing when the storm broke loose. There was thunder, lightning, and rain. Rain coming down harder and faster than Roberta had ever imagined rain could come down. She was so scared; she did the first thing she could think of. She ran over and stood underneath the one big tall tree, trying to hide from the storm. But even though she was standing under a tree, the rain was coming down so hard and so fast, she was soaking wet. Then there was a huge flash of lightning—the kind that in the middle of the night lights up the whole world like it's the middle of the day.

In that huge flash of lightning Roberta could see Jim Cravens. He was moving toward her, and moving fast. He was motioning to her like he wanted her to come toward him, and above the roar of the storm she thought she could hear him shouting, "Roberta, Roberta, get out from under that tree."

He was her stormwalker, so she ran toward him. He moved away from her and led her over to a shallow gully—not deep with water rushing, but a spot a bit lower than most of the land around. Again, he motioned to her, and she thought she heard him saying, "Get down. Get down. Keep your head down."

Roberta crouched down in the gully. But she was only seven years old; she did not keep her head down. When she lifted it, the first thing she saw was the whirling finger of a tornado drop down out of the storm, and the first thing she saw it hit was the tree she had been standing under.

Then Roberta put her head down, and she did not lift it until she heard, "Ro-o-ber-r-r-ta-a-a!"

"Ro-o-ber-r-r-ta-a-a!"

Voices she knew—her mom and her dad!

She stood up in the gully, and her parents saw her. They came running over, "Oh, Roberta, you are all right! There was a tornado, and we knew you were out here somewhere between school and home, but you are all right! And you were smart, to get down in a low spot like this. That was exactly the right thing to do, caught out in the open in a storm like that. We didn't know you knew that. You were so smart."

Roberta looked at her parents, "I wasn't smart. Jim came. He's the one who brought me to this gully. Jim was here."

Her parents just looked at her, and then her mother said, "Roberta, I know you believe what you just said. But honey, Jim couldn't have brought you to this gully. He died today, around noon. We were going to tell you first thing when you came home from school."

Roberta Simpson is all grown up now. She married a man named Lonnie Brown and changed her name to Roberta Simpson Brown. I met her because she also tells stories, and she told me this story from her life and allowed me to tell it to others. She also writes stories. Her first book, *The Walking Trees*, published by August House, contains several stories Roberta Simpson Brown made up, and one true story, "Storm Walker," where she recollects the events I've just told you about.

If you ever meet Roberta Simpson Brown, and I hope you will, you can ask her, and she will admit to you that she still does not consider herself a good stormwalker. For many years Roberta taught sixth grade English at Southern Middle School in Jefferson County, Kentucky. Even in her classroom, when it was thundering and lightning outside, her first thought was always: "Why don't I just dive under this big old teacher's desk and wait out this storm?" But she knew if she dove under her desk there would be chaos in her classroom, so even though she was afraid, she held on. But if alarms went off, she took cover right along with her students, because she knew how important taking proper cover could be.

You could also ask her, and she would admit to you that every year, at least once, she gets in her car and she travels the two to three hours it takes to go from her home in Jefferson County down to that part of Kentucky where Russell and Adair counties meet. There, she visits the grave of Jim Cravens, her stormwalker.

COMMENTARY

"Stormwalker" is a true story from the life of Roberta Simpson Brown. I first learned about these events in Roberta's life when she told about them at Tale Talk, a gathering of storytellers at the offices of the International Order of E.A.R.S. in Middletown, Kentucky. I found the events intriguing and entrancing, so I asked Roberta for permission to retell the story, not in the first person, as she had told it, but in the third person. Roberta requested that I work on my retelling, then come to her house for dinner and tell it to her so she could determine if she was satisfied with my rendition. On December 19, 1990, I went to the home of Roberta and Lonnie Brown for dinner and told her the story.[2] Roberta approved of my retelling, and I've been telling the tale ever since.

Ah, what a lovely model for how to ask and receive permission to tell a story! Well, yes; however, Roberta and I skipped a very important step. We failed to put our agreement in writing. Why would that matter? Read on.

In 1992, I created an audiocassette of several Kentucky tales, and wanted to put my retelling of "Stormwalker" on that audiocassette. By then Roberta had sold the rights to her story to August House, who published "Storm Walker" in *The Walking Trees and Other Scary Stories*.[3] Even though I had never read the published story before creating my version of it, the adaptation rights belonged to August House, so it was necessary for me to secure their permission to record my own adaptation.

Nine years later I released "Stormwalker" on my CD *Some Dog and Other Kentucky Wonders* (it included the stories from the 1992 audiocassette of the same title, plus two additional tales), necessitating another permission agreement for the different format. "Stormwalker" won a 2003 Honor Title, Storytelling World Award, Category 2: Stories for Pre-Adolescent Listeners.[4]

My brother Jeff found the recording especially useful. Like all teachers, Jeff's responsibilities included making sure his students could quickly move to a designated storm shelter area in the event of a tornado warning. He noticed his high school students considered storm safety a topic unworthy of their attention. One year, he played "Stormwalker" before talking about where to seek shelter, and his students listened to him—they really wanted to know! After that "Stormwalker" played a recurring role in his classroom.

Bringing my retelling of these events to you in this print format has required yet another round of permission negotiations. So, if I have learned something from my permission experience, it is this: Even if you are given permission to tell a story by a friend, take time to put it in writing. That small step beyond your verbal agreement could eventually save both of you from anxiety and paperwork.

I've told this story many times over the years, but at no time has a telling made a bigger difference than it did when I told it at Kentucky Crafted: The Market, 2006.[5] You see, when Roberta tells her story, she never mentions Jim Cravens's last name. She always thought of him as Jim, so that's what she calls him. But when I tell the story, I say his full name. Attending the Kentucky Craft Market that year were descendants of Jim Cravens. They heard his name, listened to the story, and began to think they might have known the specific fellow the tale talked about. They asked me how to contact Roberta, and they did. It seems the Cravens family left Kentucky shortly after Jim's death, and Roberta had been out of touch with them all those years. Roberta told me that if she had been there telling the story the connection might never have been made, but because I used Jim's full name two families who had once been neighbors became reacquainted.

Promises to Keep

1861. That was a real important year in our country's history, for in 1861 this country split in two and the North and South went to war against each other. It's a war that's come down to us by many names. The War Between the States. The War to Free the Slaves. In the North it was called the War of Southern Rebellion; in the South, the War of Northern Aggression. The Civil War.

When the war began in April 1861, young men all over the North and South looked at each other and said, "We've got to sign up. This whole shooting match will be over in three months. If we don't sign up now, we'll miss our chance."

In southwest Indiana, near the town of Winslow, one young man replied, "Can't go. I made a promise to Maggie, and I aim to keep it." The young man was Cyrus Humphrey. Maggie was Margaret Jones, a farmer's daughter whose family farm was next door to the farm of Cyrus Humphrey's family. Cyrus and Maggie had grown up together, and the summer of 1861 was the summer Cyrus had promised Maggie the two of them would be married.

So when his friends left, Cyrus stayed behind. His friends soon became members of the 24th Indiana Regiment. Cyrus stayed home, married Maggie, and the two of them set up housekeeping in a small cabin on their own farm, created from land given partly from his family and partly from hers.

Three months came and three months went. The war kept on.

By fall Cyrus and Maggie knew a child was on the way, so they felt their marriage was off to a fine start.

"Christmas," folks said, "this war will be over by Christmas." But Christmas came and Christmas went. The war kept on.

That winter Cyrus made a cradle for the coming baby. Maggie wove a coverlet for the baby's cradle, and she knitted socks for Cyrus.

She had a feeling Cyrus was going to become part of the war, and she knew all soldiers need good socks.

In April 1862 word arrived in Winslow of a battle in Tennessee, a battle that had taken place outside a small church by the name of Shiloh. The battle lasted just two days, April 6th and April 7th, but by the end of those two days thousands of young men from the North and the South lay dead and thousands more lay dying. Cyrus's friends from the 24th Indiana Regiment were there at Shiloh, but they were among the Union reinforcements who arrived after the end of the first day's fighting, so they weren't as badly hurt as the Union soldiers who had been surprised by the attack.

When word of Shiloh reached Winslow, Cyrus turned to Maggie, "Maggie, this war's going to take everybody, and I need to go do my part. But I promise you I will not leave until our crops are planted and our baby is safe in this world."

Cyrus kept his promise. After the baby was born, once Cyrus could see both Maggie and the baby were strong and healthy, he said, "Maggie, I've got to go. I've kept my promise. The baby's here. Our crops are in the ground. I've talked with your little brother. He says he'll come help you at harvest time. I promise you, Maggie, I'll tell the men I serve with that if anything happens to me, I want them to send my wedding ring back to you."

"Cyrus Humphrey! The only way I want your wedding ring back is on your hand, with you walking it through the door."

"I'll do my best, Maggie," he said, and he left. It was not long before Cyrus was a member of the 80th Indiana Regiment.

In late August word reached Winslow of General Kirby Smith's invasion of Kentucky, and Maggie felt Cyrus had made the right decision. Summer ended, fall came. Maggie and her brother began harvesting the crops.

On the afternoon of October 8th Maggie rested on her porch. Her baby slept in the nearby cradle. Maggie watched Cyrus's dogs play with each other, and she thought about her husband. As she thought, she twisted her wedding ring, and she hoped, wherever he was, Cyrus was taking as much comfort from his wedding ring as she was from hers.

It was moving on toward dark, so Maggie took the cradle inside, lit a fire, made herself a little supper, and sat down to eat. Then she heard the dogs. Oh, she knew how the dogs sounded when they scrapped with each other, but what she heard sounded like a fight. She lit a lantern and hurried outside. Sure enough, the dogs were fighting over something. Maggie moved closer, and she could see they were fighting over a hand. She had to kick at the dogs to make them let it loose. Then she knelt down to examine the hand. She saw a ring on a finger. Maggie worked the ring off and dropped it in her pocket. She picked up her lantern and the hand. She set the hand up in the fork of a tree so the dogs wouldn't be able to get at it. Then she walked into the house.

Maggie set the lantern on the table, sat down in her chair, and took out the ring. She examined it by lantern light, and then Maggie began to weep. For inside the ring she had read the initials MH and CH—for Margaret Humphrey, Cyrus Humphrey. Maggie knew she was holding Cyrus's wedding ring.

The next morning the hand was gone.

Quite some time passed before Maggie received official word that Cyrus had been among the first killed when the 80th Indiana Regiment went into its first battle—the Battle of Perryville, in Kentucky.

There were those who were amazed the ring had found its way back to Maggie. But Maggie? She wasn't amazed, for she knew she had married Cyrus Humphrey, a man who always did his best to keep his promises.

COMMENTARY

So how in the world does a story set in Indiana wind up in a book of Kentucky tales? Answer: Market forces and historical fiction.

Market forces? In 1995, I was hired to tell stories for "Literally, a Haunted House," a multi-night event at the Culbertson Mansion State Historic Site in New Albany, Indiana.[1] While brave souls waited to enter the "haunted" carriage house, others visited the formal parlor, where my job was to tell them haunting tales that were either set in or could have been told during Victorian days. So, I needed appropriate stories to tell. I had run across two versions of a Civil War–era legend about the return of a wedding ring, one collected by Michael Paul Henson,[2] the other by Berniece T. Hiser.[3] Kentucky was the setting for both versions, but other details varied, including the main characters' names. Henson reported collecting the tale from Daniel Buck, of Barwick, Breathitt County, Kentucky, in 1958. In Henson's version the main characters are named Josephine Tyler and George Thomas. George joins the Union Army, leaving when Josephine is pregnant. Josephine receives three letters from George, and in the third letter he tells her he "would see that, somehow, she would get his wedding ring if he should be killed."[4] When no more letters arrive, Josephine contacts the War Department and learns George had been killed before he could have written the last letter. In Henson's version the ring reappears in 1865.[5] In both the Hiser and Henson versions the wife finds the ring because of a ruckus raised by the dogs and the owner of the ring is verified by the initials engraved inside. In both versions the hand is gone by the next day.

Below is the Hiser-collected version of the story:

The Wedding Ring

Berniece T. Hiser

We lived [in] the last house above the head of the Creek, one of the little neighbor boys told an inquiring stranger, but even there the stork came. In those days there was no doctor for many a mile, so when one of us was to be born, my father went off through the wilderness and brought in a granny woman. I will never forget the one who come when Sister Audrey was born, for it was her that first made us aware of how horrible war can be. She was Aunt Polly Daingy McIntosh. She was then close to seventy-five, a real old withified looking soul, smoked a cob pipe, and wore a red kerchief tied around her head. We children were mortally afraid of her, and it was no wonder—the tales she and my Grandma Sally told as we sat scrounged around the fire at night! Witches, rapping spirits, tables being moved by unseen hands! Brother Oak and I set with our backs pressed to Mom's knees, trying to make ourselves as small and unnoticeable as possible, but no matter how we shrank, came the moment when Aunt Polly would say in her long mountain drawl, Old sister,—(or brother, as the case may be)—go fetch me a splinter to light my pipe wit, and one of us would have to go into the fearful dark of the new room Dad was building onto our house and get her some shavings where he was hand-planing planks for the ceilings, and you can imagine the gladness when we once more set down in front of the fire.

Bill, she would say to my father, did you ever see a hant?

Dad would say he guessed he never did; but then he would remember the time he and Uncle John Strong had ridden into Jackson Town to see Bad Tom Smith hanged and how a critter like a big dog had jumped on their horses that night and rode all the way home with them and they couldn't shoot it off.

Did I ever tell you how I got this wedding ring? Aunt Polly would ask, after a silent respect paid to Dad's tale, holding her skeletony old hand out to the fire so the gold ring would flash in the light.

Tell us, Oak and I would beg, in horrible fascination, for she had told it to us once a night since she came, chilling our marrow.

Well, sir, Bill, you know my man John and me had jist got married when the war over the colored people broke out, and made us a little log cabin off yond way on Frozen Creek, and our youngun Henderson was a baby in the cradle, when he rid off to Lexington town in the Low Country and jined up with the United States Gover'ment to be a soldier. I recollect, hit was in the spring of the year he went, and my pap tried to get me to bring the baby and stay with him; but I woultn't do er, for I was a strong young gal then and felt like I would better stay at home and raise us a corn crop, fer everybody knowed in reason the fightin would be over afore winter set in. I dug me in a puore hillside a corn and beans with pumkins and cushaws here and yander in them. I took the youngun to the field wid me and laid him in the shade and hoed for who laid the chunk, and when fall come I had as fine a crap a corn as eera man on the creek, and more shucky beans than I've ever had since. I missed my man awful, but I tended to the cowbrute and our sow and pigs and my chickens and garden sass, and played with the baby and John's two hound dogs Jip and Jep. Time passed on and it got to be winter. I had hard work then, getting in wood and feeding the critters, but I made it. When it got real bad weather, one of my little brothers would stay a night or so with me. About the middle of December it come a warm spell, you know how it'll do, Bill, and I was by myself. I put Hent in his side of the bed and set by the fire and read the three letters I'd had from John since he left. Directly, after I had almost dozed off from the warmth of the fire, the two hounds let up a clamor in the yard and I heard other dogs a-snapping and snarling around the house and yard. I boldened myself up and lit out of bed, and into the yard I went in my nightwrapper, with the fat-wood light I kept ready by the fireplace. I knowed in reason they was something big a-goin on, for I had never heared sicha afore in my life. I beat them with the broom and stuck the fat-wood light in their faces fer I seed they was a-eatin something.

And, Bill, you know what hit was? (Her voice fell to a whisper). Hit was a man's hand they was a-fightin over. They drapped it and run and I picked it up a-goin to stick it up in the forks of a sweet apple tree thare in the yard and bury it the next mornin. But when I looked closter I seed it had a wedding ring on the ring finger. I worked it off, and, Bill, hit was my man John's ring. She took it off her bone finger and held it out to the firelight. There inside air his and my letters *JM & PM*. That's how I knowed it was his'n. I laid his hand up in the forks of the tree and went inside the house. Our dogs come in by the fireside, and I took up the baby. He was a-cryin and I was too. But tears didn't bring back my John. God knows how his hand ever got thare. Hit was gone next morning and I never could hear any tell of him from the gov'ment. I got a war pension fer several years and Hent got one till he was eighteen. I got married atter a while, for a womarn can't live alone to do no good; but I've allus wore this ring, and when my second man, Jack Kilburn, died back here about twenty year ago, I took back my name of McIntosh cause I allus felt more for my John than for any othern.[6]

*   *   *

I was attracted to the tender love between husband and wife in the stories as well as the mystery of the ring's return. So, I decided to create a work of historical fiction, building on the common threads of both legends.

Growing up I had always heard that people really had thought the Civil War would end in just three months, and that there were soldiers who wanted to become involved quickly so they would have a chance to fight. The plot of both legends had begun with the war already underway, but I knew I wanted to include this bit of history in the story I told, so I decided I would begin the story at the beginning of the war. I also realized that if I started the story earlier, I could give the main character friends who left when the war began. And what better reason could he have for staying behind than love?

To meet the requirements of the job at the Culbertson Mansion, I knew the soldier would need to be from Indiana, but where? When the curator at the Culbertson Mansion mentioned that wounded soldiers from the Battle of Shiloh had been transported to New Albany, Indiana, for medical care,[7] I decided I wanted to include Shiloh in my retelling. Yet, because I did not want to lose all Kentucky connections in the story, I decided I also wanted to include Perryville, in Boyle County, site of the best-known Civil War battle in Kentucky. Fortunately, my husband, Charles Wright, is a bit of a Civil War buff and owns books that include lists of which regiments fought in which battles. Here I could learn which Indiana regiments fought at Shiloh and Perryville.[8] Armed with the list of Indiana units involved in both battles, I set out to learn if soldiers from the same part of Indiana could have been in different regiments, one fighting at Shiloh, the other at Perryville. That quest led to the Kentucky Historical Society Library, where I found a publication that listed each regiment that fought in the Civil War, including where the soldiers were from and when they were mustered in. Bingo! The 24th Indiana Regiment, Company E, who fought at Shiloh, were from Pike County, Indiana. The 80th Indiana Regiment, Company H, who fought at Perryville listed soldiers as residents of Winslow, Indiana, a Pike County community.[9] I now had soldiers from the same area of Indiana present at each battle.

Next, I wondered when the Indiana Regiments formed? Could the 24th have been early enough to be a three-month enlistment? No, I learned the 24th Indiana, Company E, from Pike County mustered in July 31, 1861, for a three-year enlistment. Now I was faced with a decision: Stick with the facts and omit the three-month reference? Or include the three-month reference and fudge the facts a bit? Without direct lecturing, I wanted to tell my audiences that predicting the length of a war is simply not possible. People have miscalculated in the past, and we are foolish if we think we can calculate it now. Because this was important to me, the three-month reference stayed. I elected to imply that the 24th might have been early enough to be a three-month enlistment without directly saying so, which would have been a contradiction of the 24th's history.

And when did the 80th muster in? Was there time enough between the formations of the 24th and the 80th for the soldier to stay behind, marry, hear about Shiloh, welcome his child, and plant crops before leaving? Yes, the 80th Indiana, Company H, from Winslow, mustered in August 19, 1862—time enough. My characters now had a home.

But the soldier still lacked a name. I knew I did not want to use the name of any real soldier, but I wanted a first and last name that fit the time. Nor did I want to use either of the two sets of names used by Hiser and Henson.[10] In my husband's books I found names of officers listed.[11] The given name of Cyrus was listed more than once. It seemed common enough then, and uncommon enough today, to evoke an earlier time. I had already been thinking of her as Maggie, for I knew Margaret with Maggie as a nickname had a long history. Surnames of Jones and Humphrey were also verified from the lists of soldiers. No, they were not common in the Winslow area, but I did not want anyone from that area thinking I was actually retelling the story of one of their ancestors; I was telling fiction, not fact.

As I began telling the story to audiences, I could see that over and over again Cyrus kept his word to Maggie. As time and tellings went on, I saw multiple opportunities to use the word promise as both verb and noun. That worked well, and finally the title rose up: "Promises to Keep."

Telling this story has greatly increased my appreciation of the skills used by those folks who perform historical material in which they must remember many, many more facts than I need for telling "Promises to Keep." I actually have a difficult time keeping some facts in my head. So I start with the first number of my house, a six, to help me recall that Shiloh was April 6th and 7th; and then Perryville was October 8th. Once I learned the 24th fought the second day of Shiloh[12] and the 80th went into its first battle at Perryville,[13] I had no trouble recalling that information, but dates? I needed the memory crutch—hooray for my house number!

The story's progression from war's beginning in April 1861, to the summer marriage, the winter work, Shiloh in April 1862, through the baby's birth that year, followed by Perryville in October 1862 I find easier to recall, probably because I am recalling images, not factual data. Although I don't include the details when I'm telling, I do picture the changing of the seasons, the winter indoor work, the spring planting, and the fall harvesting of the crops, and so much more as I tell the tale. Those images seem to have a natural progression that helps me recall the story. Facts are different. Even though I've told the story oodles of times now, I still run the regiment numbers by my husband whenever I'm thinking of telling it because his memory for specific facts is much better than mine. Thank goodness I have a Civil War buff close by!

The Gingerbread Boy

There once lived a girl who shared a home with her stepmother. Years earlier, her mother had died and her father had remarried. While her father lived, her stepmother treated her kindly. But after the girl's father died, that woman turned poison mean. She made the girl do all the work around the house and on the farm. When the girl didn't work fast enough—and most days there was no fast enough—the woman beat the girl with a chain. The girl was miserable, but she had nowhere else to go.

One morning, when the girl was around fourteen years old, her stepmother said, "Today you are going to chop the weeds out of the cotton.[1] Go on out there, and don't come back to the house until you've finished, either." She sent the girl out without any breakfast.

The girl trudged out to the shed, picked up a hoe, and walked on down to the cotton patch, where she began chopping weeds. The girl chopped and chopped. The sun beat down on her. Her stomach growled. Still she chopped. But as she worked, she thought: "I ought to just run away, but where would I go?"

The longer she worked, the more running away seemed like a reasonable idea. Finally she gave in. She hid the hoe in tall weeds under an old wagon. Then she walked into the nearby woods.

Now, even though the woods were so close that the girl could hear leaves rustle in the slightest breeze, she had never been there before. Her stepmother kept her working so hard; she'd never even had time to explore the woods right next to the fields. So in no time she was lost, but that didn't stop her. "I'd rather die out here than go back," she thought, and she kept walking.

About midafternoon she reached a clearing. In front of her stood an amazing house. The shutters were made of wafer cookies, and gumdrops studded the walls. Oh, the girl was so hungry, she couldn't stop herself. She ran up to a window, broke off a bit of shutter, and popped it into her mouth. The door of the house opened, and an old woman looked out. "Child," she said, "you must be awfully hungry if you're chewing up my house."

The girl swallowed hastily. "I'm sorry, ma'am," she apologized. "I should never have done that. I am so sorry."

"It's all right, child," said the old woman. "You've done no harm that can't be undone. Like I said, you must be awfully hungry." The old woman offered her hand. "Come on inside, and let me feed you a proper meal."

The girl went inside, and the old woman did indeed feed her a fine meal. The old woman also told the girl stories and jokes. The two of them talked and laughed together. The girl felt a joy she had not known since her mother died.

Then the old woman glanced out the window. "Oh child, it's going to be dark soon," she said. "You need to go on home now."

"Oh," sighed the girl, "Do I have to go? Couldn't I stay with you?"

"No, you need to go home."

"But—"

The old woman interrupted her. "I know you're living a hard life, but you have to go home."

"I was lost when I found your house," the girl protested. "I don't even know how to go home. Please, can't I stay?"

The old woman stood. "I'll help you find your way, child." She walked to a cupboard, opened it, reached in, and pulled out a gingerbread boy. She handed the gingerbread boy to the girl, saying, "Put this in your pocket. Eat it after you reach home." The girl put the gingerbread boy in her pocket. She was about to speak again, but the old woman raised her hand, and the girl fell silent. "Your life will be better, child," the old woman assured her. "You'll see."

The two of them left the old woman's house. In a very short time the old woman had led the girl through the woods and within sight of the old wagon. They said their goodbyes. Then the girl retrieved her hoe from under the wagon and trudged on home.

When she walked into the house she smelled freshly baked bread. Her stepmother sat at the kitchen table, knife in hand, slicing the loaf. When she saw the girl, she set down her knife. "I don't know where you've been, but you were not chopping out the cotton like I told you." As she spoke, she leaned over and picked up the chain beside her chair. "Don't think you'll be eating any of this bread."

When the girl saw the chain, she ran toward her room. Her step-mother came after her, whirling the chain. The girl ducked as she ran into her room. She slammed the door and braced herself against it. She could feel the door shudder as the chain struck it again and again. Finally the stepmother tired and returned to her chair at the table.

The girl braced a chair under the doorknob to keep her stepmother out; then she collapsed on her bed and cried. She cried for her father and mother. She cried in longing for the joy of that afternoon. She cried and cried. When she was cried out, she rolled over and felt the gingerbread boy in her pocket. She took it out, looked at it, held it by the head, and bit off an arm.

Out in the other room, the stepmother sat eating warm bread slathered in butter. Suddenly her knife flew out of her hand and—whack!—it cut off her arm. She couldn't scream. She just stared at her arm on the floor.

Back in the bedroom, the girl bit off the other arm. Whack! The stepmother's other arm landed on the floor.

The girl broke off a leg. Whack! One leg gone.

The girl bit through the other leg. Whack! Another leg on the floor.

Then the girl broke the head from the body. Whack! The step-mother's head fell to the floor.

After she finished eating the gingerbread boy, the girl fell asleep.

The next morning, when the girl walked out of her room, she found her stepmother's body in pieces. No blood on the floor—just pieces.

The girl knew just what to do. She took a shovel from the shed and she dug a grave. She had worked so hard for so many years; she had no trouble digging a hole six feet deep and three feet wide. Of course, she had no need to make it six feet long. After all, the body was in pieces!

In the years that followed, the girl lived on there in her own house. She and the old woman in the woods became fast friends and the very best of neighbors.

COMMENTARY

Leonard Roberts[2] collected this story from three sources, Billie Jean Fields, Mary Day, and Margie Day.[3] My telling was most influenced by the Fields version. In all three versions the girl is made to do all the work around the house and is mistreated by the stepparent. In both Day versions the girl visits a known witch. In the Fields version the girl visits a woman who seems to be a witch (she lives in the classic cookie house familiar to audiences from the witch in the "Hansel and Gretel" tale), but Fields never specifically labels the old woman "witch." In all three versions the old woman, witch or not, is kind to the girl. She gives her a gingerbread man in the Fields version and a candy doll in the Day versions. In the Fields version a mean stepmother is eating fresh bread and is killed by her knife when the girl eats the gingerbread man. In the Day versions a mean stepfather, while chopping wood the girl forgot to chop when she went to visit the witch, is killed by his axe when the girl eats the candy doll.

Roberts published a retelling of the Margie Day version in 1954. In the headnotes of the published story, Roberts writes, "It is also about the best and most concise example of a peculiar power of witches known as *Murder by Sympathetic Magic* (Motif D2061.2.2). The twelve year old girl who told it, Margie Day, Leslie County, Kentucky, seemed not to be aware of the force and malignant power motivating her story."[4] In the published version of Margie Day's telling, the ending reads: "The old man died and the witch come over after that. She got the house and land and lived there and the little girl lived with her forever."[5] However, in the sound recording of Margie Day telling this story, she gives it the following ending: "And the old man, he died, and she took and lived happily ever after with that old witch. She lived with the witch forever."[6] In Mary Day's telling, the girl also lives happily ever after with the witch, and in the background on the sound recording a voice that sounds like a child's voice can be heard commenting, "a fine home."[7] I have no way of knowing why Roberts would have interpreted and published the ending with the witch moving into the girl's house and taking over the girl's property, when it could just as easily have been that the girl went to live with the witch.

When I listen to the children, Mary and Margie Day, telling the story, they don't seem unaware of malignant power. Instead they seem well aware of the cruelty of the stepparent and sound fully satisfied by the ending of the tale in which the abuse is over and the child lives happily ever after. In the ending of the Fields version, not collected until 1970, there is no mention of the old woman moving in with the girl. The Fields version reads: "Now everything belonged to the little girl and she could do what she wanted. So she lived happily ever after."[8] In my retelling, I have the old woman and the girl remain good neighbors. I also picture the girl as a young teenager, not a little girl, and I imagine the story taking place when a teen living alone could have been acceptable.

Telling this story, unsettling as it is, is also lots of fun. Audience members will often seem startled by the first "Whack!" By the time I reach the last "Whack!" some cringe while others look downright gleeful. I've even had the experience of hearing audience members call out, "Now the head!" as the girl eats her way through the gingerbread boy. The first time I mentioned that the girl did not need to dig a grave six feet long because the body was in pieces, some listeners laughed. I decided to keep this bit of comic relief. Yes, audiences do teach tellers how to tell, but only if we listen to them.

My retelling of this story is no longer the only version being told by a contemporary professional storyteller. After August House published my retelling in 2009,[9] I received an email from Linda Gorham, a fantastic, energetic storyteller from Chicago. In her email, Linda wrote, "I got inspired by your story 'The Gingerbread Boy' in *The August House Book of Scary Stories*. Can I have your permission to tell it my way? I wrote a draft—attached so you can see what I did with it."[10] I read it and loved it. Here's Linda's draft:

2010 Gingerbread Boy

Linda Gorham
August 2010

Summer is fun for most kids. But not for twelve-year-old Tommy George. Each summer he was sent down south to work on his uncle's farm.

All summer, Tommy George had to work from sunup to sundown—planting, pulling weeds, picking cotton, cutting hay—the work never ended. And if he didn't do the work right or if he didn't do the work fast enough, his uncle would grab his whipping stick and beat him. Whack. Whack. Whack. Tommy George would curl up in a ball, cry, and pray for the beating to end.

One day, after a particularly bad whipping, Tommy George ran away. He didn't know where he was going. He just ran through the cot-

ton fields and into the woods. After running for a long time, he came
to a dirty white clapboard house. It's a wonder he saw it—the place
was half hidden by bushes and covered with vines. He had never seen
it before. On the front porch, an old woman was sitting on a rocking
chair—rocking real slow.

"What be your name boy?"

(*puffing*) "My name's Tommy George, ma'am."

"Well, Tommy George, why you running past here all crazy?
Seems to me you're gonna pass out from the heat.
Come on over here boy. Let me take a look at you.
You thirsty boy?"

"Yes'um."

"Come on over here.
Let me get you sweet tea. Something t'eat too."

Now Tommy George knew stuff about not talking to strangers
and all, but he was tired, he was hungry, and she seemed nice. He went
inside her house and she fixed him some cold sweet tea and a peanut
butter sandwich. Tommy George thanked her, but he didn't say much
else. Finally, after a long while, she said, "You in trouble ain't you boy?
What's wrong?"

Tommy George began to cry. Between the tears, he told the old
woman about how his uncle beat him all the time.

"Would you like those beatings to stop?"

"More than anything, ma'am."

"Are you sure?"

"Yes'um, I'm sure."

"Now let me tell you something.
Take one of these gingerbread boy cookies.
Go on, put it in your pocket.
When you get home, eat it."

"I don't want to go home, ma'am!"

"You have to boy.
Now, just do as I say and your life will get better."

"Better by eating a cookie, ma'am?"

"Just do as I say.
You hear me?!"

"Yes'um. I'll do it."

It was a long walk home. Tommy George knew his uncle would be mad. He knew another beating would come—and it did. As soon as he could, Tommy George ran to his room and shoved a chair up against the door to keep his uncle out. He lay down on the floor and cried. Then he felt the gingerbread boy cookie in his pocket.

He took out the cookie and bit off an arm. Outside his uncle was chopping wood. The axe flew out of his hand and whack! His left arm was cut off. The uncle was in shock. He couldn't even scream. He just stared open-mouthed at his arm on the dirt.

Back in the bedroom, Tommy George bit off the other arm of that cookie. Whack! His uncle's right arm fell to the ground.

Tommy George bit off a leg. Whack! His uncle's right leg came off. He fell down hard on the dirt, but he could not cry out for help.

Tommy George bit off the second leg. Whack! Left leg—off—severed in a clean cut. Then Tommy George bit off the head . . .

Tommy George finished the cookie and fell asleep. The next morning he got up early and went outside to start his chores. That's when he found his uncle's body—well, pieces of it—two arms, two legs, one body, and a head. Tommy George didn't cry. He didn't feel nothing. He just grabbed a shovel and started digging.

*   *   *

Receiving a written draft from a teller requesting permission to retell a story based on my telling sparked my curiosity. I don't write the stories down as I work on them. Oh, I may write out a portion here and there, but I rarely write down entire stories. Well sure, I'm writing them down for this book, but I've told them many times to many different audiences before writing them here. Linda seemed to begin her work with the story by writing. After all, she called the version I've included here a draft, which implies more written revisions to come. I simply do not begin with writing! So, I asked about her process.

First I assumed she would use her revised written version as a script to be memorized, but Linda wrote, "No, I couldn't memorize a story if I tried."[11] This sounded very familiar to me because I don't memorize stories either.

Nevertheless, I'll admit that when audience members or storytelling workshop participants hear this, some protest: But you know them from memory, what do you mean you don't memorize? Albert B. Lord in *The Singer of Tales* defines memorization this way: "Memorization is a conscious act of making one's own, and repeating, something that one regards as fixed and not one's own."[12] Neither Linda nor I regard our versions of this story as fixed text.

So, how does Linda use her written versions if she does not treat them as fixed texts to be memorized?

"My process works this way: first, I write out the story based on my research. I need paper to organize my thoughts and 'see' it come together. Then I need to say it aloud to get it right. I write and rewrite after saying it aloud—often adding dialogue and description. I practice on a treadmill, while riding a bike, or walking on a path. I can't practice in my house. If I sat on a chair to practice, I'd fall asleep. I need distractions to let my mind freely 'see' what I can do beyond the paper.

"I try to record any new thoughts/comments on my text although sometimes I never get new ideas back to the paper. My written versions never match what I actually end up telling. Then, after I tell a story to listeners the first time, I add new notes based on what worked spontaneously. I keep doing that for quite a while. Telling helps hone the story more than anything else. It takes me a long time to feel comfortable with a story."

Linda told me she labels her drafts by date and sometimes has five years of story revisions. So, since she's not going to treat her written versions as fixed texts, I wondered why she creates and saves them. "My written versions are my safety net. My training is as a linear thinker. When I write out a story, I use bullets, indents, color, italics, spacing— tricks to help my mind get a picture of the story. Paper gives me comfort and helps my mind 'see' the story."[13]

Then Linda compared her way of working with methods some other tellers use: "I wish my 'way' was easier. But I know we all have to find what works for us. Pictures don't do it for me. Practice in a quiet place doesn't do it for me. Practicing in front of a mirror doesn't work. I need distractions to get a story in my head. The more distractions, the better. Oh, and by the way, I almost never practice most of my facial expressions and/or movements—except for major interactive movements that are part of the story. I trust that those things will come naturally."[14]

Linda does not do all of her preparation for telling to audiences in isolation. She also talks with others as part of her research and works with a storytelling coaching group.[15] "For the Gingerbread Man, many of the new revisions reflect conversations with my husband about folks 'down south' and how they live and talk. He spent all of his summers as a boy in rural Georgia. A lot of the new imagery (names, dog, New York reference) came from those discussions."[16] Please don't worry about Linda's husband's summers in the South, because she also wrote, "My husband had a grand time. He loved the balance between city life and summer country life. No evil uncle. No working on the farm—except for the fun. No flying axes!"[17]

"Then I took the story to my coaching group for review. They helped enhance the grossness at the end when Uncle Bo's body got chopped up."[18]

Hmm? You didn't read the reference to New York? And you are wondering: What dog? What Uncle Bo? Those details have developed through Linda's continued work on her version of the story. What you have in this book is an early draft! So, to hear the latest version you'll need to watch for an opportunity to hear Linda Gorham tell stories in your area, and then make a special request for "The Gingerbread Boy," her retelling of a Kentucky tale.[19]

LITTLE RIPEN PEAR

There once lived a family—a mama, a daddy, a little girl, and a little boy. Every day, the father and son would leave the house to go work in the fields. The mother and daughter stayed home. They cleaned the house, cooked the food, sewed the clothing, tended the garden, and did other nearby chores.

One day, the mother said to her daughter, "Go to the orchard and pick pears. Now, don't you go giving even one away. If you do, I promise, I'll kill you."

The little girl left the house. She walked over the hill, through the woodlot, past the barn, and on down to the orchard. When she got there, she did not see any pears. She looked carefully at each pear tree, and finally she found one fallen pear. It was overly ripe, right on the verge of turning rotten, but it was the only one she could find, so the girl carefully wrapped it up in her apron and headed home with it.

Now the moment the little girl left for the orchard, the mama disguised herself as an old woman. She followed the little girl. And when the girl came up the hill from the orchard, there the mama was, sitting on a tree stump looking for all the world like a poor old woman.

The girl saw the old woman, and she stopped, "Good afternoon, Granny, how are you doing today?" Now, the girl did not think the woman was her grandmother; she called all older women Granny, just to be polite.

"Oh," said her mama, changing her voice to sound like an old woman, "I'm not doing too well. I'm so hungry. Would you happen to have anything I could eat?"

The little girl thought about the pear, but she remembered what her mama had said, so she lied, "I'm sorry, Granny, but I don't have a thing."

"Are you sure? Maybe you have just some little something wrapped up in your apron? I'm so hungry, I'm not sure I'm going to be able to reach my home. I had to stop here just to rest."

The girl thought about the pear, and she thought about what her mama had said. She didn't know what to do. Finally, she decided the right thing was to give away the pear. "After all," she thought, "it's almost rotten anyway, so Mama probably would not be very pleased with it anyhow. And no person should have to go hungry. It will be best if I just tell Mama there weren't any pears, and there really weren't any on the trees—I found this one on the ground."

So, she handed the pear to the old woman. The old woman thanked her, and the girl walked on toward home.

The moment the girl disappeared around the edge of the barn, the mama threw off her old woman disguise and hurried home, taking a shortcut to get ahead of her daughter.

When the daughter reached home, her mother asked, "Where are the pears?"

"Oh, Mama," the girl said, "I looked at every pear tree and couldn't find a single pear in any of them."

"Are you sure you didn't find any pears?"

"Not a one," said the girl.

"Not even on the ground?" asked her mother.

The girl hesitated. She did not want to lie to her mother, but she was afraid to tell her the truth.

"You gave away the pears, didn't you? After I told you not to, you up and gave away our pears."

The girl couldn't help herself. She told the truth. "Oh, Mama, I really didn't find any pears on the trees, but I found one pear on the ground. It was nearly rotten. Then on my way home, I met an old woman. She was so hungry, I gave her the pear. It was nearly rotten anyway, Mama, so I didn't think you'd want it. And the woman was so hungry."

The mama stared at her daughter and shook her head. Then she said, "Go out to the porch and bring in the chopping block."

"Why, Mama?"

"Because I told you to, and I'm your mama."

The girl went out and she brought the chopping block inside. "Now then," said her mama, "go get the axe."

"Why, Mama?"

"Because I said so, and I'm your mama, that's why. Now, go get the axe."

So, the girl brought the axe inside. Then the mama said, "Go upstairs to your bed and get your pillow."

The girl did as asked. When she returned with her pillow, her mother said, "Now, set the pillow on the chopping block and lay your head down."

"No, Mama, you're going to chop my head off."

"I wouldn't hurt you. I'm your mama. Now lay your head down."

"No, Mama, no! You'll kill me!"

"Don't be silly. I'm not going to kill you. I'm your mama. I wouldn't hurt you. I love you. You're my little girl."

So, the girl laid her head on the pillow, and her mother took up the axe and chopped her head off. Then the mother buried her daughter's head and body in the garden.

That evening, when the father and son came home from their work in the fields, the father noticed his daughter's absence, "Where's my little girl?"

"Oh, one of her cousins came by and invited her to visit, so she's gone over there."

"Well, will she be back in time for supper?"

"Oh no, it was one of your relatives that lives far away. She's gone off to visit for a long time. It'll probably be six weeks before she's back."

"Six weeks? Why didn't she come to the fields to tell us good-bye?"

"Oh, you know how she is when her cousins come around. She was so excited about going to visit with them, she didn't even think about taking time to say good-bye."

The father didn't think that sounded like something his little girl would do, but her mother spent more time with her than he did, so he figured she must know what she was talking about. Later that night, the father, mother, and brother ate their supper and went on to bed.

The next morning, the mother said to her son, "Run out to the garden and dig up a few potatoes. I'll fix us some fried potatoes for our breakfast."

The little boy went to the garden. He walked over to the row of potatoes, squatted down, and thrust his hands into the hill to feel for some potatoes. And then he heard singing:

Brother, Brother,
don't pull my curly hair.
Mommy killed me
over one little ripen pear.

He jumped up from the potatoes and ran back to the house.

"Daddy," he said, "I'm having some trouble with the potatoes. I need you to come help me."

The father and brother went out to the garden. When the daddy reached into the potato hill, he heard:

Daddy, Daddy
don't pull my curly hair.
Mommy killed me
over one little ripen pear.

The father and brother walked back to the house, where the father said to his wife. "There's something wrong in the garden. You need to come out here and help dig the potatoes."

The mother walked out, and the moment she reached the potatoes, she heard:

Mommy, Mommy
don't pull my curly hair.
You know you killed me
over one little ripen pear.

The mother looked at her husband and son, and she could tell they had heard the song too. Together the father and brother dug in the potato hill, and they found the little girl's head. The father looked at his wife, "What did you do to her?"

Before the mother could finish her story, he took up the axe and chopped her head off.

The father and brother buried the little girl on one side of the garden and buried the mother on the other. From the little girl's grave a rose bush grew, but from the mother's grave all that ever grew were briars.

Commentary

ATU Tale Type 780B The Speaking Hair.[1]

Leonard Roberts collected ten versions of this tale.[2] It was told by both children and adults.

Table 1 shows information from different versions.

In some of Roberts's collected versions, the little girl sings; in others she chants. The tune I use in my retelling is not based on any tunes in the collected versions because I worked on a song for my retelling using manuscripts from Roberts's collection, before listening to the field recordings. Figure 1 shows the tune I use:

Bro-ther   Bro-ther   don't pull my cur - ly hair.   Mom-my   killed me

o - ver   one   lit - tle   ri - pen   pear.

Same Tune: Father Father, don't pull my curly hair.
      Mommy killed me over one little ripen pear.

Slight change: Mommy, Mommy, don't pull my curly hair.
      You know, you killed me over one little ripen pear.

It is not elaborate. I intentionally wanted a tune a child could believably sing in a mournful, pleading way, as well as a tune I could readily sing. Yes, I'm capable of what I call "singing pretty."[3] However, when characters sing in a story, it jars my ear if they suddenly burst into song with a sound akin to that of a trained singer when all their dialogue within the story has sounded conversational.

When I tell this story, I also picture, quite specifically, the orchard I remember from my childhood. It was down a hill behind the barn that had been my great-grandparents' barn. Our house was located on adjoining property, and to reach the orchard from our house I walked up a hill into the woodlot, down a road, past what had been their house (what our family calls "the old house"). From the old house I would have walked up a slight hill to their barn, walked around the barn, and then down a hill to the orchard. I can also picture the shortcut route someone

Table 1. "Little Ripen Pear" Comparison Chart

1) Title 2) Call number or Format	About the teller	Reason given for killing child	Burial site	How the murder was discovered	How the teller ended the story
1) Little Ripen Pear 2) LR OR 003 Track 8	Rudy Spencer, age seventeen, from Letcher County, was recorded in Lige Gay's classroom in October 1949. On the recording she states she heard the story from her sister, who heard it from her mother, and she thinks her mother heard it from her grandmother.[a]	Girl sent to store for pears and warned she will be killed if she gives any away. Girl gives one pear to an old woman, who is witch stepmother in disguise.	Head chopped off and buried in garden; body cooked and served to father and brother for supper.	Brother cannot eat because body parts speak (ex.: "Don't eat my finger.") Next day, voice chants, "Don't step on my golden curls. For my stepmother cut off my head for one little rotten pear." Father and brother hear.	Father and brother kill stepmother. Girl comes back to life and they live happily ever after.
1) Little Ripen Pear 2) LR OR 017 Track 4	Jimmy Pennington, age seventeen, from Leslie County, heard the story from his grandmother. He was recorded at Berea Foundation School and College, Madison County, May 1950.	Girl sent for pears is warned that if she gives even one away, her head will be cut off. She finds only one, and gives it to an old woman in a hollow stump, who is really her mother in disguise.	Head chopped off, and girl's body and head buried in potato patch.	Sister sent for potatoes, hears, "Oh sister, oh, sister, don't pull my curly hair. Mother killed me over one little ripen pear." Another sister and a brother and the father sent for potatoes, each hear the chant.	Father makes mother dig potatoes. While she digs, a bird flies over, drops a stone on her, and kills her.
1) The Rotten Pears 2) LR OR 029 Track 1	Claudetta Maggard heard this story from her grandmother. She was recorded at Wooton in Leslie County in 1953.	Mother and girl picking pears; girl eats a rotten one and gets sick. Medicine does not make her better.	Mother chops off girl's head, and buries her in the garden.	Next day, mother, father, brother, and sister each hear chant. "Oh mother/father/ brother/sister, Oh mother/father/ brother/sister, don't pull my curly hair."	Father tells wife, "You killed the only child I liked." And then he kills her.
1) Rotten Pear 2) LR OR 055 Track 5	Faith Howard heard the story at her school when her teacher told it. She was recorded in Leslie County in 1955.	Mother tells girl to get pears. Girl meets a bear with single rotten pear, persuades the bear to give her the pear. The girl takes the pear home to mother.	Mother chops off girl's head and buries it in the potato patch. No mention of body burial.	Boy sent to dig potatoes, hits head, which chants, "Brother, brother, don't pull my curly hair." Father and mother also go dig potatoes and hear the chant. Mother returns from patch crying.	Father kills mother, "and they lived happily ever after."

Table 1. "Little Ripen Pear" Comparison Chart   (cont.)

1) Title 2) Call number or Format	About the teller	Reason given for killing child	Burial site	How the murder was discovered	How the teller ended the story
1) Three Rotten Pears 2) LR OR 016 Track 17	Mrs. Clyde Gibson, an adult, could not recall who told the story to her. She was recorded at Berea Foundation School and College, Madison County, May 1950.	Girl sent to store for pears, warned not to give any away or lose any money. On way home girl gives three rotten pears to old woman who begs and begs for them.	Mother kills girl and buries her in yard.	When father and brother are digging in the yard looking for girl, Daddy pulls hair, and hears chant, "Oh daddy, oh daddy, don't pull my curly hair. Mother has killed me over three rotten pears."	Ending unknown because recording stopped abruptly, and this story is not transcribed in Roberts's collection.
1) Old Rotten Pear 2) LR OR 099 Track 13	Bobby Boggs heard this story from his sister. He was recorded at Pine Mountain Settlement School, Harlan County, in October 1952.	Girl sent to store for pears, told if she gives any away, mother will kill her. Girl gives one pear to a beggar.	Mother kills girl and buries her behind the smokehouse.	Brother and father ask about girl. Following mother's suggestions, boy visits aunt and grandmother, but the girl is not there. Mother suggests girl is playing in the smokehouse, boy looks, not there. Father goes to search and sees hair behind smokehouse. Father pulls hair, hears song; "Papa, papa, don't pull my hair. Mama killed me over one rotten pear."	Father kills wife, boy and dad live happily ever after.[b]
1) The Rotten Pear 2) Manuscript, ca. 1950	John Miniard, from Leslie County, wrote out this version of the story.	Stepmother sends girl for pears. Stepmother disguises herself, beats the girl to pears, and then takes a pear away from the girl. When girl returns, stepmother asks about missing pear, then accuses girl of eating it and lying.	Stepmother chops off girl's head, buries her in the potato patch, but fails to cover up all of the girl's hair.	Boy sent to dig potatoes, sees hair, pulls it, and hears chant: "Oh brother, oh brother, don't pull my curly hair, for mother has killed me for one little rotten pear." Boy shows father. Father brings wife out and tells her to dig.	Father cuts mother's head off and buries her where girl was, "and he got the doctor to sew the girl's head back on, and they lived happily ever after."

Table 1. "Little Ripen Pear" Comparison Chart (cont.)

1) Title 2) Call number or Format	About the teller	Reason given for killing child	Burial site	How the murder was discovered	How the teller ended the story
1) No title given 2) Manuscript, 1956	Betty Cusick, from Evarts, Harlan County, collected the story from Olivia Cusick, a student.	Little girl, Clara, at orchard, eats three or four over-ripe peaches and listens to bird singing for a long time. Returns home and stepmother asks where she has been. Clara tells the truth.	Stepmother chops girl's head off, buries her head down in the orchard. Flowers grow where head is buried. No mention of body burial.	Father returns from work, asks about Clara, told she is visiting neighbor. He hears the bird singing and follows the song to the orchard, where he finds flowers. When he asks, his wife says the flowers are a neighbor's gift. Then the bird song changes to, "Oh father, oh father, she killed me over an old rotten peach."	The little singing bird throws a big stone on stepmother's head and kills her. Clara comes back to life.
1) The Rotten Pear 2) Manuscript, 1956	Zora Lovitt heard it from Marcella Creekmore, age fourteen, of Watts Creek Community of Whitley County.	Girl finds pear in yard. Mother says, "Lay it on trunk, but if it is rotten I will kill you." Mother cuts open pear, and it is rotten.	Mother chops girl's head off and buries it under doorstep. No mention of body burial.	When anyone crosses the threshold, the girl's voice calls, "Brother/Father, don't step on my golden hair for my mother killed me for an old rotten pear."	Father removes doorstep, finds girl's head. He cuts off mother's head and buries it beside girl's head.
1) The Three Pears 2) Manuscript, 1955	Betty Rae Nichols heard it from Vivian Gold, Harlan County, who heard it from her grandmother.	Stepmother sends Mary to store to get pears. She comes home with three, all rotten. Because stepmother thinks father pays too much attention to his children, she uses pears as excuse to get rid of Mary.	Stepmother chops Mary's head off and buries it in the garden. No mention of body burial. The next day, the brother Jud meets the same fate.	Father sent to garden to dig potatoes. Mary's voice says: "Oh father, oh, Father, don't pull my curly hair, for mother has cut off my head."	Father kills wife and buries her in garden. "Where the cruel stepmother was buried a thorn bush grew. Where Mary and Jud were buried roses grew."[c]

Notes:
[a] In the notes on this tale in his *South From Hell-fer-Sartin,* Roberts writes, "learned tales from her father, a miner" (276).
[b] At the end of the story on this recording (LR OR 99, Track 13), Roberts asks listeners, students at Pine Mountain Settlement School, if they have heard the story before. They say they have. He then asks if they have heard any different endings. They say this ending is the one they have heard.
[c] The ending of this version inspired the ending I use.

could have taken—from the barn, walking behind the old house toward a different barn, and then through an open field—to beat me back to our house if they really wanted. I can also picture how I would likely not have seen the person traveling quickly by that route because of the old house, and the hills, trees, and other vegetation of the woodlot. So, why does this matter? And if it is so important, why don't I explain it in my telling of the story?

It matters because until I can truly picture a story, I cannot tell it. Making the setting concrete by picturing the land where I grew up is one method for helping myself see the story. I know if I can see the story, and take time to see it as I'm telling it, my listeners will be able to see it too. Will they see the exact same picture I see? Absolutely not. Instead they will create their own images of the tale, using their imaginations to picture the setting, costume the characters, and bring the story to life in their minds. As storytellers are fond of saying: Put ten listeners and one storyteller in a room, and when the teller tells a story, eleven different stories will be heard.[4]

Yes, I suppose it could be possible to tell stories with such minutely detailed descriptive language that the listeners' images would be identical, or nearly identical. However, doing that would rob storytelling of what I see as its greatest strength. I don't view my life's work as telling stories. Instead I see my work as strengthening imaginations. After all, the ability to imagine forms the foundation of all planning, hoping, dreaming, goal setting, and inventing we humans do. Because humans love narrative,[5] storytelling provides an excellent vehicle for exercising imaginations. When I tell stories, I do not want to control my listeners' imaginations; instead I strive to leave plenty of room for the listener to imagine the specific details, thus providing a refreshing imagination workout—even through stories as inherently creepy (okay, possibly beyond creepy, even downright disturbing) as "Little Ripen Pear."

FLANNEL MOUTH

There once lived a woman who was so difficult to get along with no one even knew her name. Everyone just called her Flannel Mouth. Ornery as Flannel Mouth was, people still sought her out because of her fine weaving. Back in Flannel Mouth's day, if you wanted cloth you had to weave it yourself or find someone who would weave for you. Flannel Mouth traded her weaving skills for everything she needed to support herself and her small child.

One winter day, when the snow lay deep, Flannel Mouth was so busy weaving she didn't notice when the fire in her hearth died out. But her little child noticed. Her little child grew cold and began to whimper.

"Hush," said Flannel Mouth, and she kept on weaving.

But the child couldn't hush. The child was cold. The whimpers grew to cries.

"I said hush," Flannel Mouth warned.

But the child couldn't hush. The child cried and cried from the cold. Flannel Mouth stopped weaving. She turned toward her child. "I told you to hush."

When the child kept on crying, Flannel Mouth stood up. She walked over and picked up her child. She shook her child. She slapped her child. She killed her child. Flannel Mouth walked outside and pushed her child's body into a snowdrift. Then she returned to her weaving.

That night, the moment Flannel Mouth's head touched her pillow, she heard the sound of a child crying. Night after night, every time she tried to sleep, she heard a child crying. "This house is haunted," she thought. "I've got to move away from here."

One day Flannel Mouth went to see a woman she wove for often. This woman had a large house, so Flannel Mouth told her, "My house just does not suit me anymore. I was wondering if I could move in with you. I'd do all your family's weaving in exchange for food and a place to sleep. For anything else I need, I'll take in more weaving."

The woman replied, "Well, Flannel Mouth, that would be fine, but what about your child? Where is your child?"

"My child? . . . well, there was a lady came through not long ago. Saddest lady I ever met. She stayed with me awhile. I learned she was sad because she didn't have a child. So, I gave her my child. It made me feel good to make somebody so happy."

"Well then, Flannel Mouth, you go on home and start packing. We'll bring the wagon up in a couple of days and move you here."

So Flannel Mouth moved, but when her head hit her pillow at night, she still heard the sound of a child crying. Night after night, Flannel Mouth barely slept. One day she was so tired she walked over to her bed and lay down in the daytime. That was when she discovered if she slept in the day she would not hear the sound of a child crying.

After that, Flannel Mouth lit torches and worked all night, then slept all day. Worked all night, and slept all day. All was going well for Flannel Mouth, but all was not going well for the rest of the household.

One day, the woman of the house told Flannel Mouth, "You need to work during the day when we work and sleep at night when we sleep. I cannot spend time keeping my children quiet all day so they won't disturb your sleep. Besides, children are not supposed to be quiet. They are supposed to play."

"That wasn't our deal," insisted Flannel Mouth. "We never agreed to anything about when I worked and when I slept. That wasn't our deal."

The woman of the house thought a bit, and then she said, "I have an idea. We have a small cabin up the hill behind the house a ways. It's one room, just big enough for your loom, a small bed, and a chair. Not big, but it is weathertight. There's a little porch on the front. The windows are small and high up, but since you'd be sleeping during the day . . ."

"Suits me fine," agreed Flannel Mouth. She moved into the little cabin. She worked all night, slept all day, and disturbed no one.

One night Flannel Mouth sat at her loom weaving when the door of the cabin opened all by itself. Flannel Mouth looked over, thinking the wind had somehow opened the door, but into the doorway walked two big, hairy legs.

"Who are you, and what do you want?" she asked.

From the doorway, a deep voice answered, "I'm just two big, hairy legs."

Then two little child legs walked across the porch, into the doorway, and stood beside the big, hairy legs. Again, Flannel Mouth asked, "Who are you, and what do you want?"

A little child's voice whimpered, "It's cold in the snow."

Flannel Mouth sat at her loom and stared at the doorway. She saw a big, hairy body come in supported by huge hands attached to long, hairy arms. The hands climbed up those big, hairy legs and the big, hairy body settled itself on top. "Who are you, and what do you want?" she called.

"I'm just a big, hairy body, sitting atop two big, hairy legs," the deep voice answered.

A little child's body came in. Little child hands climbed up the child legs and set the body on top. "Who are you, and what do you want?" Flannel Mouth insisted.

"It's cold in the snow," the child's voice cried, "I've been so cold in the snow."

Flannel Mouth didn't know what to do. She just sat and watched the doorway. She saw a big, hairy head roll in. The big, hairy body bent down, picked up the big, hairy head, and placed it on its shoulders. Flannel Mouth could see the head had fiery red eyes. She was so frightened, she couldn't speak.

A little child's head rolled in. The little child body bent down, picked up the head, and placed it on its shoulders. "Who are you," shouted Flannel Mouth, "and what do you want?"

A little child's voice answered, "It's cold in the snow, Mama, I've been so cold in the snow."

Then the hairy creature raised its arm, pointed one claw-tipped finger at Flannel Mouth, and roared, "Woman, I have come to deliver your punishment."

Flannel Mouth thought: "I'm seeing things. That's all this is. There's nothing over in that doorway. My mind is playing tricks on me. All I need to do is run right through that open door. I'm just seeing things."

She ran for the door. When she drew near, the big, hairy creature wrapped its huge, hairy arms around her, sank its claws into her back, and pulled her close. It picked her up, turned, and walked across the porch and off through the snow. Everywhere the creature stepped, the snow melted all the way to the ground and smoke rose from the footprints. A little child's voice could be heard calling after them, "I'm not cold anymore, Mama, I'm not cold anymore."

COMMENTARY

This is my retelling of a story Nora Morgan Lewis used to tell her children and nieces and nephews.[1] I've been unable to determine whether it is a tale she invented or one that she heard growing up. It has the feel of a folktale. There are many stories of murdered people returning for revenge. But I've never run across any other versions of this particular tale.

In the summer of 2003, I met Jack Lewis, son of Nora Morgan Lewis, at Berea College in Berea, Kentucky. I also met some of Nora's other children and nieces and nephews. They were visiting Berea College because they were related to Jane Muncy, who Leonard Roberts had collected several stories from in 1949 and 1955 during Muncy's childhood and teen years. I was one of a group who had gathered in Berea to study the Leonard Roberts Collection in a project directed by folklorist Carl Lindahl, of the University of Houston, Texas, in association with Indiana University, Bloomington, Indiana.

At a reception I talked with Mrs. Lewis's relatives, and when they mentioned their mother had told stories, I asked about her storytelling. The story they all seemed to most remember was "Flannel Mouth." It was a tale that frightened them as children, but they had loved to hear it anyway. One of Nora Morgan Lewis's relatives laughingly commented that Lewis may have told "Flannel Mouth" as a form of child control because she told it when all the cousins were together, the children all sleeping in the same room at family gatherings. The story was told at bedtime, and after hearing it the children huddled close to each other, and not a single one of them wanted to get up for any reason whatsoever![2]

When she was getting on in years and in poor health, Nora Morgan Lewis wrote down the stories she had so enjoyed telling. Her family members told me no one in the family had carried on her storytelling at the time she wrote her tales, but she thought they might want the stories someday, and she wanted them to outlive her. In the summer of 2003, her family donated copies of her stories to the Southern Appalachian Archives, thus assuring her stories would indeed be available to a wider audience. Nora's son, Jack, wrote of her stories, "I believe it was my mother's most profound desire to have them made into book form."[3] I'm honored to participate in making her desire reality.

I did not memorize the words Lewis wrote, but retell the story in my own words. Given the change in time periods between her telling and mine, I felt the need to say a little more about why people would have been weavers, and specify the use of the wagon to move Flannel Mouth from place to place. I mostly stay with the same plot and images, but use somewhat different wording. Here's how Nora M. Lewis wrote the story down:

Flannel Mouth[4]

Once there was a woman so mean she did not like anyone, not even her own baby. She said so many mean things and cuss words people called her Flannel Mouth, and by that name and no other was she known.

Old Flannel Mouth worked for the folks around her to support herself and her baby. At that time everyone wove their own cloth to make their clothes. Flannel Mouth was a wonderful hand to weave so she wove day in and day out never caring for her baby.

One day as the snow lay deep, real deep on the ground, she had been weaving and let her fire die out. The baby became cold and began to cry. This made her angry, so she killed her baby and hid it in a big snow bank.

Every night she could hear crying under her pillow, so she could not sleep at all. She left her home and went to hire to a woman. The woman asked her where her baby was. She said, "I gave it to a kind woman who wanted a baby very much."

Her job with this family was weaving. She wove and wove of a day but as soon as she went to bed something began to cry. She got up and wove all night by candle light for she could not bear to hear that crying any longer. She cussed the crying and cussed everything, but cussing did not do any good, the family got tired of her working all night and sleeping all day.

One day the mistress of the house told her she could not keep her because she stayed up all night, but that they had a cabin up a branch and that she could stay there. Flannel Mouth was glad to get by herself again.

For a few nights everything was so quiet, she sat down by her fire and fell asleep. Something woke her and in the door stood one big hairy leg. She cried out, "What are you here for?"

But it answered and said, "I am just one big leg. I am just one big leg."

In come a little white leg and stood by the large leg.

"Why did you come here? Oh! Why did you come here?"

The little leg said, "I was cold in the snow, Mother, I was cold in the snow."

In came another big hairy leg, and stood by the other one. All she could say was, "Why have you come here? Oh! Why have you come here?"

The answer was the same, "I am just two big legs. I am just two big legs."

In came another little leg and sat by the other leg.

"Oh! Why did you come here?"

"I was so cold in the snow, Mother, I was cold in the snow."

By this time the door was full of legs and she could not pass them. In came a large hairy body and got up on those legs.

"Why did you come here?" she said.

The answer was the same, "I am one big body, I am one big body."

In came a little body, and got on the little legs. By this time Flannel Mouth could not speak, but the body said, "I was cold in the snow, Mother, I was cold in the snow."

In came a big head with red eyes and arms so long with claws so sharp, and two horns on its head. In came two small arms and the small head and got on its body. The mean woman tried to pass by, but the big hairy body with the horny head grabbed her and said, "To mile [mete] out your punishment. You owe me a debt that has to be paid."

And the baby said, "I am not cold in the snow, Mother, I am not cold in the snow any longer."

The baby smiled, but the hairy head only grinned and took her away so fast he left his tracks smoking.

*   *   *

I can attest the story has staying power for audiences today, just as it did for the children and nieces and nephews of Nora Morgan Lewis. Several years ago eighth graders at St. Romuald Interparochial School in Hardinsburg, Kentucky, used the story to humorously complain—and lucky me, one of their teachers told me about it! I had told stories there early in the school year. One day in winter, the heat went out. Teachers kept the classroom doors closed and space heaters were brought in to provide heat. That left no heat in the halls. While younger students spent most of their day in the same classroom, older students changed rooms each class period. The teacher reported eighth graders entering her classroom moaning, "It's cold in the hall, teacher, so cold in the hall," duplicating the tone and timing from the refrain in "Flannel Mouth." More than once I've been speaking in a different context, only to have someone say, "Oh, I know you. You're the 'It's cold in the snow, Mama' [imitating the plaintive way I say this during the telling] person, aren't you?" I love it when that happens, and it is a special treat when the person tells me how long it has been since they heard the story! Yep! It's a tale with staying power.

THE BLUE LIGHT

Near the edge of a large forest lived a woodcutter and his three beautiful daughters, Emily, Ella, and Lisa. All three girls had hair like their mother's, as fine and pale as the tender silks on the corn that grew in the family garden.

When Lisa, the youngest, was just a toddler, her mother died. Nevertheless, she and her father and sisters managed to live well. Every day, the father and daughters ate breakfast together. On weekdays, the father took up his axe and walked into the forest to work. The daughters worked around the house and in the garden, and they fixed dinner. Then Emily, the oldest, carried her father's food into the forest. Emily never knew exactly where her father would be working, so she followed the sound of his axe. At the end of the day she helped him carry wood home. On weekends, the father and daughters carted the wood to the nearby town and sold it in the marketplace.

One day, the woodcutter returned from the forest alone. "Why didn't Emily bring my food?"

"She did," said Ella. "She left hours ago."

The woodcutter hurried back into the forest to look for Emily. He searched and searched, but could not find her. When he returned home it was dark.

The next morning the woodcutter told Ella and Lisa, "I'm going to keep looking for Emily today. Both of you stay home. I'll find her and be back before dark."

Ella and Lisa completed their usual chores. By the time they ate their dinner, they could hear the faint sound of their father's axe. "Oh," said Ella, "Daddy must have found Emily. I hear him working. She must be hungry. I'm going to take them food." She packed a pail of food and left.

Late in the afternoon the woodcutter returned home alone. When Lisa saw him coming, she ran from the house calling, "Where are Emily and Ella?"

"I couldn't find Emily," her father answered, "and what do you mean where is Ella?"

"We heard your axe, so we knew you'd found Emily," Lisa explained. "Ella took you food." Again the woodcutter searched the forest until dark. Again he returned home alone.

The next morning the woodcutter said, "Lisa, stay home." He left without eating breakfast. Now Lisa was a good girl. She really tried to stay home. She cooked and ate breakfast. She washed the dishes. She swept the floor. She pulled weeds in the garden. She tried to keep herself busy, but she had never been home alone all day before. By noon, she was bored. She cooked her dinner. As she sat on the porch eating, she heard the sound of an axe in the woods. She thought: "That's Daddy working. I know he told me to stay home, but he must be hungry. He didn't even eat breakfast. I'm not a baby; I know I'm big enough to take him food, and Ella and Emily will be hungry too." She packed food in a sack and walked into the forest.

Carefully, she followed the sound of the axe. When the axe stopped, she stopped walking and waited. When she heard the axe again, it seemed to come from a slightly different direction. She walked toward the sound. Again it stopped, and again she stopped. Each time the axe began again, Lisa changed her direction ever so slightly to walk toward the sound. Eventually she began to fear she would never reach her father and sisters, for the sound always seemed the same distance away. Again the axe stopped. Lisa waited and waited, but the sound of the axe did not return. Only then did Lisa realize the forest was growing dark. She had walked all afternoon.

She started walking again, hoping to find shelter as the forest darkened around her. Finding nothing, she sat with her back against a large tree trunk and hungrily ate the food she had packed. She feared wild animals would find her, but she didn't know what to do.

When the forest grew fully dark, Lisa could see a faint blue light shining through the trees. "Good," she thought, "a light means people." She carefully walked through the darkness toward the blue light. Eventually she reached a clearing. A house stood in the clearing, and from a window a blue light shown. Lisa hurried to the door and knocked. When a man opened the door, she said, "Hi, my name's Lisa. I was lost in the woods, and I saw your blue light."

"Come in," the man said as he opened the door wide. He motioned

Lisa over to his kitchen table. He placed a steaming bowl of soup in front of her. "I was just about to eat," he said. "Please, join me." As they ate, he said, "Hmm, I believe I recognize you. Aren't you one of the woodcutter's daughters?" Lisa acknowledged she was. "Well, I know where you live," the man added. "You aren't too lost, but it's way too dark to travel now. Tomorrow, I'll show you the way home."

After supper the man took quilts from a cedar chest and made a sleeping pallet near the fire in the kitchen for Lisa. Then he went to another room for the night.

The next morning the man cooked Lisa a fine breakfast. Then he said, "I've got some errands I need to get done before I take you home. While I'm gone you just stay around the house. You can go out on the porch if you want to, but don't go in my storage sheds." Then he left.

Lisa appreciated the man's kindness, so she washed their breakfast dishes. She found a broom in a closet, so she swept his floor. She sat on his couch and waited for his return. She grew bored, very bored.

She carried the broom outside and swept the back porch. She noticed a line of storage sheds in the back yard. "I wonder what he keeps in those," she thought. She finished sweeping, sat on the porch steps, and stared at the sheds. The longer she looked at them, the more curious she grew. Then she remembered: "He told me not to go in the sheds. He didn't say I couldn't look in."

She walked over to the sheds. Locked—they were all padlocked. "I don't know why he told me not to go in them," she thought. "I can't go in anyway." She returned to the porch, picked up the broom, walked inside, and placed the broom back in the closet. She was just about to close the closet door when she saw a large silver ring hanging from a nail on the closet wall. From the ring hung a single key. She grabbed the silver ring and headed for the storage sheds. Again and again the key slipped into the padlock, but would not turn. At the last shed, the key turned and the lock popped open. Quickly Lisa removed the lock and placed it in her pocket. She opened the shed door a crack and peeked inside.

The shed was so dark, she could see very little. The floor looked damp. Near the door was a basket. Lisa could see corn silk glinting in the faint light. "Now, why would anyone store a basket of corn silk," she wondered. But as her eyes grew accustomed to the darkness, she could see that beside the corn silk was something else. Skin? She opened the door wide to let in more light, and stepped inside. She saw her sisters' heads resting side by side in the bottom of the basket. She gasped and looked away. In the dim light she could see her sisters' headless bodies fastened to the back wall of the shed.

Lisa stepped back from the shed. She was trembling, but she managed to close the door and fasten the lock. Then she ran back to the house and returned the silver key ring to the closet.

She paced. She did not know what to do. She worried: "I don't know the way home. Besides, if I leave and he finds me in the woods, he will know something is wrong because I didn't wait for him. I locked the shed. If I don't say anything he'll never know I looked." She was still pacing when she heard footsteps on the front porch. Quickly, Lisa sat down on the couch.

When the man opened his door, he asked, "Well now, have you been a good girl?"

"I sure have," Lisa replied, keeping her voice strong and steady, "I even did the dishes and swept the floor for you."

"Did you go in my sheds?" he asked.

"You told me not to," she said.

"But did you?" he persisted.

"I told you, I did the dishes and swept the floor. I even swept your porch too. You told me not to go in the sheds."

"So, you are a good girl." He smiled; then he walked over to her and stood before her. "Hold out your hands," he demanded.

Lisa held out her hands. He inspected them, and smiled again. Then he pulled over a chair and sat in front of her, "Now, hold out your feet," he ordered.

Lisa lifted her feet. When the man saw her feet, he muttered. "There's a bloodstain on your right foot. You are not a good girl. You were in my storage shed." He rose from the chair and walked toward the kitchen saying, "Now I need my knife."

Lisa jumped up and ran from the house. The man called after her, "Come back here, bad girl. You're just like the others, a bad, bad girl." Lisa could hear him running after her. He knew the forest; she didn't. She ran this way and that trying to stay ahead of him. She tripped on a tree root. She scrambled to her feet, but he caught her.

He dragged her back to his house and out to the last storage shed. There he killed her. He placed her head in the basket and fastened her body to the back wall beside her sisters.

By now it was near dark. He returned to his house, cleaned himself up, and washed his knife. Then he took vegetables from his storage bin and chopped them for soup. By the time the soup began to cook, it was fully dark. He lit the blue light and placed it in his window.

The soup was almost ready to eat when he heard a knock on his door. He opened it, and there stood a girl. Her short hair, black as a crow's wing, curled over her head. "Hi," she said. "My name is Susan. I was lost in the woods, and I saw your blue light."

COMMENTARY

ATU Tale Type 312 Maiden-Killer (Bluebeard)

My retelling comes from "The Blue Light," collected by Leonard Roberts from either Mrs. Dicie Hurley of Majestic, Pike County, Kentucky, or Mrs. E. McClanahan of Freeburn, Pike County, Kentucky.[1] What most attracted me to the story is the ending. In most tale type 312 Maiden-Killer (Bluebeard) variants, the girl survives and the man is punished. In this ending he is still out there, making it a much more chilling tale than most. Listeners who enjoy returning movie characters, such as Jason in the *Halloween* movies and Freddy Krueger in the *Nightmare on Elm Street* films, also appreciate the open-ended close of "The Blue Light." I have encountered a storytelling colleague or two who protest, "You can't kill off the third sister." Oh, but you can, and the story chills.

Roberts collected another Bluebeard variant, "The Three Girls and an Old Man,"[2] from Chrisley Day of Polls Creek, Leslie County, Kentucky. It includes checking the girls' feet for bloodstains. I deliberately incorporated this image in my retelling, especially after hearing an audible gasp from a listener during a WOW Storytelling Weekend[3] when I included the bloodstained foot for the first time.

Other changes I'm aware of between the collected version of "The Blue Light" and the version as I retell it include reducing the number of sisters from four to three, sending the father out to search for the lost daughters, using the sound of the axe as the method the girls typically use to locate their father at work, having the man feed the girl and treat her with kindness the evening she arrives, changing the prohibition to "don't go in" instead of "not to look into," which then makes the bloodstain on the foot more chilling, since she seems to have gotten away with her actions until the man inspects her feet. In the typical Bluebeard story, as in the Roberts-collected text, the keys are dropped into the blood. By describing the sisters' hair, I've managed to weave in their mother and use the desire for a closer look at the corn silk in the basket as the reason for the third sister to step into the shed, thus acquiring the bloodstain. Describing their hair also helps distinguish the dead girls from the girl who arrives at the end of the story. In some early retellings, a few audience members interpreted the last girl as a sister returned to life or as a ghost of one of the dead sisters.

My retelling developed through my working on this tale at a WOW Storytelling Weekend, telling it to many different audiences, making subtle changes, and then intentionally keeping what seemed to work best. In short, I've done what I was taught to do as a storyteller: I've reimagined the story and retold it from the images I created in my imagination.

Here is the Roberts-collected text, as I found it in the archives, including the paragraphing and the inserted paragraph symbols:

The Blue Light[4]

Once upon a time there was a woodsman who had four daughters. Each day this man went far into the forest to cut wood and the eldest daughter took him his noonday meal. One day the eldest daughter prepared her father's lunch and started on the long journey into the woods. As evening turned to night the father came home. He was very angry because no one had brought his lunch to him. His daughters told him that his eldest child had went off into the woods with his lunch early that morning and had not returned.

The next day the next oldest daughter went into the forest to take her father's lunch. That evening the father came home and wanted to know what had happened to his lunch and they told him that it was sent to him by the next eldest daughter. ¶The same thing happened the next day. ¶The man had only one daughter left and he didn't want her to go into the forest. The man went back to work and left his daughter to tend the house. The daughter became lonely there by herself and she decided to take her father's lunch to him even though her father had told her not to go into the forest. She set out through the woods to find her father and as she walked, she didn't notice how thick and dark the forest had become. When she did she had lost her way and it was getting late. She had traveled some distance when she saw a blue light shining through the forest. When she had gotten to the source of the light and she saw a small cabin in a clearing. She knocked on the door and a huge man opened the door and let her in. She told him that she was lost and could not find her way home. He told her she was not to look into any of the locked rooms or outside buildings. ¶She agreed and the next morning she decided to clean the house while the man worked in the forest. She had clean[ed] most of the house when she spied a set of keys on a chain hanging on the wall of the cabin. She remembered what the man had said about not looking in the locked rooms but her curiosity got the best of her so she took the keys from the wall. She tried all the doors but the keys wouldn't fit so she went outside and tried the buildings. When she came to the last one she tried the keys and the lock snapped open and the girl almost screamed for there was three headless girls. ¶She stepped inside and saw the rings on the fingers of the dead girls and she knew that they were her sisters. As she turned around she dropped the keys on the floor in the blood. She picked them up and wiped them hastily. When the man returned he noticed the keys and he told her that she had disobeyed him and for that reason she must die too. ¶He started toward her with a long sharp knife and as he came closer she ran out of the door and through the woods. As she ran blindly she tripped and fell. Before she could get up the man had found her. He dragged the screaming, crying girl back to the cabin where she received the same fate as her three sisters. ¶When he had cleaned up the blood and locked the door of the outside building he heard a knock at the door. It was a girl who had lost her way and was attracted by the blue light.

THE OPEN GRAVE

A long time ago, when it was night it was *dark*. You may be thinking: so what? It's dark at night now. But in the time I'm talking about the most frequent light anybody had to travel by was moonlight, and on the night I'm telling you about there was no moon. But there was a fellow traveling home through the darkness on that moonless night. He decided to take a shortcut through the town graveyard.

There he was, walking along through the cemetery, and whoosh! He fell into a newly dug grave. Well, he did what most of us would do, he tried to jump out. He'd jump up, get a fingerhold, and then dirt would give way and he'd slip back down. Jump up, get a fingerhold, slip back down. Jump up. Slip down. Over and over again he tried to jump out, until he was exhausted.

Then he began calming himself down, "I'm going to be all right. I'm just going to have to spend the night here, that's all. People don't dig graves for no reason. Tomorrow, there's bound to be a funeral. After the funeral folks will come out here for the burying. They'll find me. They'll fetch a ladder and help me out." He breathed slowly and deeply. "I'm going to be all right. Just spend the night here. That's all." In the darkness, he felt his way down to one end of the grave. Once there, he sank down into the corner and curled in on himself to keep warm. Finally, he did indeed feel warm, and he drifted off to sleep.

Later that same night there was a second fellow headed home in the darkness. As fate or luck would have it, that second fellow made the same decision as the first fellow: "I believe I'll take a shortcut through the town cemetery."

There he was traveling along when whoosh! He fell into the very same newly dug grave. Just like the first fellow, he tried to jump out. He'd jump up and get a fingerhold. The dirt would give way and he would slip. He too tried over and over again until he was exhausted.

But then, he didn't work on calming himself down like that first fellow had. No, that second fellow took to hollering, "Help! Help! I've fallen in a grave. Somebody come get me out of here! Help! Help, help, help!"

He made such a racket that he woke up that first fellow who was sleeping down in the end of that grave. When that sleeping fellow woke up, he peered through the darkness in the direction all that racket was coming from and said, "No sense yelling and hollering like that. You can't jump out."

He was wrong. (Ending 1)

When the fellow who was hollering heard that voice in the darkness, he gave one jump, "Aaah!!!" and he was out of that grave and on his way home. (Ending 2)

I understand he was moving real fast too. (Ending 3)

COMMENTARY

Related to ATU Tale Types 1313A* In the Open Grave and 1313B* The Cold Grave

I first encountered this story as "The Men in the Open Grave," in *Ghosts Along the Cumberland* by William Lynwood Montell.[1] He reported four versions of this tale, one each from Mercer County, collected by John Short in 1965; Monroe County, collected by Lynwood Montell in 1958; Green County, collected by Jerry Powell in 1964; and Clark County, collected by Viola Burgess in 1964.

In my retelling of the story, I did just as most folks will do. I kept the core of the story. I chose to avoid drinking as a reason for either person to fall in, as given in two of the reported versions. I also emphasize the darkness of the night in the time before security lights became common, as they are in many town and rural cemeteries today. My audiences are contemporary, often students or school-age children and their parents, so most of my listeners have grown up when very few cemeteries are poorly lit.

You no doubt noticed I marked three endings for this story. I vary the endings depending on audience reaction. Ending 1 was inspired by John Benjamin, actor, director, and arts education program coordinator for the Kentucky Arts Council, who heard me tell the story using the second ending. In 2010 John told me his great uncle Will Agnew, who was originally from Virginia but lived in Atlanta for the last years of his life, told it to him. John recalled:

> The punch line was that the man who fell into the grave tried and tried to get out, but to no avail. Exhausted, he crumbled to the ground to catch his breath. From the other end of the grave came a voice, "It's no use. You can't get out."
> But he did.[2]

John had told me about hearing the story several years before our 2010 email exchange. I remember him saying that when he first heard the story he was so young he had to think about what that meant. Later, he could delight in the understatement as he heard the story again and again over the years. When I first began using the "He was wrong" ending, I thought I was using the exact ending John told me he had heard growing up. Based on our correspondence, I'm now inclined to believe the "He was wrong" ending was more inspired by (instead of taken from) John's discussion of the tale. Most adult audiences react to this brief ending. It also works well in most mixed-age audiences.

Ending 2 was the ending I used before John told me about his experience with the story. Now, I use the first ending, pause, and add information if there is little to no reaction or a mixed reaction from my audience. Usually, I also accompany the telling of the man leaving the grave with a gesture—picture starting with hands held horizontally, palm to palm, at around waist level. The lower hand stays in place to serve as the ground at the bottom of the grave. The upper hand rises quickly to illustrate the man jumping in fright. Once the hand rises, the arm can also be extended to suggest the man making a quick getaway. The timing goes something like this: During the "Aaah!" the hand goes up. The arm extends during the "and on his way home" (said at the same time as the arm extends). Sometimes I'll even use these gestures after the first ending, but not say a single word during the gestures.

Ending 3 is for audiences in need of a little more information before they begin laughing. I deliver it as a very understated afterthought. For audiences of elementary school children, this detail is sometimes just the bit of confirmation they need to help them accept the picture in their minds and laugh. My experience has been that listeners in homogeneous-aged audiences often react differently than the same aged listeners in a mixed-age audience.

Yes, listeners do indeed make a difference in how a story is retold. Sometimes they give me information, as John Benjamin did, which results in better future tellings. Other times, my observations of their reactions as they listen prompt the change needed to make the telling suit the particular audience in front of me.

TALL TALES
AND
OUTRIGHT LIES

Tall tales "weigh the delicate balance between truth and untruth in favor of untruth"[1] and rely on outrageous exaggeration and lying for comic effect.[2]

In this section, you'll find stories about real people—Daniel Boone, Otis Ayers, Ivan Petrovich Pavlov, and my four brothers. You'll find stories about real events—the Meade County Fair, Halloween, and presidential elections. You'll find stories that take place in our real world—in the woods, on the farm.

Most importantly, for tall tales, you'll find stories with truth stretched to impossibility. And if after reading them you believe them, "go stand on your right eyebrow."[3]

DANIEL BOONE ON THE HUNT

Back in Daniel Boone's day, if you wanted meat to eat you had to go hunt it yourself. Fortunately Daniel Boone was a skilled hunter and an intelligent man.

One day Daniel Boone was out hunting, and he met up with a bear. Now Daniel Boone was not hunting for bear, so he was not especially pleased to see a bear. From what I hear, the bear was not especially pleased to see Daniel Boone either. That bear charged Daniel Boone. Fortunately Daniel was about fifty yards away from the bear when it charged, so he figured he had a head start. He turned his back on that bear and he began to run.

Now you may doubt my claim that Daniel Boone was intelligent when I tell you he ran from a bear. Rest assured, he knew people cannot outrun bears, and he was not trying to outrun the bear. He simply figured those fifty yards would give him enough time to find a tree he could easily climb, and that's what he did. Daniel Boone swung himself up into a tree and started climbing.

"Now, wait just a minute," you may be thinking, "bears can climb trees." You are correct. Bears can climb trees, and Daniel Boone knew that—I told you he was an intelligent man. As Daniel climbed up the tree he knew it would not be long until the bear would be climbing up after him, so he prepared. Daniel Boone was not only a skilled hunter and an intelligent man; he was also a resourceful man.

Daniel Boone didn't do a thing but sit straddle on a limb with his back to the trunk of the tree. Then he wrapped his legs around the tree trunk and dropped forward beside the limb, so he was hanging from the tree—upside down, legs holding onto the trunk, arms dangling. Daniel watched, and sure enough, it wasn't long before the bear reached the tree, took one look up at Daniel, and started climbing toward him.

Daniel Boone was not only an intelligent man and a resourceful man; he was also a patient man. He held his hands up near his shoulders and he watched the bear climb closer and closer. Oh, he was a patient man!

Finally the bear was within biting distance of Daniel, and when the bear opened its mouth to take a big bite out of Daniel Boone, folks say Daniel Boone didn't do a thing but run his fist down the bear's throat, all the way through the bear, and out the other end. Daniel Boone grabbed the bear's tail, gave it a big yank, and turned that bear inside out. Then he let go, and the inside out bear ran right down the tree.

I've heard those inside out bears don't live long, so Daniel Boone never needed to worry about that bear again.

COMMENTARY

ATU Tale Type 1889B Hunter
Turns Animal Inside Out

I have been completely unsuccessful in locating the source of this tale or remembering how the tale came to be in my telling repertoire, and yet, I am quite confident I did not make it up, but read a tale of the inside out bear somewhere. I can verify the basic tale exists in Kentucky folklore because there are at least four versions in the Leonard Roberts Collection.[1]

While I'm not sure how I first encountered the tale, I do know that the repetition built on stating an attribute (skilled hunter, intelligent, resourceful, and patient man), then following with an action that calls the attribute into question, developed over time in front of audiences. In the telling, when I call an attribute into question there are inevitably nods of agreement in the audience from folks who are having that same thought. This pattern developed based on a telling at a school when I heard audience members whispering, "But bears can climb trees!" and I responded to that whisper. Eventually, I began to incorporate the audience doubt into the telling deliberately. It makes for a fun, yet subtle, give and take between teller and listeners.

FARMER BROWN'S CROP

Folks say Farmer Brown was a pretty good farmer, and like most farmers he was also a practical man. One year, he decided to plant his corn and his pumpkins in the same field. The way he saw it, he and his hardworking plow horse would have a bit less ground to plow, and the leaves on the pumpkin vines would shade out the weeds so there would be no need to hoe out the corn either.

That spring he plowed his cropland. Then he planted corn and pumpkins. Oh, good fortune was with him! The ground stayed warm. Soft spring rains came, and Farmer Brown knew corn and pumpkins were sprouting. One day, he saw tiny green shoots poking up out of the ground. He was delighted. Every few days he visited his field. Soon he noticed that all the shoots were just alike. They were all pumpkin plants, with no corn in sight. But he didn't give up. He just figured the corn needed more time to sprout than the pumpkins. Day after day he watched. The pumpkin vines grew rapidly, but the corn never appeared. Farmer Brown considered replanting his corn. But he soon realized that if he worked through his field replanting his corn, he would trample the vines and destroy the pumpkins. So, he decided he would simply be satisfied with growing pumpkins instead of corn.

Those pumpkins grew and grew. Farmer Brown was justifiably proud of his fine crop of pumpkins. Finally harvest time came. One morning Farmer Brown hitched his plow horse to the wagon and the two of them headed out to the field to harvest the pumpkins.

By noon Farmer Brown had harvested a whole wagonload of pumpkins. When he headed to the house for dinner, he left the wagon by his corncrib. He figured after dinner he'd put his pumpkins in there. After all, he'd grown no corn and he needed a good place to store his pumpkins. But he selected one pumpkin to take up to the house so Mrs. Farmer Brown could make him a pumpkin pie for supper.

After dinner, Farmer Brown headed out to his corncrib to unload pumpkins. Mrs. Farmer Brown took out her largest kitchen knife and some old newspapers. She spread the newspapers on her kitchen table and set the pumpkin on top. Then she cut off the top of the pumpkin. But instead of slimy strings of pumpkin innards and pumpkin seeds, she discovered the pumpkin was filled with corn. Not corn on the cob, mind you, but shelled corn.

She ran for the porch, hollering, "Farmer Brown, Farmer Brown, come back up here. You are not going to believe what's in your pumpkin!"

Don't you know every single pumpkin from that crop contained nearly two bushels of shelled corn! It ended up being one of the best corn crops Farmer Brown had ever grown.

Mrs. Farmer Brown's pumpkin pie won a blue ribbon at the county fair that summer. The judges declared it "pumpkin through and through with just a hint of corn." When her friends asked her for her recipe, she told them about Farmer Brown's corn crop, but they simply refused to believe it. They said, "If you don't want to share your recipe, just say so. There's no call for you to make up such a big lie." Poor Mrs. Farmer Brown! Even now a couple of her former friends do not speak to her because they believe she lied rather than share the real secret of her prize-winning pumpkin pie.

COMMENTARY

"Farmer Brown's Crop" is retold from "The Bushel of Corn,"[1] collected by Leonard Roberts from J. B. Calton of Mary Helen, Harlan County, Kentucky. The story as collected runs three short paragraphs, as follows:

The Bushel of Corn

One day there was a farmer who planted his corn and pumpkins together. His pumpkins came up big and fat, but the corn never came up.

He picked the pumpkins and put them in the storehouse but the corn never came up.

One day he wanted pumpkin pie, and he cut one of the pumpkins open and there was a bushel of corn in each pumpkin.

*   *   *

How I moved from those three paragraphs to the story I now tell, I do not know. I do know that my audiences for this story are mostly school children who are not living on farms, and so do seem to benefit from a more detailed description of the planting and growing process. I also recall that the first time I ever mentioned "Mrs. Farmer Brown" someone laughed, so she became a keeper. In addition, from growing up on a farm, I am well aware that shelled corn would be even more valuable than corn on the cob, and would make an even more amazing lie.

The story also has two endings. Sometimes I will end it with the statement about every pumpkin containing shelled corn. Other times, when the audience seems especially interested in Mrs. Farmer Brown and time permits, I'll add the segment about the pumpkin pie contest.

HUNTING ALONE

One morning, a man took his gun and his dog and he went hunting. He'd been out quite a while when he and his dog heard some rustling in the underbrush. They looked and spotted a possum heading home. Well, the dog dove right through a thicket following that possum. By the time the man had made his way through the thicket, the possum had sought refuge in a hollow log. There the man's dog stood, at the big end of the log. He looked up at the man, then into the log, then up at the man again, and barked, as if to say, "Shall I go get it?"

The man sized up the log and thought: "I'm skinny. I can scoot into this log and get it myself." So he sent his dog down to guard the small end of the log. The man leaned his gun up against a tree, got down on all fours, and crawled into the log.

He could hear the possum up ahead of him. The scurrying grew louder, so he knew he was gaining on it. But the log became a bit smaller, so he had to hunker down more, moving along on his elbows, but he could tell he was gaining on the possum, so he kept right on going. Then he stretched one arm out, and he grabbed the possum's tail.

But just as he grabbed the possum's tail, the possum scrunched up and pulled his tail right out of the man's grasp. The man thought: "Oh no, you are not getting away from me that easy." He pushed with his feet and pulled with his fingers, inched himself forward, and again he grabbed the possum's tail.

This time he got a firm hold on that possum. "Gotcha! You're not getting away from me now," and the man started to back out of the log. It was then he made an important discovery: "I'm stuck. I am stuck."

And sure enough, the man was indeed stuck. No matter how hard he tried, he could not back out of that log. All he could do was lay there thinking: "I am in big trouble. My wife always told me not to go hunting alone, but I've always told her hunting alone is the best way to make sure you won't get shot. Now, here I am.

"No one knows I'm in here but my dog. That dog's no Lassie dog; he'll just go on home when he gets hungry.

"Even if someone happens to find my gun, they won't think to look inside this log.

"My wife is going to be so mad at me. She's going to think I've run off. But I'm going to die here. This is pitiful.

"Someday this log will disintegrate and here I'll be, the skeleton of a man hanging on to the skeleton of a possum. It's pathetic."

He thought about all he had done during his life. Then he remembered how he had voted in the last presidential election, and that memory made him feel so small he just stood up and walked right out of that log.

COMMENTARY

My telling is retold from the story "Half Pint,"[1] collected by Leonard Roberts from Walton T. Saylor of Whitley County, Kentucky, in 1956. Saylor reports that it was told by Uncle Charlie Day of Lida, Laurel County, Kentucky. "Half Pint" includes another incident establishing the intelligence of Charlie Day's dog Old Trail (able to smell the trail of a rabbit from a year before and track it down) before the incident with the possum in the hollow log. In the collected story, Uncle Charlie thinks of the benefits of catching the possum before entering the log. Once stuck he recalls all the mean things he had done, with the topper being "he had crossed over and voted the democrat ticket." Another version of the tale, collected by Lena Ratliff from Wrigley, Kentucky, in 1960 from Boon Hall, also from Wrigley, does not include politics. Instead the fellow simply thinks of all the little things he had done in his life, and those little things make him feel small so he shrinks.[2]

In my retelling, the hunter thinks about various aspects of his life, makes a reference to Lassie that baby boomers in my audience react to, and simply remembers how he voted in the last presidential election. As a life-long McGovern-style Democrat, I just could not have him feel bad about voting for the Democratic ticket, but I also wanted the story to be enjoyed by all, so not mentioning the specifics of his vote gives everyone in the audience room to interpret his actions their own way. Of course, I can also vary the election mentioned from presidential to gubernatorial, depending on the place and time of the telling. One of the most fun parts of telling the story in person is the time spent holding one arm outstretched beside my head, mimicking the position of the man in the log while recounting his past memories. Just holding that position also adds to the humor for the listeners.

A few years ago, I told this tale in Florida[3] and met a former Kentuckian, Alson Adkins. Adkins was born in 1942 and grew up in McKee, Jackson County, Kentucky. He had heard a version of the story about 1953, when he spent some time traveling with his grandfather, visiting his grandfather's customers. Alson said it was his grandfather's farewell tour, but as a youngster he had not realized that his grandfather knew he was near death at the time. In the version Alson heard on that journey, a raccoon ran up inside a hollow tree and the person got stuck climbing up after it. When the man recalled voting for Adlai Stevenson for president, he felt so little he fell out.

OTIS AYERS HAD A DOG—TWO STORIES

1

Folks say Otis Ayers had the best quail-hunting dog around. One day Otis and his dog were out hunting when a covey of quail fluttered up and took shelter in an old hollow stump. His dog ran over, jumped up, put his paws over the exit of that stump to block the quail in, and then looked up at Otis and grinned.

Otis was delighted, "Oh, Dog, we're going to have us a fancy hunt! When I say, 'Pull!' you let one loose."

The dog woofed in agreement.

"Pull!" yelled Otis. His dog let one quail loose, and Otis shot it.

"Pull!" Again the dog let a single quail go.

Over and over, "Pull!"

Bang!

"Pull!"

Bang!

"Pull!" But the dog didn't move. Otis was surprised. He knew there were more quail in the stump. So he said, "Oh, come on Dog. We've been having a good time. I said Pull." Still the dog would not move.

Then Otis noticed his dog was not looking at him, but seemed to be looking at something just behind him. Otis turned around and standing there was the game warden. Sure enough, Otis had shot the legally allowed limit of quail, and that dog of his was not about to let Otis get himself in trouble with the law! Now, that's a good dog.

2

Folks say one time Otis Ayers had a real good bird dog, but he lost it. It seems he and his prize bird dog were out hunting, when the dog disappeared. Otis looked and looked for his dog, but could not find it.

Finally, he had to give up and head on home. He figured the dog would surely come home when it got hungry, but it didn't.

The next year, Otis went out hunting in that same area. He was making his way through some tall weeds when he came upon his dog. Or, at least, he came upon the skeleton of his dog, bones still standing, still holding a point. Otis followed his dog's point, and sure enough, he found the skeletons of a whole covey of quail.

COMMENTARY

Both stories related to ATU Tale Type 1920F* Skillful Hounds

Tale 2 also related to ATU Tale Type 1889N The Long Hunt

I heard both of these tales from Butch Thompson, who was working the sound at an event at Doe Run Inn, in Meade County, Kentucky, in 1992. He heard these stories from Otis Ayers, who was a retired river boat captain who had worked for American Barge Lines.

Otis and his wife, Susie, were good friends of Butch's parents. Otis and Susie had no children, but they always did lots of things for Butch. Susie even gave Butch his nickname. Both families had houseboats, camped on weekends together, and liked to pull practical jokes in a respectful way. As a teenager, Butch reports, he enjoyed being around them. Butch heard Otis tell these stories many times over the years. Butch also heard stories about Otis's adventures on the river and other hunting escapades. While all the stories were tall tales, Otis always told them with an absolutely straight face, as if reporting facts.

I could tell from talking with Butch that Otis Ayers must have been a fine storyteller. When I asked about variations in the telling, Butch acknowledged that Otis always kept the gist of the story, but naturally varied the words some from telling to telling.[1]

Another version of the first "Otis Ayers Had a Dog" story can be found in *The Harvest and the Reapers: Oral Traditions in Kentucky*, by Kenneth and Mary Clarke. The story is recounted as an example of a tale told "in the big lie tradition." In this version, a beagle herds quail into a groundhog hole and lets them out one at a time. There is no mention of the game warden episode. According to the book notes, this narrative would have come "from the Western Kentucky University

Folklore and Folklife Collection or from the authors' manuscripts of Kentucky folktales."[2]

Another version of the second "Otis Ayers Had a Dog" story was reported to Leonard Roberts by Cleadia Hall, of Knox County, Kentucky, in 1956.[3]

Before working on this book I would have told you that I retell these stories pretty much the way Butch told them to me. However, when I interviewed Butch, I learned the person who owned the dogs was Otis Ayers, not Otis Haynes—the name I had mistakenly been giving him. I've now changed back to the real name because, as Butch observed, it would be wonderful for these stories and Otis Ayers, the man who delighted in telling them, to be remembered. I agree.[4]

SOME DOG

When I was a child growing up on the farm in Meade County, it seemed to us that city folks were all the time taking kittens and puppies they didn't want and dropping them off at the end of farmers' driveways. We couldn't imagine why city folks thought we wanted their pets if they didn't want them, but boxes and bags of kittens and puppies showed up so often we just thought: must be how city folks' minds work.

So, it's not surprising that one day, when my daddy and my four brothers, Steve, Alan, David, and Jeff, were on their way in from the fields, there at the bottom of the driveway was a cardboard box. My brothers started begging right off, "Oh, Daddy, can we keep it? Can we keep it?"

Daddy said, "Boys, let's see what's in the box first. Then we can decide."

On this particular day, the box held four pups. My daddy looked them over, and he could see those pups had paws that were extra large for their bodies. He knew that meant those pups were part hound dog, and that meant that at least one of them might grow up to be a halfway decent hunting dog. So he said, "All right, boys, if you can divide them up without fighting over them, they're yours."

My four brothers were as pleased as any four boys have ever been. Each one of them had his very own pup. Then tragedy struck. First, my oldest brother Steve's pup disappeared without a trace. Next, Alan's. Then David's. Gone. My youngest brother, Jeff, was panic-stricken. He went to my folks saying, "Please, please let me bring my pup inside. I've got to sleep with it. I've got to be with it every moment of every day or something's going to happen to it. Please? Please, let me bring it inside."

Daddy said, "Jeff, you are growing up on a farm. And you know how it is here on the farm. Animals are not allowed inside this house. Well, maybe a sick calf or a little runt pig could move into the basement to be bottle fed until it's well enough to go back out, but cats and dogs are not allowed inside this house."

Jeff knew that was true, but he couldn't give up. He started in begging and pleading, pleading and begging, begging and pleading, pleading and begging, begging and pleading, pleading and begging, begging, pleading, pleading, begging, begging, pleading, pleading, begging—are you getting tired of reading¹ this? Then you know why this works on some parents. Finally, it even worked on my daddy.

"Jeff, if you are willing to take one of Mama's throw rugs, throw it down there on the basement floor, and sleep on that rug with your pup, it can come inside. But Jeff, if that pup so much as whimpers and keeps any of the rest of us awake, back out it goes."

Jeff was pleased. He got himself one of Mama's throw rugs, threw it down on the basement floor, and slept on that floor with his pup. Those first few nights Jeff just patted his pup, and patted it, and patted it, until it drifted off to sleep without making a sound. Then Jeff remembered how he liked to read to help himself go to sleep, so he started reading to his pup. It didn't take long for Jeff to figure out his pup's favorite books were books about dogs. So Jeff started going to the library and checking out every dog story he could find. He read dog story after dog story to his pup, and when the dogs in the books were doing brave exciting things, that little pup's tail would just wag, wag, wag, and he would drift off to sleep, dreaming all kinds of brave, puppy dog dreams.

One night, our whole family was awakened by "Arooo, aroo, aroo, aroo!"

My daddy jumped out of bed. He headed downstairs, "Jeff, I told you—" and he stopped. There on that rug was my little brother, Jeff, tears just streaming down his cheeks. Sitting right there beside him was the pup, looking equally pitiful. Daddy saw the book Jeff had been reading to his pup that night was none other than *Old Yeller*. He shook his head, "I tell you. That pup is going to grow up to be some dog." Then he went on back upstairs.

Jeff said, "Pup, did you hear that? Daddy says you're going to grow up to be some dog. I believe that's a name you could grow into. What do you think?" The pup stuck out his tongue, licked a tear off my little brother's cheek, and that is how Some Dog got his name.

Some Dog really was some dog. Jeff and Some Dog stayed together all day every day. One day they were playing in the tall weeds on the

hill between the barn and the pond down below, when Jeff lost sight of
Some Dog. And then he heard, "Aar! Aar, aar, aar!" Jeff came running,
and there was Some Dog, his toenails dug into the bank of the pond
trying to hold himself on shore. Hanging on to the other end of Some
Dog, pulling hard on Some Dog's tail, was a gigantic turtle.

Jeff ran down there, grabbed hold of Some Dog, and started pulling against that gigantic turtle, yelling, "Help! Help, help, help. Help!"
David ran down and grabbed a leg of the gigantic turtle to keep it on
shore. Alan ran down and he, too, grabbed a leg to keep the gigantic
turtle on shore.

Steve ran down, sized up the situation, and yelled, "Hang on boys.
I'll get the tractor. We're going to need chains." Steve drove the tractor
down to the pond. They wrapped chains around the legs of the gigantic
turtle and pulled with the whole weight of the tractor to try to keep
the gigantic turtle from making off with Some Dog. Now, my brothers
did everything they could think of to try to make that gigantic turtle
let go of Some Dog, and it is a disgusting thing to have to tell you, but
finally they had to take an axe and behead the turtle. Yes, it was messy,
but Some Dog was saved. Oh, his tail was a bit mangled, but he was
going to be all right.

Now, I don't know what kind of family you grew up in, but I did
not grow up in a wasteful family. With that gigantic turtle we had one
huge harvesting and eating problem. You might think eating up a gigantic turtle would be sort of like trying to use up all the leftover turkey
after Thanksgiving, but it's worse. It's more like dealing with zucchini
in August. But we were up to the task.

My mom, my sister, and I got out our recipe books and we started
cooking and eating our way through the gigantic turtle. We ate turtle à
la king, broiled turtle, turtle croquettes, turtle dip, turtle étouffée, fricas-
seed turtle, turtle gumbo, turtle hash, turtle ice cream. We put up about
a half-dozen jars of turtle's foot jelly. We've been kind of afraid to taste
that jelly, but we weren't wasteful; we've still got all six jars. One day,
we took sticks, sharpened up the ends of them, slid on a chunk of turtle
meat, green pepper, onion, turtle meat, green pepper, onion, turtle meat,
green pepper, onion, and put one of those little cherry tomatoes on the
end. Then we fired up the grill and grilled ourselves turtle kabobs. They
were delicious. My mama made several recipes of turtle loaf, and she put
them in the freezer so we could eat them come winter. We ate Mornay

turtle and turtle noodle bake. Many a morning, we sat down to turtle omelets. At suppertime, we ate turtle pot pies. When company came over, we fed them all turtle quiche—they did not know the difference. We ate roast turtle, turtle soup, turtle turtles. One night we got real fancy—put tablecloths on the table, lit candles, and sat down to turtle under glass. We preceded that with some kind of cold, soupy looking stuff called turtle vichyssoise. We didn't like it, but we tried.

My daddy, a near genius, harvested out of that turtle a lifetime supply of Turtle Wax. My mama, another near genius, harvested out of the turtle a lifetime supply of turtle extract. It's one tiny bottle, no taller than three inches, but since we have yet to locate a recipe calling for turtle extract, we remain confident that one tiny bottle does indeed constitute a lifetime supply. On the mornings we didn't sit down to turtle omelets, we got out the blender and whirled up turtle yogurt breakfast shakes. They were delicious. And we contributed to the demise of our second greatest harvesting problem by devising a recipe for turtle-stuffed zucchini.

The shell of the gigantic turtle was recycled into a boat. When their chores were done my four brothers and Some Dog would float on various ponds on the property in their turtle shell boat. One day, they were floating on the very pond where Some Dog almost met his maker, when all of a sudden their whole turtle shell boat started to lift up out of the water. Alan was the first to assess the gravity of the situation. He yelled, "Boys, we best abandon ship!" They all headed for shore, Jeff hanging on to Some Dog for all he was worth. They climbed out on the bank and looked back just in time to see the head of an even larger turtle grab their turtle shell boat in its mouth and pull it underneath the water.

My brothers went up to the house. They told my daddy what they had seen. Daddy studied on it a bit. "Boys, sounds to me like the turtle that grabbed your turtle shell boat must have been the mama of the turtle that almost made off with Some Dog. I reckon that mama had been looking for her child. And when you all were out there today, she must have looked up and thought: 'There's my child. Just got itself turned over and can't flip back. I'll go help it.' And I reckon now she's taken that child of hers down to the nest to be with its brothers and sisters."

My four brothers thought about what Daddy had said. And if it was as true as it appeared to be, it meant that pond was the most dangerous place on our entire farm. Since they were the ones who uncovered the danger, they felt it was their responsibility to make that pond safe. They considered a wide variety of options and concluded that going head to head in combat with gigantic turtles was not one of the better ones. After much consideration, they decided the proper course of action would be to clear-cut every bit of vegetation a good distance back all the way around the circumference of that pond so those gigantic turtles wouldn't have any cover. So that's what they did.

Every day my brothers would take their hoes down to the pond. Three of my four brothers would be chopping back everything in sight while the fourth stood watch for gigantic turtles. One day, at noontime, when my brothers went up to the house for dinner, one of those boys left his hoe down there at the pond resting blade up. I don't know which one because not a one of them has ever owned up to it.

Now, I don't know if you've ever done any farming or gardening, but one of the first things you learn is that you ought not leave a hoe resting blade up. If you have to leave a hoe out in the open, you lean it up against the side of a building or up against a fence post—somewhere where you will remember where you left it. If there's nothing to lean it against, you leave it resting blade down. My brothers knew that, but one of them forgot.

After they'd eaten their dinner, they headed back down to the pond to work. Some Dog was with them. He was always with them. There he was running along, intent on being the first one back down there, and before anybody could see what was going to happen, holler "stop," or take any other preventive measure, Some Dog had run right through that upturned hoe blade. He sliced himself from the end of his nose right through to the tip of his tail, and there he was in two pieces.

Jeff was the first one to come up on him, and he started wailing, "Oh! Look what happened to my dog! Look what happened to my dog!"

David was next, "Jeff, I'm going to be an animal doctor when I grow up, and I'm going to be a good one. I just got my first patient. Alan, give me your shirt." David slapped Some Dog back together, took Alan's shirt, wrapped it around Some Dog, picked Some Dog up, and headed for the house. He stopped off at the tobacco barn. Old folks will tell you that tobacco on the outside cures just about anything. David took big, long tobacco leaves, wrapped them around Some Dog, and then slid him inside a burlap bag.

Next David stopped off at the kerosene barrel. Old folks will tell you the same thing about the curative powers of kerosene. He dunked Some Dog in the kerosene a few times, slid him inside another burlap bag, and then headed on into the house. "Mama, Some Dog has suffered a serious injury. He's got to take up residence in the basement again." And Some Dog was back downstairs.

David would sit by that burlap bundle and say, "Some Dog, I'm going to be a veterinarian when I grow up, and I'm going to be a good one. You're my first patient. You've just got to get well. Come on Some Dog, you've got to make it." He was sure he could hear a faint, "ouw, ouw-ouw."

Jeff would go downstairs. He would sit by that burlap bundle and read books about brave dogs who survived tremendous hardships. And when those dogs were at their bravest, he was pretty sure he too could hear a faint, "ouw, ouw-ouw."

At last the day dawned when David declared Some Dog was as well as Some Dog was ever going to get, so our whole family assembled for the great unveiling. Now, I need to take a moment here and tell you my brother David really did grow up to be a veterinarian. He was part of a practice in Hardinsburg. That's in Breckinridge County, just one county over from Meade County where we grew up. He was a real good veterinarian, and folks there still do miss him. For reasons I won't go into here, he left his veterinary practice and became a people doctor, and now he lives in E'town, where he delivers babies. Now, I'm not telling you all this to brag on my brother, even though going to both veterinary school and medical school is quite an accomplishment. Instead, I'm telling you this because I don't want you to hold what I'm going to tell you next against him. Some Dog's injury was serious, and David hadn't had any medical training at the time. He actually wasn't even in high school yet.

Let's take a moment away from the story here so you can ask yourself: Are you certified in first aid? Do you know how to put on a Band-Aid? Those of you who could only answer yes to that second question have skills approximately equal to David's at the time of Some Dog's injury, so I know you'll understand how this next part of the story happened.

Some Dog's injury was serious, and it seems David must have panicked and worked just a bit too fast. Yes, he saved Some Dog's life and got him back together, but with two legs pointing up and two legs pointing down. Yet, this was not a tragedy.

Some Dog won the most unusual pet contest at the Meade County Fair three years in a row. That third year he was the only contestant—wouldn't anybody else pay any entry fees to enter their pets. Some folks went to the Fair Board and complained, "That dog those Hamilton boys are entering is not unusual. That dog is unnatural, and there is a difference!"

Well, the Fair Board had to agree because they weren't collecting any entry fees, so they presented Some Dog with a lifetime unusual pet certificate and named Some Dog the leader of the Meade County Fair Pet Parade. Some Dog proved an excellent pet parade leader. You see, previous pet parade leaders would sometimes take a notion to rest, and go sit on the curb a spell. It doesn't take much imagination to see how that could ruin a parade. But Some Dog? He never needed to rest. If the two legs he was walking on got tired, he'd just flip himself over and keep going on the other two.

The same untiring quality that made Some Dog a superb Meade County Fair Pet Parade leader also made Some Dog an outstanding hunting dog. He could stay out on the hunt longer than any other dogs. He could stay out longer than any of my brothers really wanted to be out with him. But then they discovered that as much as Some Dog liked to hunt, he still liked stories more. All they had to do was take a book, shake it in his direction, and call, "Some Dog, come on over here. I'll read you a story," and Some Dog would come right in off the hunt.

About this time, the oldest of my four brothers, Steve, headed off to Meade County High School. About this same time, Meade County High School decided to upgrade its social studies curriculum by offering a class called psychology. Now Steve had always been real smart and he figured a class that ended in -ology sounded like something a smart person ought to take, so he signed up. Really early on in that psychology class, Steve learned about a person by the name of Pavlov. It seems this Pavlov fellow had himself a bunch of dogs, and every time he fed his dogs he would ring a bell. It got so Pavlov could ring that bell and his dogs would start to slobber even if there wasn't any food there. Now Steve thought it was pitiful, pitiful, that anybody could get to be world-wide famous, the way this Pavlov fellow did, for teaching dogs how to slobber. I don't know how dogs are where you live, but in Meade County slobbering is an inborn doggie gift—no training required. Nevertheless, Steve grasped the training principles and decided to use them to teach Some Dog.

Because Some Dog was so untiring, Steve set his first goal as teaching Some Dog how to hunt independently. Some of you may be thinking, so what, dogs hunt independently all the time. You would be correct, except the human hunter is only allowed to shoot the animal that is in season for hunting at the time. So Steve would hold up a picture of an animal, "Some Dog, you see this picture?"

Some Dog would look at the picture, "Woof."

"This is the animal that's in season. You go get it, and run it back by the back porch. We'll wait for you to run it by."

Some Dog would say, "Woof," and then he'd run off, and he wouldn't come back until he could run by the back porch the animal that was in season at the time.

Some Dog did so well with the pictures that Steve took to gluing the pictures on a calendar. He would hold up a calendar and say, "Some Dog, you see this square. That stands for today."

Some Dog would say, "Woof."

"And you see back here, this square with the picture on it. That's the animal that is in season. It's going to be in season until you see it on this other square with a big X over the top of it."

"Woof."

"So, this is today. This animal is in season. Now, you go get it. We'll wait for you to run it by."

Some Dog would take off, and my brothers would wait for him to run the right animal by. Some Dog did so well with the pictures on the calendar, my brothers put one of those huge wall chart calendars down on the wall inside Some Dog's dog house. When Some Dog would come up to the house of a morning, one of my brothers would say, "Hey Some Dog, you want to hunt? Go ahead; I'll wait for you to run something by."

Some Dog would say, "Woof." He'd run down to his dog house, check his calendar, see what was legal, "Woof." He would take off and not come back until he could run the right animal by.

Everything went real well until along about November 1st or November 2nd. Some Dog came up to the house one morning. One of my brothers said, "You want to hunt? Go ahead. I'll wait for you to run something by."

Some Dog went down to his dog house, checked his calendar, and he took off. Several hours later we received a phone call from a farmer who lived a good distance away. "You all need to come get your dog. Now, I know it's yours. It's got two legs up and two legs down and nobody else around here has a dog like that. I don't know what's wrong with it, but I believe your dog has lost its mind. It's out here barking at the remains of my pumpkin patch and carrying on something awful."

We all went to get the dog, and for a while everybody sat on the back porch staring at everybody else, until somebody said, "Why don't we go check his calendar?" Remember I told you this happened along about November 1st, November 2nd? Sure enough, back on October 31 for Halloween Day there had been a picture of some pumpkins. Some Dog was just hunting what he knew to be legal.

My brothers said, "Oh, it's a good thing we figured this out before Thanksgiving. Turkey farmers would have been upset with us."

"And look yonder, on Christmas Day, there's a picture of an evergreen tree. I'd hate to think how Some Dog would have tried to herd home a tree." My brothers took little pieces of paper, covered up all those holiday symbols, and Some Dog didn't have any more trouble.

Some Dog was smart. He could hunt independently, in season, so Steve decided to raise his training one more notch by teaching Some Dog how to hunt by specified size. My brothers did this by leaning up against the back porch wall the pelt board that corresponded to the size of the animal Some Dog was to bring back. Smaller pelt boards for smaller animals. Larger pelt boards for larger animals.

Some Dog would come up to the house of a morning. If he saw a pelt board leaning up against the back porch wall, he'd know it was a hunting day. He'd note the size, "Woof." Then he'd go down to his dog house, check his calendar, "Woof." Then off he'd go, and he wouldn't come back until he could run by the back porch the animal legally allowed to be hunted and of the size specified by the size of the pelt board leaning up against the back porch wall.

It was a superb system, and it would have been foolproof too. Except, one hot July day my mama decided it was entirely too hot to do her ironing inside the house. Now Some Dog was brilliant. I know if my mama had set her iron on the back porch first, or strung her extension cord out the kitchen window first, Some Dog would never have been confused. But the first thing my mama carried out to the back porch was her ironing board. And she didn't set it up for ironing. No, she just leaned it up against the back porch wall in the very spot where my brothers usually set their pelt boards.

Some Dog came up to the house that morning. He saw the ironing board and thought it was a pelt board, "Woof!" He ran down to his dog house to see what was legal. Folks, in Meade County, Kentucky, in the middle of July the only animal legally allowed to be hunted are groundhogs. Some Dog said, "Woof?!?" and he took off.

Now, none of us were on the back porch to see which way he went. We managed to piece together what had happened when he turned up missing and we realized where the ironing board had been. So, far as I know, he could be all the way to where you are by now. If you should happen to see him, now he is going to be easy to spot, he's got two legs up and two legs down, not many dogs are like that. If you should happen to see him, please call him off the hunt. Remember, all you have to do is get a book, shake it in his direction, and say, "Hey, Some Dog, come on over here. I'll read you a story." And if you don't mind, we'd really appreciate it if you'd make the book you choose be something like *Lassie Come-Home*, so Some Dog will be reminded of us. We sure do miss him.

COMMENTARY

ATU Tale Type 1960 The Great Animal or Great Object

ATU Tale Type 1889L The Split Dog

Some Dog is a story I developed in 1991, in preparation for potential bookings during Kentucky's bicentennial celebrations in 1992. I knew that if I wanted to present programs that reflected the variety of Kentucky's narrative traditions, I needed a tall tale in my repertoire. Tales of amazing dogs and incredible hunting exploits are the common Kentucky-collected tall tales, not the tall tales of human heroes like Pecos Bill and Paul Bunyan I had learned about in elementary school. Fortunately, I found the tall tales of amazing dogs especially appealing. But I struggled with the tall tale telling tradition of first-person storytelling. Although I did indeed grow up on a farm, I've never hunted in my life. Also, Kentucky-collected tall tales were usually told by men. One day it dawned on me that I have four brothers. The hero dog in the story could belong to them, which would allow me to tell the story in first person while talking about what happened to my brothers and their dog. That decision got me over my only major hurdle in developing this tale.

After spending time reading and thinking about many Kentucky-collected tall tales, there were two that really captured me. One was a gigantic turtle segment of a much larger tale, attributed to Ted Middleton.[2] The other tale was a brief mention of a dog so smart it could hunt by specified size given the size of the pelt board set out for it. One day when an ironing board was put in the pelt board's place, the dog ran off and was never heard from again. This was attributed to high school students in Whitesburg, Letcher County, Kentucky.[3] The longer story of the big turtle first recounts the tale of a catfish so huge you could not see all of it at once, but you could know which pool of water in the creek the fish was in because the water level changed depending on where the fish was. Attempts to catch this fish, first with a high-powered rifle, then with a three-foot fishhook made from a wagon rod attached to fishing line made of bailing wire, eventually succeeded. In the story an amazing ox used to try to drag the catfish (which turns out to be the turtle) from the creek almost drowns and has to be rescued by the narrator. A second ox is brought in and before the turtle can drown both of them, the oxen manage to haul the turtle out and wedge it between two trees. Folks use logging chains to hold the turtle and a crosscut saw to behead it.

The meat from the turtle is described as follows:

"You know turtles have all kinds of meat in them, chicken, duck, fish, cow, hog, and every kind of meat there is, and make awful good eating. We had every kind of meat for weeks after that, eat chicken meat 'till we got tired of it, then have beef, then fish, then quail, just whatever we took a notion to have. We give lots of it to neighbors, everybody had every kind of meat 'round there the rest of the year."[4]

The shell of the turtle becomes a boat:

"Well, you know, that turtle shell laid 'round there on the bank of the River for a long time, possums and other wild animals eat it out clean. I was down there one day and saw it would make a good boat. I got four or five of the boys who lived 'round up there to help me, and we turned it over and put it in the River. It was the best and biggest boat ever on Poor Fork. Twenty people or more could ride in it. It was really too big for Poor Fork, big as it was even in them days."[5]

Later, when using the boat, the following happens:

"... and all of a sudden like something started pushing it up outten the water, and then it started pulling it down under the water. Me and Bill jumped outten it and swum to the bank to save our lives. When I got to the shore I looked back and saw something grab it in its teeth and pull it under the water, and it was gone. Never saw it again."[6]

When one of the loafers listening to Middleton tell the story asks if he has any idea what took the shell underwater, Middleton offers this explanation. "... turtles hatch out early in the Spring. They don't get their growth for a long time, and the mother turtle looks after them just like anything else 'till the young 'uns get big 'nough to look atter themselves. That was a real young turtle we caught, he wasn't weaned, and his mother had been looking for him, and when she saw that shell turned upside down she thought the baby turtle had got over on its back and couldn't turn back over. She straightened it out, and took it back to the nest where the other young 'uns was. Taint no way ever knowing how big its mother was, I just saw its head when it took the shell in its mouth."[7]

Those were the segments from the turtle tall tale that fit my sense of humor and captured my imagination. I laughed over the idea of different kinds of meat. Then I told an early version of "Some Dog" to other storytellers at Tale Talk, a monthly storytelling group I participated in when I lived in Louisville.[8] One of the listeners commented that he had always heard that different parts of a turtle taste like different other kinds of meat. I thought: "Shoot, I thought every bit of that was exaggeration, not just the quantity of meat." So, I rejected using the different types of meat and replaced that with the turtle recipes. To come up with the various turtle dishes, I sat down with my cookbooks and poured over the indexes, until I had an A–Z list. Go back and look in the story—you'll see that's exactly what it is, with elaboration developed through repeated telling. By the way, this happened before the *Forest Gump* film came out in which one character frequently lists various shrimp dishes! I have been asked if I got the idea for the turtle recipes from the movie. No, I didn't. Did someone from the movie get the idea from me? I seriously doubt it!

When I read about the mama turtle retrieving the turtle shell boat, my mind immediately went to *Beowulf*, and I thought: "Whoa! This is just like Grendel's mother coming for revenge!" And I knew the "shell into boat with mother turtle retrieving it" was an idea I had to incorporate.

As mentioned earlier, I also liked the pelt board story, but how to connect it with the segments from the big turtle story? I had been aware of the split dog story for years.[9] I'd heard and read many versions of it, and I could verify that it had also been collected in Kentucky.[10] In most versions the dog runs fast and can bark from both ends. For a long time I resisted incorporating the split dog tale. Eventually I realized I could tie the two traditional tales I liked together if I would just allow myself to insert the split dog story in the middle. Yet, I was determined to come up with something different to say from what I'd read and heard in the past. After all, I knew the storytellers in my audiences would see the split dog segment coming from miles away, and I wanted them to have some payoff for not abandoning me during that segment. Somehow, the idea of an unusual pet contest hit me, and I was off and running with the three traditional tales woven together.

What about the rest of the "Some Dog" development? I really do have four brothers, and they act pretty much true to the personalities depicted in the story. In fact, I called each one up and told them the story as I worked on it to be sure they were okay with how they were being portrayed. During the phone call with my brother Steve (and yes, he is smart), he came up with the idea of Some Dog going after pumpkins, confused by holiday symbols on a giant wall calendar. I tried it; it worked, so I kept it. My brother David really was a veterinarian when the story was in development. He has since become an obstetrician. The setting is the farm I grew up on, so it is also real, complete with a tobacco barn and kerosene. Pets were never allowed in the house, only weak calves or runt pigs. And yes, some folks really do abandon their pets on farmers' driveways. So many of the story details are true—in keeping with the tall tale telling tradition of lies laced with just enough truth to keep listeners coming along.

There really is a Meade County Fair,[11] with a Fair Board, but no unusual pet contest or pet parade. I remember having to stop the story once and explain that there really was no such thing as either event. Why? I had an audience of school children from Meade County in front of me, and they started whispering to one another, very concerned that they had never heard of these events even though they'd been attending the Meade County Fair all their lives. After I stopped talking, acknowledged their sharp observation skills, then reminded them that the story was a tall tale, so I was supposed to lie, the telling could continue. From a teller's standpoint, it was truly fascinating to see almost an entire audience leave the world of the story because it came a bit too close to real life!

Some Dog really got his name one night when I was driving home from another Tale Talk gathering where I had told another work in progress version of the tale. While driving I thought: "Wonder how Jeff kept that dog quiet at night? I know. He could read to it. And wouldn't it be something if the dog liked books about dogs? Oh, and what if he cried when Jeff read *Old Yeller*? That would be some dog. That's it— Some Dog is the dog's name!"

Of course, once the idea of the dog understanding books entered the story, it was just too good to use only once. More books to call him off the hunt and *Lassie Come-Home* to finish out the story seemed natural fits and provided a thread to help pull the segments together.

As for Pavlov? I don't recall the circumstances that generated the Pavlov section; however, the people I grew up around value common sense just as (if not more) highly as book learning. While I know Pavlov's salivating dogs were actually part of an experiment he conducted that supported his observations about conditioned reflexes, it struck me that any country person worthy of claiming that title would surely see Pavlov's work as somewhat wasted because dogs possess a natural inclination to slobber! I mean, if Pavlov's work resulted in dogs being conditioned to do something, why not something much more worthwhile, like hunting independently?

Although I had not considered it during the story's development, the insertion of Pavlov has paid off again and again in school performances. When telling "Some Dog" to upper elementary and middle school audiences, I can say something like, "While I know most of you have never heard about Pavlov, I can assure you all your teachers have. In fact, they don't let folks become teachers without making them learn about Pavlov." Usually some, if not all, of the teachers are nodding at this point. The students notice their teacher's acknowledgment of Pavlov as real, so they accept that he is indeed "world-wide famous." The teachers generally shake their heads and laugh over my brother's interpretation of Pavlov too. So, Pavlov became one of those points in a story where it works well to somewhat step out of the tale narrative and talk even more directly with the audience before stepping back in to continue the telling of the story.[12]

So "Some Dog" developed the way many of the stories I tell have. It began with a desire to add a tale to my repertoire. I identified folktales I wanted to use. Feedback from my brothers and from other storytellers helped me develop my retelling. Then ongoing feedback from audiences over the years keeps feeding into the story, helping me keep the telling fresh time after time.

Sometimes an audience can even come to a teller's aid. In 2000, I was in Nevada telling stories for the By the Light of the Moon Storytelling Festival, sponsored by the Las Vegas–Clark County Library District, and I almost completely lost my voice. I could speak, barely. Barking was beyond my ability, yet I had been asked to tell "Some Dog." The audience, made up of all ages of listeners, quickly caught on to my difficulty, so I asked them to bark. They did, eagerly! I soon learned all I had to do was hold up my "paws" (both side by side, or one up and one down, depending on the portion of the story) and they would bark. When a bit of suggestion for the tone of the bark was needed, all I had to insert was a single word (ex. "Some Dog was amazed" [paws gesture] and the audience provided a bark of amazement). While I felt stressed telling with little voice, the audience participation made that telling of "Some Dog" one I will always remember.

When I am teaching about the art of storytelling, "Some Dog" has also proven a good example of the need to match story with audience. I've learned I can tell "Some Dog" successfully to a mixed-age audience, as long as only a very few preschoolers are in the mix. The story also works well for all-adult audiences. For other homogenous age group audiences, other factors come into play—especially experience with rural life. Multiple tellings have taught me that rural audiences as young as third and fourth grade readily enjoy "Some Dog" because they pick up on the humor early. The more removed that school-aged groups are from rural life, the older I find they have to be—sometimes up to tenth grade—before really grasping that the gigantic turtles are humor, not a real-life Kentucky farm report! This is not a sign of intelligence or lack thereof on the part of different audiences, but instead relates to one of the questions tellers have to be aware of when matching stories with audiences—what must my audience know in order to understand this story? So, why does it work with mixed ages and not with homogenous groups? Because in those mixed-age audiences, the children will look to their adults for guidance on what is and is not funny during the telling and the children also know they can always ask the adults questions later for clarification.

"Some Dog" is also one of those stories that adapts well to different time segments. I can shorten the turtle recipes, leave out the excessive begging and pleading (which developed from eye-rolling feedback I received from high school students in Tennessee, so I kept it up until they were nearly squirming, then added the comment about it working on some parents—they reacted with nods and laughter, so this became another keeper), leave out the pumpkins segment, and shorten other descriptions when I have only a short time to tell.

Once in a while it can even grow. Some audiences have heard about people who have told me about how much they like my brother David—relating how they recall his saving their dog when they were little, then how much they appreciated his recent work in helping deliver their first child. An audience or two have heard about ballet classes being conducted using our combine as a mirror because the surface is so shiny from all the Turtle Wax. Responses have been mixed (some laughter; some no reaction at all), so those additions have not become keepers, but once in a while they will still crop up in a telling.

Much to my delight, I've even met folks who report that after hearing the story they named their very next dog Some Dog. So, while I never once had a dog by that name, I love knowing Some Dog really lives!

MORE KENTUCKY FOLKTALES

Here are some Kentucky folktales that don't exactly fit the earlier categories of tall tales and lies or haunting, frightening, and creepy tales. So, now that you know what they are not, let me tell you what they are. In this section you will find:

- a formula tale, a story with a very repetitive, highly predictable plot—so it is also going to be exceedingly easy to recall and retell, should you have a mind to.
- a tale with a catch or trick—enough said, or I'll be giving away the trick!
- a couple of folktales of the realistic sort—stories that in all likelihood never ever happened, but are set in a world such as ours with events possible in our world, so perhaps they could have happened after all.
- a fairy tale, a type of story also called a wonder tale or by the German word märchen. Lindahl writes, "The märchen is an invitation to imagine the impossible."[1] I heartily agree. But wait, you may be thinking, the tall tales in the previous section contained impossible events. Yes, they did, but tall tales take place in our real world. A fairy tale invites you into an imaginary world, even when the characters and their emotions may be oh so very human. Like most fairy tales, there are no fairies in this fairy tale, but there are magical creatures with amazing powers.

I'll leave it to you to decide just which tale is which!

THE ENORMOUS BEAR

Once upon a time, a grandma, a grandpa, a little girl, and a little boy all lived together in a small house. Next to the house a squirrel lived in a tree. The squirrel enjoyed watching the people and even thought of them as his family.

One day the grandma said to the little boy, "We are all out of bread and milk, so I need you to go down to the store and come back with bread and milk."

The little boy headed for the store, singing to himself,

Bread and milk, bread and milk
Going to the store for bread and milk
Bread and milk, bread and milk
Going to the store for bread and milk
Bread and milk, bread and milk
Going to the store for bread a—

Up ahead he saw a bear. The little boy thought: "That bear's big. Nope, that bear's huge. Nope, that bear is enormous!" He called out, "Hey, Bear, how'd you get so fat?"

The bear walked toward the little boy, and growled,

"I ate five pounds of meat, and an ice cream treat.

"And I'm gonna eat you!" Chomp. Gulp!

The bear swallowed the little boy.

Meanwhile back at the house, Grandma grew tired of waiting on the little boy, so she said to the little girl, "Sugar, go on down to the store. Find that brother of yours, and the two of you come on home with some bread and milk."

The little girl said, "Yes, ma'am, Grandma!" She headed for the store and she, too, was singing:

Bread and milk, bread and milk
Going to the store for bread and milk.
Bread and milk, bread and milk
Going to the store for bread and milk
Bread and mi—

She met the bear. "Oh," thought the little girl, "that bear's big. No, that bear's huge. No, that bear is enormous!"

She called out, "Hey, Bear, how'd you get so fat?"

The bear walked toward that little girl, growling:

"I ate five pounds of meat, and an ice cream treat,

"A little boy,

"And I'm gonna eat you!" Chomp. Gulp!

The bear swallowed the little girl.

Meanwhile, back at the house, Grandma grew tired of waiting again, so she said to her husband, "Honey, please go down to the store and get some bread and milk. And look for those grandkids. Bring them home with you too."

Now Grandpa had been out doing his chores. He had just come in and sat down in his favorite chair. He didn't want to move, but when he saw how tired and worried Grandma looked, he knew he had to go. So, without saying a word, he pushed himself up out of his chair, made his way over to the door, lifted his hat off the hook, set it on his head, and then he stepped outside. As he walked toward the store, he was grumbling:

Bread and milk, bread and milk
Going to the store for bread and milk.
Bread and milk, bread and mi—

He met the bear. Grandpa thought: "Now that bear's big. No, that's not right—that bear's huge. No, that's not right either—that bear is enormous!"

And Grandpa called, "Hey, Bear, how'd you get so fat?"

The bear walked toward Grandpa, growling:

"I ate five pounds of meat, and an ice cream treat,

"A little boy, a little girl,

"And I'm gonna eat you!" Chomp. Gulp!

Meanwhile, back at the house, Grandma was still waiting on the bread and milk, and she was getting rather annoyed with the rest of her family. "Hmpf!" she said, "Can't anybody in this family find their way home!"

So Grandma headed for the store, singing:

Bread and milk, bread and milk
Going to the store for bread and milk.
Bread and mi—

She met the bear.

"My goodness," Grandma thought, "that bear's big. No, that bear's huge. No, that bear is enormous!"

Grandma called out, "Hey, Bear, how'd you get so fat?"

The bear walked toward Grandma, growling:

"I ate five pounds of meat, and an ice cream treat,

"A little boy, a little girl, an old man,

"And I'm gonna eat you!" Chomp. Gulp!

Meanwhile, back at the house, the little squirrel had watched all of his people leave their house. And when they didn't come back he went to look for them. Now, he had heard the song they were singing, so he sang it too:

Bread and milk, bread and milk
Going to the store for bread and mi— Uh-oh!

The squirrel saw the bear and thought, "That bear's big, Uh-uh, that bear's huge. Uh-uh, that bear is enormous!"

The squirrel called out, "Hey, Bear, how'd you get so fat?"

The bear walked toward the squirrel, growling:

"I ate five pounds of meat, and an ice cream treat,

"A little boy, a little girl, an old man, an old woman,

"And I'm gonna eat you!"

The bear lunged for the squirrel, but the squirrel ran up a tree. The bear looked up that tree and said, "Huh, if your little feet can take you up that tree, my big feet can take me up that tree." So the bear climbed up the tree. The squirrel ran way out on a teeny-tiny limb and jumped over to another tree. The bear watched, "Huh! If your teeny-tiny feet can take you all the way out that teeny-tiny limb and over to another tree, my great big feet can take me out that teeny-tiny limb and over to another tree." So the bear started walking out the teeny-tiny limb. The limb broke. The bear crashed to the ground. And when he hit, he split wide open.

Out jumped Grandma saying, "Whoop-de-doo! I'm out."

Out jumped Grandpa, "Whoop-de-doo! I'm out."

Out jumped the little girl, "Whoop-de-doo! I'm out!"

And the little boy, "Whoop-de-doo! I'm out!"

The little squirrel looked at all his people, and he said, "Well, whoop-de-doo! I'm out too, and I was never in!"

COMMENTARY

ATU Tale Type 2028 The Devouring Animal That Was Cut Open

For many years, I told "Sody Sallaraytus,"[1] a variant of this folktale. Although I had read the Kentucky-collected variants published by Leonard Roberts ("Cheese and Crackers,"[2] "The Bad Bear,"[3] "The Greedy Fat Man,"[4] and "Fat Man, Fat Man"[5]), they simply were not as appealing to me as the "Sody Sallaraytus" story. Audiences enjoyed "Sody Sallaraytus" and I had fun telling it, so I did not add a Kentucky-collected variant of the tale to my repertoire.

Then I was awarded an Appalachian Sound Archives Fellowship from Berea College. During the fellowship, I listened to sound recordings of over three hundred stories Leonard Roberts collected from people ranging in age from young children to the very elderly. At first I was tempted to skip the variants of "Sody Sallaraytus." After all, I had already read several and knew I had no interest in adding a different version of the story to my telling repertoire. But then I reminded myself that one reason I had applied for the fellowship was to see what I could learn from hearing the stories instead of reading them, so I made myself listen to variations on this tale. The more times I heard different tellers tell it, the more I looked forward to the next opportunity. Over the course of the fellowship I listened to versions from eight different tellers, and I fell in love with the story.[6] Table 2 shows some details from the stories I heard.

Table 2. "The Enormous Bear" Comparison Chart

1) Title 2) Call number	About the teller	Who?	Left home why?	Foods eaten	How bursts	Characters' exit comments	Other notes
1) Fat Man 2) LR OR 055 Track 4	Lena Day reported hearing the story from Lorriane Howard of Polls Creek, Leslie County, and added that she did not know who told it to Lorriane.	Woman, man, boy, girl, squirrel, fat man.	To town for groceries.	"I eat five pounds of meat, and I'm going to eat you."	Follows squirrel up tree, steps on rotten limb, and falls.	"I'm out." Squirrel: "I'm out and never been in."	Meat also makes exit comment.
1) Fat Man 2) LR OR 029 Track 13	Billy Joe Lewis, recorded in the Big Leath-erwood Creek area of Perry County in February or March 1950.	Man, woman, little boy, little girl, squirrel, fat man.	To store for milk and bread.	No prior food mentioned. "I'll eat up all your bread and milk, and I'll eat you too." Each person responds: "No you won't. I'll run."	Follows squirrel up tree and falls out.	"Whoopdee, doopdee, I'm out!" Squirrel: "Whoopdee, doopdee, I'm out, and I was never in." (more accurate spelling could be "Hoopdee Doopdee.")	Fun, high-pitched voice for the squirrel on "No you won't. I'll run."
1) Teller says could not remember title 2) LR OR 003 Track 7	Estill South, age eighteen, from Perry County, who reported hearing it from a teacher in his hometown. Recorded in Lige Gay's classroom in October 1949.	Old man, old woman, little boy, little girl, rabbit, squirrel, bear.	To the country store for a can of kraut.	"I'm gonna eat you up." Each person responds: "No you're not."	Squirrel is in tree when Bear eats rabbit. Bear sees it and decides to go after it too. When squirrel jumps from limb, bear jumps after it and falls.	"Ha, ha, I'm out." Squirrel: "Ha, ha, I'm out, 'cause I was never in."	

Table 2. "The Enormous Bear" Comparison Chart (cont.)

1) Title 2) Call number	About the teller	Who?	Left home why?	Foods eaten	How bursts	Characters' exit comments	Other notes
1) Greedy Fat Man 2) LR OR 005 Track 10	Harold Joseph, age fourteen, of Leslie County, who told it during a recording session at Polls Creek, Leslie County.	Man, woman, girl, boy, rabbit, squirrel, fat man.	To store for a piece of fat meat.	Fat man at store: "I'm going to eat you, fat piece of meat." Then to each person: "I eat a fat piece of meat, (inserts all others eaten so far), and I'm gonna eat you."	Squirrel runs up tree. Fat man follows, steps on rotten limb, and falls.	"I'm out." Squirrel: "I'm out, and I've never been in."	Fat piece of meat makes exit comment. Fun asides on who fat man could swallow whole and who he had to chew because they were fat too.
1) Dozen Eggs 2) LR OR 099 Track 14	Bobby Boggs, recorded at Pine Mountain Settlement School, Harlan County, October 1952.	Old man, woman, girl, boy, baby, squirrel, bear.	To sell one dozen eggs each.	No prior food mentioned. "I'm gonna eat you up." Each person responds: "No you won't. I'll run back home."	Follows squirrel up tree and falls.	"Tee hee I'm out." Squirrel: "Tee hee I didn't get in to get out."	Old man takes a switch with him because he intends to switch the rest of them for not coming straight home.
1) Old Fat Man 2) LR OR 099 Track 15	Bobby Boggs, recorded at Pine Mountain Settlement School, Harlan County, October 1952. (Yes, the same teller told two variants in a row.)	Man, woman, boy, girl, baby, monkey, fat man.	To store for a loaf of bread and a can of beans.	"I eat a bowl of gravy, drank a glass of milk, and I'll eat you too."	Monkey runs into a drain pipe. Fat man follows, hits a sharp rock, and bursts.	"Tee hee I got out." Monkey: "Tee hee I didn't get in to get out."	
1) Title unknown 2) LR OR 061 A, Track 12	Lila McVey, from Knox County, recorded April 16, 1958.	Man, woman, girl, boy, squirrel, bear.	Out to sell eggs.	People: "Want to buy some eggs?" Bear: "No, I want you."	Squirrel runs up bush. Bear follows and falls back and bursts.	"Pee, pee I'm out." Squirrel: "Pee pee I'm out, and I never was in."	

Table 2. "The Enormous Bear" Comparison Chart (cont.)							
1) Title 2) Call number	About the teller	Who?	Left home why?	Foods eaten	How bursts	Characters' exit comments	Other notes
1) Fat Man, Fat Man 2) LR OR 032, Track 49	Birchel Couch, thirteen years old, recorded in Harlan County in 1952.	Man, woman, boy, girl, monkey, fat man.	To store for a loaf of bread.	"I ate a bowl of gravy, drunk a cup of coffee, ate a loaf of bread, (inserts all others as they are eaten), and I'll eat you too if I can catch you."	Monkey climbs up a tree. Fat man falls and bursts open.	"Tee hee, I got out." Monkey: "Tee hee, I didn't get in to get out."	

Note:
The numbers below each title refer to the location of the tale in the Leonard Roberts Collection Sound Archives in the Hutchins Library Special Collections at Berea College.

From my previous telling of "Sody Sallaraytus" I've kept the same characters, I've retained the swallowing gesture and audible gulp, and I've kept the jumping from tree to tree ending segment. From Lena Day's version I used "five pounds of meat," to which I added "and an ice cream treat" because it completes a rhyme and adds humor. I'm sending characters to the store for bread and milk, selected from Billy Jo Lewis's version, because bread and milk are the items people commonly make a quick stop at a store for today. I also loved Lewis's use of "Whoopdee, doopdee," but I discovered I simply could not say "Whoopdee, doop-dee," so I shortened it to "Whoop-de-doo." Then, through repeated tellings I discovered the squirrel could rhyme, "Whoop-de-doo, I'm out too." Lewis was also the inspiration for the high-pitched voice I use for the squirrel. I added the progression of big, huge, enormous for its audience participation potential.

The song I've included came about through trial and error. I knew I wanted the characters to sing because I enjoyed that aspect of telling "Sody Sallaraytus." From June to September 2010, I played around with the song enough that a melody and rhythm settled. I have fun, and my audiences readily join in on the fun, as we sing the song with a slightly different sound for each character. Here is the melody I use:

Bread and milk   bread and milk.   Goin' to the store for   bread and milk.

When I reflect on how "Sody Sallaraytus" became part of my telling repertoire, I recall that I first encountered it as a told story, not a written story. I'm not sure who I first heard tell it. Perhaps I heard Barbara Freeman of The Folktellers,[7] the storytelling duo of Barbara and her cousin Connie Regan-Blake, who I first heard in 1979 or 1980? Or, maybe it was Ed Stivender,[8] a storyteller from Philadelphia, who I first heard tell this tale about that same time? What I do know is that after hearing both of these folks tell the story, then reading it in Richard Chase's *Grandfather Tales*,[9] I began retelling it in programs I was presenting when I worked as a children's librarian in Grand Rapids, Michigan—a job I held from 1979 to 1983. So, why would I have found those versions compelling enough to want to retell the story, but not have been attracted by the Roberts-collected versions I read, even though I had a desire to enhance my repertoire with Kentucky-collected tales?

One reason may relate to what was actually being published in the written versions I read. In his notes to *Grandfather Tales* Richard Chase states that he created the tales he published from multiple retellings of the stories.[10] Although he includes a frame story of sorts that places the tale in the mouth of a specific storyteller, and he attributes this tale to a single person,[11] the tale is not actually a transcript of a single telling. Chase created a retelling to be read and admits, "For me, the writing down of these tales has often been a difficult and tedious process."[12]

On the other hand, Leonard Roberts published specific told versions, each collected from a single individual in a specific place and time, not a new version created to be read after being changed by many oral retellings. Like Chase, Roberts also told stories; but unlike Chase, Leonard Roberts approached his story collections as a folklorist—working to capture a single storytelling event, so his published tales range from exact to nearly exact transcripts of the audio recordings he made while listening to the storytellers.

An even more compelling reason why "Sody Sallaraytus" captured my attention when the Roberts-collected published variants did not hinges on the nature of the art of storytelling itself. Donald Davis, a North Carolina–based storyteller, writes about the five languages of storytelling: gesture (not hands alone, but facial expression and all nonverbal body language), sound, attitude, feedback, and words.[13] My first encounters with "Sody Sallaraytus" had been encounters with all five languages in use. Both Freeman and Stivender made use of gesture and sound in a variety of ways (vocal inflection and pacing changes for different characters, sound effects, and much, much more). I had been present in the audience, not listening to sound recordings, so I was also able to absorb their positive attitudes toward the story and toward the opportunity to tell it to the particular audience at hand. Both had enjoyed the feedback from the audience and had engaged us in playfully joining in on singing the "sody, sody, sody sallaraytus" song each character sang on the way to the store. And yes, they had used words. I vividly imagined the tale as I listened to Freeman and Stivender because they made full and delightful use of all five languages of storytelling. With my reading of Chase following shortly after hearing Freeman and Stivender, I suspect I was able to bring memory of their tellings to that reading as well.

Through my Appalachian Sound Archives research, I was able to enjoy the Roberts-collected stories through not just words, but with the language of sound restored. Occasionally, I could even enjoy a glimmer of audience feedback because I could hear Roberts laughing as he listened to some of the tellers. Hearing them told finally brought these Kentucky-collected versions to life for me.

This folktale tends to die on the page—it is so very repetitious—but it thrives when told in person. Each character has a distinctive way of speaking. When I tell it, the little boy sounds capable, confident, and somewhat serious about his task. The little girl is a bit higher pitched than the boy, just as capable but a bit more carefree in her attitude. The grandpa's voice is older, deeper, and he is not happy about making the trip. The grandma's voice is also older, but higher pitched than grandpa's and she is annoyed that she has to perform a task so simple any of the others could have done it, if they had just taken it seriously. The bear has a deep, huge voice. He brags as he talks about what he has eaten, and he shows no pity on any of the other characters. The squirrel has the highest pitched voice—somewhat surprisingly so to many listeners, who first look surprised when the squirrel talks, then amused at the sound of his voice (inspired by Billy Jo Lewis's squirrel voice). When the squirrel interrupts his song with "Uh-oh," it is not necessary for me to even tell them he saw the bear—they know.

In my retelling here, I have compensated a bit, but only a bit, with words to make up for the loss of other languages. In an in-person telling, I don't need to tell my audience the bear is walking toward the other characters while growling. They can see through my body language that the bear is moving toward the other character, and they can hear that he is growling. Only when the little boy meets the bear do I actually need to tell my audience that the traveling character sees a bear.

Through body language, I show my audience the specific character as the character sings on the way to the store, and each character's stance and facial expression varies just as the sound of their voices vary. My audience sees each character stop abruptly when they encounter the bear and they know right away what the character is seeing. In a recent small audience, a child actually gasped, then said, "That bear's still there!" when the little girl stopped singing.

In this same audience, the children joined in so much I soon did not need to say each character's "no, that bear is . . ." as they changed their perception of the bear's size. Instead the audience chimed in with every "no" and again on the size words "huge" and "enormous," said with a drawn out sound, making the saying of the word enormous too.

I don't need to use phrases like "the little girl thought" in the telling. Instead, a character's thoughts can be spoken aloud with only a very slight change from the sound of actual speech to convey that these are the inner musings of this character.

Once I establish that the bear has eaten the little boy, I don't need to announce that the bear has successfully eaten each additional character. The audience knows this is what happened.

There is a rhythm in the interplay of sound and gesture in the bear's chant that works well in the telling, and is nearly impossible to show with words alone, but I'll attempt an explanation here. The bear's last line is always, "And I'm gonna eat you!" Chomp. Gulp! The telling works like this: "And I'm gonna eat (pause) you!" On "you" the bear grabs the victim. This is followed by a gesture in which the bear lifts the victim to his open mouth, which then closes over the victim with a "haaawm" (biting without the click of teeth?) "Chomp" sound. That sound is followed by a loud, single gulp. So "Chomp. Gulp!" in the text is onomatopoeia doing the best it can for a printed word to replace the actual sound. In telling, the timing is more like, "And I'm gonna eat (pause) you!" (pause) clap, clap, with "haaawm/Chomp" on the first clap and "Gulp!"on the second clap.

When the bear follows the squirrel out the small limb of the tree, the words I've written hardly begin to show what happens in the face-to-face telling. Instead, once the bear heads out the limb, I just keep the bear moving, one step at a time. Meanwhile I watch my listeners because I know someone is going to begin shaking a head no, or saying, "uh-uh" or "uh-oh" or "It's gonna break" or "He's going to fall." Someone in the audience will be unable to resist revealing they know what's going to happen, and then the conversation is on! I can respond to their comments by repeating their comments and asking why? Then listeners (sometimes one in a small group; often many at once in a larger group) will call out the reason why the bear will fall. Sometimes listeners go straight to "He's too heavy." Other times they will call out "the limb broke!" Then I have the chance to call back, "the limb broke! Why?" Eventually my listeners are orally connecting the breaking of the limb with the heaviness of the bear, so I can call out, "You're right! That limb did break. The bear came crashing to the ground, and when he hit . . ." and we are off and running with the ending of the story.

Storytelling is an ephemeral face-to-face art. No two tellings of any story will be exactly the same, and each different audience changes the telling too. With some stories, like this one, the audience impact is readily observable; with others the audience impact is more subtle. Yet all stories thrive in the telling when all five languages of storytelling are in action. Because "The Enormous Bear" dies a bit on the page, especially when I've chosen to capture a telling in words, without adding many, many more words to offset the loss of the other four languages of storytelling, I hope you will let your imagination go to work on it, and bring it to life again using all five languages of storytelling.

THE FARMER'S SMART DAUGHTER

One morning a king stood in his doorway. He looked out on all the land he owned, and he had but one thought: "I want more."

The land next door to the king's land was owned by a farmer. So the king sent for the farmer and said, "Well sir, I have decided to increase my land holdings, and your farm is the land I'm going to increase my holdings by. Now, I am the king, so I could just take your land, but I believe in being fair. I am going to ask you three questions, riddles you might call them. If you can come back here in the morning with three real fine answers to these questions, you can keep your land. If you don't come back with three real fine answers, your land becomes part of my land.

"Here are your three questions: First, what is it that's fastest in all the world? Second, what is it that's richest in all the world? Third, what is it that's sweetest in all the word? Now, go on home. I'll see you in the morning."

The farmer went home. He could not believe what had happened. He sat at his kitchen table, head in his hands, moaning, "I should have seen this coming. I should have seen this coming." You see, at one time there had been several farms between the farmer's farm and the king's land. But one by one, each of those other farms had become part of the king's land. "This must be how it happened. This must be how it happened." There the farmer sat, feeling miserable, when his oldest daughter walked in.

"Daddy, you look awful! What's wrong?"

The farmer told his daughter all about the king wanting the land and the king's three questions. The farmer's daughter thought a bit. Then she said, "Daddy, I can give you answers to those questions. To-morrow morning, you go tell the king the fastest thing in all the world is nothing but the light from the sun itself. There isn't anything moves faster than that, Daddy.

And as for the richest thing? Well, that would have to be the earth itself. And if the king doesn't believe you, tell him I could come up there and prove it to him. Why, there isn't a single thing the king owns that if we ask the questions: What's that made of? Where did that come from? And what's that made of? And where did that come from? Anything he owns, Daddy, if we ask those two questions and follow it back, we'll get back to the earth itself. And if everything comes from the earth, the earth must be the richest thing in all the world.

As for the sweetest thing? Well, Daddy, he is a king, and kings have to make a lot of decisions. I'll bet there are times when those decisions just weigh on his mind and trouble his sleep. Oh, even a king would have to agree there is nothing sweeter than a peaceful night's rest when your mind is troubled. Go tell him that, Daddy. See what he has to say."

The next morning the farmer went to see the king. He told the king those answers his daughter had given him. "My," said the king, "those are real fine answers. I was pretty sure you were not going to come up with answers as fine as that. Tell me, did you have help figuring out your answers?"

The farmer admitted his daughter had helped him. "Ah ha!" crowed the king, "I may be able to have your land yet. I did not say you were allowed to have help!" Then the king thought a bit, and he had to admit, "Of course, I did not say you were not allowed to have help either. Here's what we'll do. Since that daughter of yours is the one who gave you the answers, you tell her it's now going to be her job to save your land. You tell her I want her to show up here tomorrow morning, and I want her to be not riding and not walking either. You tell her I want her to be not dressed," and when he saw the farmer's face, he quickly added, "but don't you worry, I don't want your daughter to be going around naked either. And I want her to bring me a present that won't be a present." The king thought about what he had said, smiled, and then he sent the farmer on his way with, "Remember, tomorrow morning, not riding and not walking, not dressed and not naked, and bringing a present that won't be a present. Let's see what that smart girl of yours has to say about that!"

The farmer went home. Again he could hardly believe what was happening. He sat at his kitchen table, head in his hands, and that's where his daughter found him. "Daddy, what's wrong? Didn't the king like the answers I gave you?"

"Oh, he liked them, but you won't believe what he's decided you have to do now."

When the daughter heard the king's commands, she smiled and said, "Oh Daddy, I have always wanted to meet the king, and this sounds like a perfect opportunity."

The next morning the farmer's daughter woke up early. She took a bird cage, went out to where she knew a quail's nest was, caught a quail, and put it inside the cage. Then she took that cage and an old quilt out to the barn. In the barn she took off all her clothes and wrapped herself up in the old quilt. Then she picked up the bird cage and walked over to the goat. She threw one leg up over the goat's back, and with her other foot hopping along on the ground, she started off for the king's house.

The king woke up early too. He was real eager to learn what the farmer's daughter would come up with. There he was standing in his doorway, looking off down his lane, when he saw the farmer's daughter approaching. With one foot over the back of the goat, and her other foot hopping along on the ground, she wasn't walking and she wasn't exactly riding either. He could see her bare legs dangling out below the quilt, and he thought: "She's not dressed, but wrapped up in that quilt, she can't properly be called naked either. But I just know she can't bring me a present that won't be a present. I know I got her on that one."

When the farmer's daughter reached the king's house, she stepped from the goat and said, "Good morning, King, I brought you a present." She opened the bird cage, reached in, and pulled out the quail. As she handed the quail to the king, she opened her hand, saying, "Here's your present." And the quail fluttered off.

The king shook his head in amazement, smiling to himself, and then he said, "Young woman, you have saved your daddy's land. But now, I have something else I'd like to talk with you about. You see, I have never married. Now, the reason I never married is because I always promised myself I was not going to marry unless I could marry a woman who was real smart. You have got to be the smartest young woman I have ever met. How would you like to marry me?"

She set the bird cage down and glared at the king, "Are you going to leave my daddy's land alone?"

"Marry me, or don't marry me, I will never touch your daddy's land. You have already seen to that."

"In that case, Your Majesty, if there is one thing I've always known about myself, it's that I would be a fine queen. Sure, let's get married."

Wedding plans were made. All the friends and relatives were invited. A preacher was called up. But just before he said his I do, the king looked at her and said, "One more thing. I cannot tolerate a wife who goes butting into my business. You've got to promise me you won't ever go butting into my business."

She looked at him, smiled, then said, "We'll have to see about that."

He liked her smile so much, he went ahead and said his I do anyway.

Those two were lucky. They got married after knowing each other just a teeny-tiny bit of time, but she fell absolutely in love with him, and he fell absolutely in love with her. Most of the time they agreed on things. But no matter how much two people love each other, no two human beings are going to agree on everything 100 percent of the time. But when these two disagreed, they were able to talk and listen, listen and talk, talk and listen, listen and talk, until they could find that part of their disagreement that they could indeed agree upon. They were having a wonderful marriage.

But one day, as part of his work of being king, he made a decision that was so poor, she couldn't help herself. She went right ahead and she butted into his business. When he found out, he yelled, "I told you. I told you on our wedding day I would not tolerate a wife who went butting into my business. That's it. This marriage is over. Just go on back to your daddy's house. Leave!"

She said, "All right, but before I go, could we have one last meal together? And could I look around and choose just one thing—something I could take with me to remember what it was like to have been queen and all?"

"Oh, one meal. One keepsake. That's all you want. Fine."

She went to their cooks (after all, they were a king and queen, so other people cooked their food for them). She asked the cooks to fix up all the king's favorite foods for supper that night. And when he came to the supper table, there it was loaded with all sorts of real rich, real sweet foods—all of his favorites. When the king sat down to eat, she didn't do a thing but pour him a glass of wine to drink. And every time he drank the least little bit, she refilled his glass. He'd drink, and she'd fill it. He'd drink, and she'd fill it. Drink. Fill it. Drink. Fill it. Drink fill it drink fill it drink fill it drink fill it. (You get the idea.) And pretty soon the combination of all that rich, sweet food and way more wine than anyone ought to drink at any one meal and the king was passed out right there at the table. Oh, his breathing was good. She knew he was going to be all right, but he wasn't going to be waking up anytime soon.

She had the cooks help her pick him up. They carried the king outside and loaded him up in the wagon. She hitched the horses to the wagon, climbed up in the driver's seat, flicked the reins of the horses, and drove on down to her daddy's house. Once there, her daddy helped her carry the king inside. They dumped him in the bed that had been hers as a child. Then she climbed into bed next to her husband and slept till morning.

The next morning, the king woke up. His head hurt so much he could barely move it. When he looked over and saw his wife in bed beside him, he said, "What are you doing here? I am pretty sure I told you to go on back to your daddy's house. Now why are you here?"

She smiled at him, then suggested, "Honey, maybe you ought to take a look around and see where you are."

Carefully and slowly, the king looked around the room. "I'm not home. Where am I anyway?"

"Don't you remember? You told me I could look around our place and choose one thing to take with me to remember what it was like to have been queen. Well, what I liked most about being queen was living with you, so I brought you on back to my daddy's house with me."

The king was absolutely tickled to think that with all the fancy things they owned in that great big house of theirs, the one thing his wife wanted most was him. So he said, "Honey, I am sorry I hollered and carried on like I did last night. I suppose if every once in a great long while you feel a pressing need to go butting into my business, I might be able to get used to it. Let's go on back home."

And going on back home is exactly what they did.

COMMENTARY

ATU Tale Type 875 The Clever Farm Girl

This folktale is told in a wide variety of different cultures. I had heard so many different versions of the story over the years that I was quite familiar with the basic plot before I ever encountered this variant. In

1991, I spent lots of time looking for Kentucky folktales so I could add a wide variety to my repertoire before Kentucky's bicentennial in 1992. Yes, this was a marketing strategy on my part because I knew there would be increased interest in Kentucky stories that year, and I wanted to be ready with stories from different genres and for many different ages. I was thrilled to encounter a Kentucky-collected version of a tale I already knew I would enjoy telling.

My retelling is based on a version of this story collected in the early twentieth century by Marie Campbell from Doc Roark, a traveling doctor in the Letcher County area of southeastern Kentucky.[1] In her notes on the story, Campbell writes, "The version given above as No. 10 is close to 'The Innkeeper's Clever Daughter,' pp. 95–97, Ausubel's *A Treasury of Jewish Folklore*."[2] Indeed, the story is culturally widespread. In D. L. Ashliman's guide to folktales, he lists twenty-six versions of this tale, including ones from Chile, Italy, Greece, Norway, Russia, Israel, Germany, and West Virginia.[3]

In my retelling I have used my own words, but kept faithful to Campbell's Kentucky-collected plot. I did deliberately make several changes.

Campbell's version answers the second riddle with, "The richest thing in creation is the earth."[4] I elaborated on that by having the daughter explain that everything comes from the earth, so the earth is the richest thing of all.

At this point in the story, I will sometimes step out of the story by saying something like, "You know, she was right, too. Anything in this room would work the same way. Take that T-shirt you are wearing . . ." and I'll find out what someone's T-shirt is made of. It's almost always cotton or cotton and polyester. Most audiences readily acknowledge that cotton comes from a plant that comes from the ground. When I tell them petroleum is used in the creation of polyester, they readily agree that petroleum comes from the earth too. I tend to use this digression in school settings.

I changed the bird she catches from a pigeon to a quail because it seemed to me a ground nester would be easier to catch. The daughter wraps herself up in a quilt, not a net, in my version because in the part of Kentucky where I grew up fish nets were not common, but everyone had quilts.

The idea of her marrying someone after knowing them such a

short time disturbed me, but I believed such a marriage—if a good marriage—could work. So, I added my description of a good marriage.

Campbell writes, "She kept on pouring out wine for the king till she got him dead drunk."[5] My "Drink. Fill it. Drink. Fill it. Drink fill it drink fill it drink fill it drink fill it" repetition usually lights up the eyes of my listeners. It also provides a bit of comic relief that somehow softens this use of alcohol. (Several other variants of the story have her use a sleeping potion.)

In Campbell's version, the king asks the farmer if his daughter can marry him, and the king tells his wife she may take one thing with her when he tells her to leave. Well, in retelling a folktale, the story gets filtered through the teller, so in my version the king addresses his marriage proposal directly to the daughter, not to her father. In addition, she is the one who asks for a final meal and the opportunity to take one thing with her.

I clearly see her as a very independent, smart, and clever woman, and yes, I admire her spunk. I also see the king as regretting sending her away the moment she does not protest but instead asks for just one meal and one keepsake, because they truly are enjoying a good marriage. However, his pride cannot allow him to back down.

In addition to just enjoying this story, I also like telling it because I am a farmer's daughter. Trust me when I say the typical story featuring a farmer's daughter sleeping with the traveling salesman was never a plot I found appealing. Insulting? Yes. A tale I wanted to bring to my audiences? Absolutely not!

The Fortune Teller

One evening, several years ago, I was wandering along the midway at the Meade County Fair. I walked past the Ferris wheel and Tilt-A-Whirl. I walked along a row of booths. I saw the ring toss, the baseball throws, and the shooting gallery, all offering the possibility of winning huge stuffed animals. Then I saw the sign: "Fortunes Told. Past Lives Revealed. $1."

My first thought? What a hoax! My second thought? Aaw, what the heck, why not?

So I paid my dollar and walked inside.

The woman who greeted me certainly knew how to dress the part. She wore layers of skirts and shawls. Gold bangle bracelets adorned her arms. Huge gold hoop earrings hung from her ears. A silky print scarf held her dark curly hair away from her face. She led me over to a table with a chair on each side. Even in the dim light, I could see the table was covered with at least three different printed tablecloths, each a bit smaller than the one beneath. On top a crystal ball rested on a deep midnight blue stand. She motioned me into one of the chairs, and she sat in the other. Well, I thought, I'm getting my dollar's worth in costuming and decorating if nothing else.

The woman looked into my eyes. Then she stared into the crystal ball for what seemed like a very long time, although in reality it was probably well under a minute. When she looked up, her eyes looked troubled, even sad. And then she spoke, "I can't see anything about your future," she said, "but I do see your troubled past."

Oh man, I thought, this is such a rip-off. Who doesn't have some trouble in their past, and how convenient her crystal ball won't reveal my future. What better way to discourage me from finding her at next year's fair and proving her wrong!

"In your past," she said, "and I mean in your past life, not the past of your current life." She hesitated, then said, "I'm not sure how to tell you this, but you were a dog."

"A dog?"

"Yes, and even worse, you were severely mistreated. In fact you were murdered. Shot."

"Yeah, right. I was a dog, and I was shot," I scoffed.

But she looked at me kindly. "I know this is not easy to believe, but you were shot, and even in this life your body bears the mark of the bullet."

When she saw how skeptical I looked, she told me where the bullet struck me, and she was right. I've always had a strange indentation right here.

COMMENTARY

At this point in the story, I usually gesture to my collarbone, because there is an area there where I can make it look as though my finger is going into my skin a bit. I keep talking about that indentation, and how strange it was that she knew that. Usually one of my listeners asks to touch the spot. If no listener asks, I will add something like, "I know you may find this hard to believe, but the spot is right here. If you want to touch it, I don't mind." When someone from the audience comes up to touch the spot, the moment they touch me, I bark, fast and loud.

Yep, it's a trick story. It works well one time with each small audience! It's a fun story to tell, but it demands the teller be able to keep a very straight face and serious demeanor throughout the whole set-up.

I learned this story from Mr. Patrick Black, a math teacher at T. K. Stone Middle School in Elizabethtown, Hardin County, Kentucky. In January 2009, I was conducting a Kentucky Arts Council–supported arts residency with T. K. Stone sixth graders. One day I was eating lunch in the teachers' lounge when Mr. Black walked in. He asked another teacher, Mrs. Jennifer Upchurch, "Has Jesse recovered from the story yet?" They both chuckled and began telling what had happened.

It seems Mr. Black had noticed that Mrs. Upchurch's high school-age son, Jesse, had been doing his homework in her room every day after school. Jesse worked hard each afternoon, taking his studies very seriously. Mr. Black suggested to Mrs. Upchurch that he could walk in, tell her the story, and trick her son into touching the spot. Black knew he needed Upchurch cooperating in the set-up or Jesse would suspect a trick. (Mr. Black has a reputation for keeping things lively.) So, Black went to Upchurch's room, talked about different things, and then steered the conversation to the incident in the story. As planned, Mrs. Upchurch touched the spot and commented on how strange it felt. That prompted her son to touch it too. Mr. Black reported that when he barked, Jesse's math book flew one direction, his calculator flew another, and he jumped back against a desk with such force, it turned over too!

Mr. Black first heard this story in his mid-twenties on a triple date with friends on Halloween Eve. They were traveling from one haunted house to another. Mr. Black was driving, and one of the other fellows told the tale. While Mr. Black no longer remembers who told it, he does remember thinking—Mine! Immediately, he not only knew he wanted to retell the story to others, but he also had ideas about *how* he wanted to tell it.

The first time he remembers telling it was when he was a teacher on an eighth-grade class trip to Charleston, South Carolina. The students had been on a ghost walk and were riding back to their lodgings in a dark bus. To Mr. Black, they seemed primed for this story. He did not tell it to the entire bus, but just to a few eighth-graders sitting near him. He still remembers how they shrieked, and how in the dark he had not realized just how close the student's hand was to his neck when he started barking—so close he almost bit it! Even now, Mr. Black is delightedly remorseful when he talks about the incident.[1]

Mr. Black and I use different details to pull our listeners into the story. I enjoy setting up how cynical I was about the prospect that someone could tell me anything about my future or past. As I mention details of the fortune teller's booth, I can see my listeners sometimes nodding in agreement that she looks the part, and that revealing a "troubling past" is clever of her. When Mr. Black tells the story, he sets it up with some of his buddies encouraging him to see a palm reader. They've already had their palms read, and they think he should too. When he refuses to waste his money, his buddies insist on paying for him. The palm reader comments on Mr. Black's having more than one life line—one line matching his current life, the other a short broken line indicating a previous life cut short. The palm reader eventually reveals that Black was once a dog who died from a gunshot. When Mr. Black refuses to believe her, she proves it to him by telling him where his scar is located. Both Mr. Black and I work to assure our listeners that, like them, we are not easily taken in. Then, when we appear to have heard something surprisingly true, our listeners are more willing to believe because, like them, we began as skeptics until we had the proof that turned us into believers.

Telling this tale has indeed been fun for me. I only tell it when I have a small audience, no bigger than a single class-sized group. One gift I've given my nieces and nephews is to visit their classrooms once a year to tell stories. My brother Alan's children, two high school students and one fifth grader, all had me tell this story to their classmates shortly after they first heard me tell it at a family gathering. It really set up the story well when they suggested I "tell about what happened at the fair." In a class of juniors at Franklin County High School, where my niece Kate was a student, so many volunteers wanted to touch the spot that I had to squelch an argument by promising they could take turns. By that time Kate's eyes sparkled so much, I could no longer look at her for fear of breaking out laughing. The young man who touched first jumped back so quickly when I barked, he landed on the floor and slid backward across the room! Yes, I believe he intentionally exaggerated his reaction, but we all had a good laugh together, including the young man.

I'm lucky to have encountered Mr. Patrick Black, one of those natural storytellers who are also wonderful teachers. In fact, Mr. Black was Kentucky's Middle School Teacher of the Year in 2003. I suspect the ability to tell a story serves him well in his classroom, even though this particular story is not likely to show up in mathematics class.

The Princess Who Could Not Cry

A long time ago there once lived a princess who could not cry. Her mother, the queen, said, "Darling, that you cannot cry would not matter if you didn't laugh at everything." The king and queen became so worried about the princess, they offered a huge bag of gold to anyone who could make her cry.

A wise man arrived at the palace with a plan to make the princess cry. "Feed her nothing but bread and water for a full week. She'll be crying then."

The queen protested, "Bread and water? I'm afraid she'll starve. Couldn't we feed her bread and milk instead?"

"No! Bread and water! You do want her to cry, don't you?"

The king and queen wanted the princess to cry, so they commanded that she be fed nothing but bread and water for a full week. At the end of the week the queen went to see the princess.

"Hi, Mama, watch this!" The princess kicked her foot, and her shoe sailed off her foot and hit the wall on the far side of the room. "Isn't that something? My foot's so skinny my shoe just flies right off! Want to see me do it again?" The princess laughed and laughed.

The queen cried.

And then she commanded the princess's usual diet be restored.

Another wise man offered to make the princess cry. Now, this wise man had studied all the cultures of the world to learn how to make every ugly face and every ugly sound there was. He was certain he could make the princess cry.

For a full day the wise man was locked into a room with the princess. At the end of the day her parents came to check on her. The princess sat laughing and laughing. The exhausted wise man was sent home.

"Oh, Mama, he was funny. How soon can he come back?" the princess laughed and laughed.

The queen cried.

More wise men tried, and more wise men failed. The princess laughed and laughed. The queen cried and cried. At last every wise man in the world had failed.

In this same kingdom there lived a poor mother and daughter. The mother was ill but could not afford the medicine that could make her well. Most of the time she was too ill to work, but they ate the food from their garden and managed as best they could. The girl was smart. She had heard about the gold to be won from making the princess cry, so she had been thinking about how she could win it. One morning, the daughter said, "Mama, I think I can make the princess cry. And with the gold I could buy your medicine."

"Oh, honey," said her mother, "you can't make the princess cry. All the wise men in the world have tried and failed."

But the smart girl had an idea. She walked to the kitchen for a knife, and then to their garden for an onion. She put both into a sack, put the sack in her bike basket, climbed on her bicycle, and pedaled to the palace. Once there, she announced, "I've come to make the princess cry."

The queen said, "Oh, it is lovely of you to want to try, but we've consulted all the wise men in the world without success. You need to go home."

"Couldn't I at least try?"

Her request sounded reasonable to the queen, so the girl was taken to see the princess. The princess laughed to see a girl wearing such patched clothing, for she had never seen such clothes before, and she was happy to be visited by a child about her own age. She invited the girl to play with her toys. The two of them played and played together.

Then the girl took the knife and onion from her bag. "What's that?" asked the princess.

"It's an onion, and I want you to use this knife to cut it into little pieces."

The princess laughed, "That sounds like fun." The girl showed the princess how to safely use the knife, and the princess began cutting the onion. Soon tears rolled down her cheeks.

When the king and queen arrived to check on their daughter, the princess was crying. They were so happy they laughed until tears rolled down their cheeks too. The queen presented the girl with a huge bag of gold, saying, "Just think of all the toys you'll be able to buy with this!"

"Oh, thank you, your Majesty, but I'm not buying toys. My mother is sick. With this gold I can buy all the medicine she needs."

The queen was surprised. "Your mother needs medicine, and does not have it? I don't understand. In our kingdom, everyone buys health insurance. It's the law."

The girl responded quickly, "Oh, my mother and I do have health insurance. We are law-abiding citizens, your majesty."

When the queen looked puzzled, the girl explained, "We purchase car insurance too, as required by law. But your majesty, just as having car insurance does not mean we can always afford to pay a mechanic to keep our car running, having health insurance does not mean we can always afford to pay for health care. But rest assured, your majesty, my mother and I do obey all kingdom laws. And now I'll be able to buy her medicine, and she will be well enough to work again!" The girl curtsied, saying, "Thank you for the gold, Your Majesty."

The bag of gold was so large and sat so high in her bike basket the girl had to walk her bike home, for she knew she would never have been able to see over the gold while pedaling!

The queen retired to her study. She called her advisors and told them what the girl had said. "Is it true?" she asked, "that even though everyone now has health insurance, the people of my kingdom still do not all have health care?" The advisors had to admit the girl had indeed told the truth.

The girl bought medicine for her mother, and her mother's health was restored.

The princess begged permission for the girl to come play again, and the two of them became friends. After she had cried that first time, the princess even discovered there were times she cried without cutting up an onion.

The queen and king turned their attention away from making the princess cry. Instead they put their attention on making sure all of their subjects had not just health insurance, but health care. Within a year, everyone in the kingdom enjoyed the same complete health care as the king and queen. And in such a kingdom, led by rulers such as these, it's no surprise that everyone lived happily, and healthily, ever after.

COMMENTARY

In 1949 in Hyden, Leslie County, Kentucky, a girl named Agnes Valentine told "The Princess That Could Not Cry" to Leonard Roberts.[1]

On the field recording, Agnes can be heard saying she heard the story from her sister. Listening to Agnes tell was a joy. Her voice for the princess works especially well because the princess sounds so unaware of the effect her comments will have on her mother.

As I listened to the story, I thought it seemed vaguely familiar. Sure enough, I found a version in a book by Pleasant DeSpain published in 1993. That version is one DeSpain and school children created cooperatively when he observed that many stories featured princesses who could not laugh, but not princesses who could not cry. He invited the students to suggest ideas for making a princess cry without hurting her.[2] Cutting an onion provokes tears in DeSpain's story too, but the attempts at making the princess cry vary from Valentine's version.

DeSpain's version awarded land and gold; Valentine's awarded gold. I awarded gold, but during the editing process for this book I learned that I might have awarded too much gold. Too much gold? Yes, gold is heavy. The amount I described would have crushed her bicycle, and most likely no cloth known could create a bag sturdy enough to hold that much. In keeping with my practice of paying attention to audience feedback, I will recalculate, reimagine, and reshape that portion of the story before I tell it again.

Will the reward be a smaller bag of gold? Will the queen send twenty servants each carrying a bag of gold home with the girl to deliver her reward? Will an especially strong armored car be brought round to deliver the gold? To find out, come hear me tell stories and request "The Princess Who Could Not Cry."

The references to health insurance are mine, although Valentine's version does include the need for unaffordable medicine as the motivation for the girl to try her hand at making the princess cry. Yes, in this story my thoughts on the health care issue, one visited and revisited by political powers with seemingly little progress, are included. The references to health care work especially well for mixed-aged audiences. Most children are not aware of the controversy, so the references sail over their heads. All adults in my audiences are aware of the controversy, but haven't always considered whether having health insurance is truly the same as having health care.

I am self-employed, and I have no employees. Before I married—becoming eligible to purchase health insurance through my husband's employer's group insurance plan—the best health insurance I could afford had a $5,000 yearly deductible that I had to meet before an 80/20 co-pay began. And I qualified to purchase that plan only because of my excellent health! Fortunately, my health did not deteriorate, so I could always afford the very few medicines and doctor visits I needed. Now, I pay only slightly more to purchase health insurance through my husband's employer. My current health insurance plan requires a small co-pay for medicine and doctor visits and no yearly deductible.

Truly, all health insurance plans are not the same. Buying health insurance does not guarantee affordable health care any more than buying car insurance guarantees a person can afford to pay a mechanic for changing the oil, replacing worn brake pads, and other services needed to keep a car running.

Of course, the story could be told without any references to current events. However, story can be a means of addressing issues that are difficult to bring up and address more straightforwardly. Yes, I'll be the first to admit I've been more blatant than subtle in my insertion of issues in this tale. Some would contend my insertion of those issues is downright awkward! I look forward to the day when this story seems strangely out of date because efficient, effective, and affordable health care is always readily available for everyone.

Rawhead and Bloody Bones

A little girl once lived with her daddy. Her mama had died. Not far away another little girl lived with her mama. Her daddy had died. These two little girls knew each other and got along well. Over time their parents fell in love and married each other. For a while all was well, but then the mother began to make a difference between the two girls.

She noticed that her husband's girl was prettier than her daughter, so she began to dress her husband's daughter in old worn-out clothes and dress her daughter in new pretty clothes. Whenever her husband asked why the girls' clothing looked so different, she said, "Oh, that girl of yours is just hard on her clothes. They start the same, but hers look ragged in no time." But even dressed in rags, the pretty girl was still prettier than her daughter. So the mama began to give the pretty girl harder chores than her daughter, but even the hard work did not keep her from looking prettier than her own daughter.

At first her daughter noticed her mama's meanness and tried to make it up to her stepsister by being nice to her. But then the daughter began to enjoy her new clothes, and she liked being assigned only the easiest jobs, so it became easier and easier for her to be just as mean to her sister as her mother was. And the meaner she was to her stepsister, the more her mama praised her. The pretty girl couldn't imagine what she had done to cause such meanness to come her way, but she understood how bad it felt to be treated so mean, so she promised herself she would always treat others with kindness. Because she was so kind to everyone, people liked her better than her sister too.

When the mother saw that her stepdaughter was not only prettier but also better liked than her daughter, she grew determined to get rid of the girl. She went off to visit a friend of hers who knew how to cast spells, saying, "Tell me what I can do to get rid of her."

By the time she left for home, she had a plan. When she reached home, she told her daughter, "I want you to get in the bed and pretend you are sick, even near dying." The daughter did. Then the mama began wailing and crying like her heart was near breaking.

The kind girl heard her cries and came running. When she learned her sister was sick, she immediately asked, "Is there anything I can do to help her?"

This was just what her stepmother had known she would say. "Oh," said the woman, "I've been to see a friend of mine who's real good at healing, and she says can't anything cure her but a bottle of water from the well at the end of the world."

"Give me a bottle," said the girl, "and I'll go fetch the water."

So, the stepmother gave the girl a small bottle and sent her off with a few dried crusts of bread to eat on her journey. Now, the stepmother never expected to see the girl again, for her friend had promised to cast spells that would send wild animals out to trample the girl to death along the way. Of course, the girl knew nothing of this. She walked through the nearby village and kept walking right into the woods, where wild animals lived. She hadn't gone far into the woods when she stopped to eat. Then she saw an old man walking along. He seemed to be leaning heavy on his walking stick, and the girl thought he looked hungry too. "Hello," she said, "would you like to share my food? It's not much, just some dried crusts of bread, but I'd be happy to share it."

The old man sat down beside the girl and shared her food. Then he said, "I know you are going on a long journey, and I want to give you my walking stick to help you along your way. Whenever you have trouble, just strike the ground with the stick and say—Stop! Stop!—and you'll be safe." The girl took the stick, thanked the old man, and went on her way.

She hadn't gone far when she heard a rumbling sound. It grew louder and louder. Then the trees and even the ground under her feet began to shake. She saw a cloud of dust coming toward her through the trees. It was the wild animals the witch woman had sent to trample her. The girl was frightened, and at first she didn't know what to do. Then she remembered what the old man had told her about the stick. She struck the ground, "Stop! Stop!" The dust cloud parted as the wild animals ran around and past her.

The girl walked on through the woods. At last she came to a clearing. She saw a fence. On the gate of the fence was a sign that read: Well at the World's End. "Hmm," thought the girl, "I've found the right place." So she opened the gate and started to walk through. But the gate shut on her and tried to pinch her in two. She remembered the walking stick. She struck the ground with it, "Stop! Stop!" and the gate let her through.

Sitting on the edge of the well was a bucket with a long rope. The girl lowered the bucket into the well, but when she brought it up, instead of water, in the bucket was a rawhead and bloody bones. "Wash me and dry me, and lay me down easy," pleaded the creature. So the girl carefully removed the rawhead and bloody bones from the bucket. She took out her handkerchief and used it to wash it. Then she carefully laid it in the sun to dry.

Again she lowered the bucket into the well, but again she hauled up a rawhead and bloody bones. "Wash me and dry me, and lay me down easy." Again the girl carefully washed the creature and placed it in the sunlight to dry.

A third time she lowered the bucket, and a third time she hauled up a rawhead and bloody bones. She washed it and gently placed it with the others. When she lowered the bucket a fourth time, she hauled up clear water. She took out the bottle her stepmother had given her, filled it, and headed for home.

As the girl walked out of the clearing, the first rawhead and bloody bones said, "She was kind. I wish she'd be ten times kinder—so kind that everyone will even see the kindness oozing off her."

"She smelled good too," said the second rawhead and bloody bones. "I wish by the time she reaches home, she smells ten times better."

The third rawhead and bloody bones said, "Her clothes looked sort of ragged. I don't think she has much. I wish that when she combs her hair silver and gold coins will fall from her head."

The girl walked back through the woods. As she walked, she smelled so good the animals came to find out what the wonderful smell was. Butterflies landed on her, and birds flew in close just to enjoy the wonderful fragrance.

By the time she reached the village, the smell coming from her was so wonderful all the villagers opened their doors and windows. And when they saw the kindness oozing from her, the parents called their children from play, woke up toddlers from their naps, and lifted the babies from their cribs and held them up so no one would miss seeing her walk by.

By the time she reached home, her head felt so heavy she wanted to just lay her head down. But first she gave her mother the bottle of water. She noticed her stepsister wasn't sick in bed anymore, but was up playing. "Oh," said her mother, "I guess my friend was wrong. She started feeling better just as soon as you left."

The girl felt tired out from her journey, and her head was even starting to itch, "Mama," she asked, "could I lay my head in your lap while you comb my hair?"

"No! I don't want your filthy head near me. Comb it yourself!"

So the girl sat down and began combing her hair. When she did, gold and silver coins began falling out. The stepmother noticed right away. "Oh, sugar," she said, "I must be tired to talk so hateful to you like that. I am so sorry. Here, lay your head in my lap, and I'll comb your hair for you." So the stepmother combed the girl's hair until she had all the coins she wanted. Then she pushed the girl away.

The next day the stepmother said to her daughter, "You need to go to that well at the end of the world and come home with gold and silver in your hair like she did." The girl didn't want to go, but the mother gave her a bottle to fill with water, fixed her wonderful sandwiches to eat, and sent her on her way. Her sister even gave her the walking stick and told her how to use it if she encountered trouble.

The girl trudged off through the village and into the forest. She hadn't walked far into the woods when she sat down to eat. An old man came along. His clothes were ragged. He moved slowly. He saw the girl had his old walking stick, so he spoke to her. "I see you have my old walking stick. You must be the sister of the girl I gave it to."

The girl looked at him and frowned, "You say this is your stick. Well, I'll give you your stick!" and she hit him with it. The old man moved away from her as fast as he could. The girl called after him, "And I don't have a sister." To herself she mumbled, "I have a stepsister, and there is a difference." Then she sat back down and ate her sandwiches.

After eating she walked on through the woods. No wild animals bothered her because no spells had been cast to send them after her, so she had no trouble reaching the clearing. But when she started through the gate that guarded the well, it nearly pinched her in two. She kicked at it, yelling, "Stop! Stop!" and in the midst of her yelling and kicking and hitting the gate with the stick, she also managed to strike the stick on the ground, so the gate let her through.

She dropped the bucket in the well, and hauled it up. Inside the bucket was a rawhead and bloody bones. It pleaded, "Wash me and dry me, and lay me down easy."

The girl took one look, "You nasty thing. What are you doing in my bucket? I'm not going to wash and dry you," and she threw it out of the bucket. It rolled over into a ditch.

Again she lowered the bucket, and again she hauled up a rawhead and bloody bones. "Wash me and dry me, and lay me down easy." The girl threw it into the ditch too.

Again she lowered the bucket, and again she hauled up a rawhead and bloody bones. She yelled, "Again! I'll teach you to bother my bucket." She emptied the bucket onto the ground and kicked the rawhead and bloody bones over into the ditch with the others.

Then she lowered the bucket, brought up water, filled her bottle, and started walking home. As she left the clearing, the first rawhead and bloody bones said, "Oh, she acted ugly! I wish her inside ugliness would just ooze all over her outside."

"Yes," said the second rawhead and bloody bones, "and she smelled bad too. By the time she gets home, I wish she'd smell ten times as bad."

The third one added, "When she gets home and combs her hair, I wish all kinds of snails, slugs, lizards, snakes, and awful creatures would come spilling out."

The girl walked back through the woods. She smelled so bad, the animals ran away and the birds flew as high as they could up into the sky, except the buzzards. They flew in close, trying find whatever it was that smelled so dead. Flies began hovering around her looking for a good place to lay their eggs.

When she walked into the village, she smelled so bad, people went to close their windows to shut out the smell. But when they saw the inner ugliness oozing all over her, all the grownups rushed outside, gathered up any nearby children—not just their own children, but any nearby children—and hurried them inside to keep them safe. So she walked through a village with every door and every window shut tight against her smell and all the window shades and curtains pulled tight against her ugliness.

Now, she could smell an awful smell, but no matter how hard she tried, she just couldn't seem to get away from it. She brushed her hands in front of her nose. She tried walking faster, but she just could not get away from the awful smell. When she reached her home, her mother smelled an odor that almost took her breath away, and when she went to look, there was her daughter oozing ugliness. Well, you know that woman rather liked acting ugly, so she didn't mind ugliness, and she figured one good bath would wash that smell right off her girl, so she called, "Come over here, honey. You must be tired. Just lay your head in my lap and let me comb your hair for you."

When that woman began combing her daughter's hair, all kinds of creatures came tumbling out—snakes, snails, slugs, lizards—they all tumbled out by the dozens. Then this huge monster fish-like thing came out, swallowed the mother and her daughter, and they were never heard from again.

As for the kind girl? She lived happily ever after.

COMMENTARY

ATU Tale Type 480 The Kind and Unkind Girls

I tend to think of this type of story as an equal opportunity tale in which two characters go on the same journey and meet with the same situations, but because of their actions they end up with different results. I can't even recall when I first encountered a version of this story. I've been familiar with versions from a variety of cultures for years.[1] Leonard Roberts collected several versions of the story in Kentucky, both stand-alone versions and stories where this tale is part of a longer tale.[2] This tale was also in the repertoire of Nora Morgan Lewis.[3]

Having the opportunity to listen to multiple versions of this tale through the Appalachian Sound Archives Fellowship I received in 2010 influenced my telling decisions. By listening to "Rawhead and Bloody Bones," not just reading it, I noticed that the "heads"—whether described as skeletons, or foxes, or rawhead and bloody bones—never sounded threatening when they asked the main characters to wash and dry them and lay them down easy. In some instances they even came very close to sounding kind. If I had encountered the tale in print only, it would have been easy to imagine that the heads should sound threatening, or needy, or eerie, or even evil. But after hearing teller after teller make a nonthreatening choice, I accepted that the heads, strange as they may be, are essentially not threatening. The vocal characterization I use when they speak during my telling is in keeping with what I heard from teller after teller in the Leonard Roberts–collected field recordings.[4]

In my first few tellings of the story, I simply said one girl was kind and the other was mean; however, the persistent voice of a young child (first grade or kindergarten) in South Bend, Indiana, led me to rethink that approach. While I was telling the story during a Grades K–5 school assembly, he kept asking, "Why is she so mean?" Contemplating that child's question led me to showing how the girl began to enjoy the unearned privileges she received from her mother, and how receiving praise whenever she acted ugly reinforced her behavior. I imagine she has simply not lived long enough to gain the understanding that what a parent teaches is not necessarily right, nor has she been fortunate enough to encounter anyone who took time enough to help her develop empathy. Of course, if she had developed empathy there would be no story!

Every version characterized the two girls as outwardly pretty and ugly, with the heads wishing that the girls would grow more pretty or more ugly. However, since I am more interested in inner beauty and ugliness than outer beauty and ugliness, I retell the tale with the emphasis on kindness and inner ugliness that is so extreme it can be seen. Acting ugly is a phrase I first encountered years ago when I heard my sister-in-law Jackie King Hamilton say, "Stop acting ugly" to a misbehaving child. Even though we had both grown up in Meade County, Kentucky, the phrase "acting ugly" was not one I had heard growing up. The similar "Stop acting up" phrase was familiar to me, but not "Stop acting ugly." "Acting ugly" clearly works better in this tale.

All versions, except the version from Dave Couch, included the difference in the smell of the two girls. When I was telling my husband about the Nora Morgan Lewis details of the birds flying down from the trees and the butterflies coming in close to the pretty girl and the birds flying away from the ugly girl, he quickly suggested buzzards could begin circling and flies could swarm in, looking for a place to lay their eggs. I tried it, and it worked well.

The fish at the end of the story comes from Patricia McCoy's retelling.[5] Most versions have awful things coming from the second girl's hair—snakes, frogs, snails, lice—but only McCoy's version has the fish that swallows the girl and her mother. I chose not to mention lice because head lice infestations are simply way too common in schools. I would never want a child in my audience to mistakenly think of head lice as a punishment for acting ugly.

I also deliberately inserted the descriptions of folks waking up toddlers from their naps and lifting babies from cradles to show the importance of exposing children to kindness. In contrast, I chose to include adults grabbing all children from the streets and taking them to shelter, not just their own children, when confronted with the need to spare children from the horror of inner ugliness made manifest. I believe keeping children safe from harm is not a responsibility that lies solely with a child's parents, but rests with the greater society as well. Like most storytellers, my beliefs creep into my storytelling. Sometimes I deliberately include details that reflect a particular stance, blatantly in "The Princess Who Could Not Cry" and more subtly in this story. Other times, I might tell a tale for years, unaware that particular details I've imagined reflect my deeply held ideas.

Beyond Kentucky Folktales

Here I've placed three folktales that, as far as I know, have not been collected in Kentucky—yet! While I've usually been able to tell you who collected a story, and often who the collector heard it from, and sometimes even who that person reported hearing it from, it would be a falsehood for me to claim all the Kentucky tales in this book were transmitted orally, and only orally, before various collectors heard them and recorded them or wrote them down. Some probably do come from long-thriving oral traditions within individual families. Others were probably read, then told, and eventually became a story passed along orally. It would also be a falsehood for me to claim the tales had never been told outside of Kentucky. I called them Kentucky tales in this book because they were all collected in Kentucky.

Because I tell stories all over my home state (in 99 of the 120 counties so far), it is possible that a story from this section might be heard when I tell it, or even read in this book, and then told and retold at home or at school to listeners who then tell and retell it to others. Eventually the story could become a tale heard so often it is well-known and comfortably retold by some Kentuckian in the future. Such a tale might even be retold over enough time that the memory of it once being read in a book or of it once being heard from a stranger who called herself a professional storyteller is long forgotten. And maybe in that distant future, a folktale collector will hear the story and classify it as a Kentucky folktale.

For now, here are simply three more stories I love to tell and thought you might enjoy reading and reading about. You'll find another fairy tale—this one even has fairies as characters. You'll find a folktale handed down in a family and then sent to me through the U.S. Postal Service. And lastly, you'll find a pourquoi tale—a story explaining how something came to be—that is also an animal tale and a trickster tale.

KATE CRACKERNUTS

The day of Princess Kate's birth marked the beginning of five years of happiness for Kate and her mother and father. But then Princess Kate's daddy died. For the next three years, Kate, missing her daddy, followed the men of the kingdom. From the horsemen she learned how to ride. From the woodsmen she learned how to walk in the forest and never get lost, and which berries and plants were safe to eat and which were not. She grew so sturdy and so strong she could crack nuts open with her bare hands. So, everyone began calling her Kate Crackernuts.

In a nearby kingdom, there lived a princess named Annie whose life was almost exactly like Kate's. For five years she and her mother and father lived happily. But then Princess Annie's mama died. For the next three years, Annie, missing her mama, watched the women of the palace. She watched them sew. She watched them embroider, and she watched them dance. She hoped she could learn to create such beauty, even without a mama to teach her.

When Princess Kate and Princess Annie were eight years old, Kate's mother and Annie's father fell in love and married. Kate Crackernuts and Annie became stepsisters—sisters joined by marriage who quickly grew to love each other more than most sisters joined by blood.

Time passed. When Kate's mother decided it was time to teach Kate the womanly arts of sewing, embroidery, and dancing, she thought she might as well teach Annie too. Annie loved the lessons. Between lessons she practiced her growing skills. Kate suffered through the lessons. When each lesson ended, she hurried outside to walk in the woods.

"Kate," her mother scolded, "you must develop your skills. You are a princess. Without skills you'll never find a husband. No prince wants to marry a princess who cannot sew, embroider, and dance."

"Oh, Mama, I won't marry a prince who cares about sewing, embroidery, and dancing. I'll marry a prince who wants to walk in the woods, never get lost, and never feel hungry."

Kate's mother thought, "No such prince exists."

More time passed. Kate and Annie grew old enough to attend dances. Whenever the two sisters arrived at a ball, all the young men flocked around Annie.

"Promise me a dance, Annie."

"Save a dance for me, Annie."

"Annie, may I have a dance with you?"

Not until Annie had the name of a prince written beside every dance on her dance card did the young men turn their attention to Kate. Kate didn't care. She enjoyed watching the young men hover around Annie because she knew Annie loved dancing.

Kate's mother watched, and Kate's mother worried: "How will my Kate ever find a husband with Annie so beautiful and so graceful. Kate simply does not have a chance. Annie is much too beautiful. . . . Perhaps I could destroy Annie's beauty?"

One day Kate's mother went to see the henwife, a woman known for creating spells, and she arranged a spell to destroy Annie's beauty. The next morning Kate's mother said, "Annie, go see the henwife for me. She promised me something."

"I'll go right after breakfast."

"No, Annie, go now. It's very important." As Annie walked through the palace, she stopped at the pantry and grabbed a crust of bread to eat on her way. When she reached the henwife's home, the henwife said, "Good morning, Annie. Come in. See what's in this pot."

Annie lifted the lid of the pot. Nothing happened.

"Annie," asked the henwife, "have you eaten this morning?" When the henwife learned about the crust of bread, she said, "Take this advice to your stepmother—keep your pantry better locked." Annie took the advice home.

The next morning, Kate's mother walked Annie all the way to the door of the palace. "Hurry to the henwife's for me, Annie."

As Annie walked to the henwife's she saw gardeners picking peas. She stopped and talked with them. They offered her fresh peas to eat, and she ate them. When she lifted the pot lid at the henwife's house, again nothing happened. When the henwife learned about the peas, she said, "Take this advice to your stepmother: The pot won't boil when the fire's away."

Annie took the advice home. "She said to tell you the pot won't boil when the fire's away." When Kate's mother heard this, she knew she needed to go with Annie.

The next morning, Kate's mother said, "Annie, dear, come to the henwife's with me." This time, when Annie lifted the lid of the pot a sheep's head rose into the air, flew over to Annie, and pushed itself down over her beautiful head, covering it completely. Annie tried to pull the sheep's head off, but it was stuck fast to her shoulders. She tried to call for help, but all she could say was, "Baaaa, baaaa."

"Oh, Annie, let's go home!" said her stepmother.

When they neared their palace, Kate's mother called, "Kate, Kate, come see what happened to Annie."

Kate ran from the palace. When she saw her sister, she cried, "Annie, oh Annie, what happened?"

Annie's frightened eyes peered from the eye sockets of the sheep, but all she could say was, "Baaaa, baaaa."

"Oh, Kate," her mother gushed, "Isn't it wonderful! Now all the young men will pay attention to you. You'll have your pick of princes. I can't imagine there's a prince in the entire world who will want to marry a young woman with a sheep's head."

"Mama, you caused this?"

"I did it for you, Kate, I did it for you. Isn't it wonderful!"

"Oh, Mama, no. No!" Kate ran into the palace. Soon she returned carrying traveling cloaks and a fine linen cloth. Gently, she wrapped the cloth around Annie's head. Kate made sure Annie could see and breathe easily, yet no one would be able to see the sheep's head. Then Kate took Annie by the hand, turned away from her home, and walked toward the woods.

"Kate?" her mother called, "What are you doing? Where do you think you're going? I'm your mother, Kate. Come back here."

Tears streamed down Kate's cheeks, but she held fast to Annie's hand.

"Kate? Come back here! You needed my help, Kate. You'll see. You needed my help!"

Kate kept crying, and Kate kept walking.

For days Kate and Annie traveled through the forest, but they were never hungry. At night, they slept side by side, bundled in their traveling cloaks. One day they walked out of the forest and into another kingdom.

In this kingdom, the king and queen had two sons. One prince was said to be handsome and healthy. The other lay sick and dying and no one knew the cause or the cure. The king had proclaimed, "Anyone who spends the night with my sick son will receive a pound of silver." Many tried to spend the night with the prince, but all who tried were never heard from again.

"A pound of silver?" thought Kate. "Annie and I will need money. I must try." So, Kate and Annie went to see the king.

"I'll spend the night with your sick son in exchange for the pound of silver and a safe place for my sick sister to rest." The king agreed. He took Annie to a fine room, and then he led Kate to his son's room.

The prince slept in his bed. Kate watched and waited. Night came. Nothing happened. But when midnight arrived, the prince opened his eyes, climbed out of bed, and walked past Kate as if he could not even see her. Kate followed him from the palace and out to the stable. The prince saddled his horse. When he mounted his horse, Kate Crackernuts jumped up behind him and they rode away into the forest. As they rode by trees, Kate grabbed nuts and dropped them in her apron. They rode and they rode. At last the prince stopped in front of a green hill and called, "Open, green hill. Admit the prince and his horse."

And in a voice Kate hoped sounded like the prince, she added, "And his lady."

The green hill opened. Kate and the prince rode into another world. In this world, they rode on a broad path edged by tall trees. The path ended at a magnificent house. When the prince stopped his horse, Kate Crackernuts slid off and hid in nearby bushes. The door of the house opened, and fairies ran out, calling, "Oh, it's the prince—our dancing partner!"

The fairies dragged the prince from his horse and pulled him into the house. Kate slipped into the house behind them, taking care to hide in the shadows. Kate watched as the fairies danced with the prince. They danced and danced and danced with him. They would not let him eat. They would not let him drink. They made him dance and dance.

Only when a cock crowed the coming morning did the fairies let him go. The prince stumbled outside and struggled onto his horse. Kate slipped out and jumped up behind him. Back they rode to the palace, where the prince fell into his bed.

When the king arrived to check on his son, he found the prince asleep in bed and Kate Crackernuts sitting in front of the fire cracking nuts open with her bare hands. "I've learned what ails the prince," she said, "but I don't know how to cure him. I will spend another night with him for a pound of gold." The king agreed.

That night, Kate didn't watch the prince dance. Instead, she crept in the shadows, listening to the fairies, and this is what she heard:

"Any news from the palace?" one asked.

"Sheep's head Annie is visiting," another laughed.

"Oh, what a wonderful spell that one is!" said a third, "Ugly, ugly, ugly."

"Oh yes, effective, but simple," said another. "Why, three stokes of any wand, even the one the baby's playing with—would break that spell."

Kate thought, "Where's the baby? That wand is mine." Kate crept in the shadows until she found a fairy baby playing with a wand. She took nuts from her apron and, one by one, she rolled the nuts past the baby. The fairy baby acted just like any human baby. The baby watched nut after nut roll by. Then the baby laughed, dropped the wand, and crawled off after the nuts.

Kate snatched the wand, hid it in her apron, and then slipped out to await the prince.

When she returned to the palace, Kate hurried to Annie's room. Three times she stroked the sheep's head with the wand. The sheep's head vanished—Annie's beauty restored!

"Now, Annie," said Kate, "I understand there is a handsome, healthy prince living in this palace. Why don't you see if you can meet him? I'm off to make another bargain with the king."

When the king came to his son's room, Kate was waiting for him. "I still don't know how to cure him, but I'll spend another night with him, if I may marry him." The king agreed.

That night Kate again crept in the shadows and listened to the fairies talk:

"Just think, three more nights of dancing and the prince will be ours."

"Oh, that's right," another fairy gloated. "He'll never return to the palace and no one will know what happened to him. He'll be our dancing partner forever and ever."

"It is a complicated, time-consuming spell, but it's nearly complete."

"Oh yes! The only way to interrupt it now would be to feed the prince a stew made from the little yellow birdie the baby's playing with . . ."

Kate thought, "Where's that baby?" She crept in the shadows until she found the baby playing with the birdie. Again she rolled nut after nut. Finally the baby laughed, let go of the birdie, and crawled after the nuts. Kate snatched the yellow birdie, hid it in her apron, and slipped out to await the prince.

When they returned to the palace, the prince fell into his bed. Kate wrung the yellow birdie's neck, plucked off all its feathers, dropped it into a pot of water, and began cooking yellow birdie stew. The aroma from the cooking pot drifted over to the sleeping prince. He opened his eyes, "Oh, what is that wonderful smell?"

"Yellow birdie stew," said Kate. She filled a bowl and carried it to his bed. Gently Kate lifted the prince's head and spooned yellow birdie stew into his mouth.

"More," said the prince, and he propped himself up on his elbows. Kate fed him more.

"More, please," said the prince, and he sat up in his bed. Kate fed him more.

"More, please," he said, and he stood up. Kate Crackernuts handed him the entire bowl.

When the king came to check on his son, he found Kate Crackernuts sitting in front of the fire, cracking nuts open with her bare hands. Beside her sat the prince, helping himself to yellow birdie stew, laughing, talking, and falling in love with Kate Crackernuts.

Annie and the other prince fell in love too.

In time, a grand double wedding was held. After the wedding ceremony, celebrations lasted for days and days. Annie and her prince attended every celebration and danced every dance. Kate and her prince attended every celebration and danced the first dance at each one—just to be polite. Then they slipped away for walks in the woods.

Kate's prince never did like dancing. He had no idea why he did not like dancing, he just thought, "I don't enjoy dancing." But he loved walking in the woods, never getting lost, and never feeling hungry, because he walked beside his beloved Kate Crackernuts.

COMMENTARY

ATU Tale Type 711 The Beautiful and Ugly Twin Sisters

I first encountered this tale in the version retold by Joseph Jacobs in *English Fairy Tales*, where he included this source note: "Given by Mr. Lang in *Longmans' Magazine*, vol. xiv. (not xiii as cited in *Folk-Lore* below) and reprinted in *Folk-Lore*, Sept. 1890. It is very corrupt, both girls being called Kate, and I have had largely to rewrite."[1] Andrew Lang in *Folk-Lore* included the following citation: "Collected by Mr. D. J. Robertson of the Orkneys. Printed in *Longman's Magazine*, vol. xiii."[2]

Here is the Joseph Jacobs retelling:

Kate Crackernuts

Once upon a time there was a king and a queen, as in many lands have been. The king had a daughter, Anne, and the queen had one named Kate, but Anne was far bonnier than the queen's daughter, though they loved one another like real sisters. The queen was jealous of the king's daughter being bonnier than her own, and cast about to spoil her beauty. So she took counsel of the henwife, who told her to send the lassie to her next morning fasting.

So next morning early, the queen said to Anne, "Go, my dear, to the henwife in the glen, and ask her for some eggs." So Anne set out, but as she passed through the kitchen she saw a crust, and she took and munched it as she went along.

When she came to the henwife's she asked for eggs, as she had been told to do; the henwife said to her, "Lift the lid off that pot there and see." The lassie did so, but nothing happened. "Go home to your minnie and tell her to keep her larder door better locked," said the henwife. So she went home to the queen and told her what the henwife had said. The queen knew from this that the lassie had had something to eat, so watched the next morning and sent her away fasting; but the princess saw some country-folk picking peas by the roadside, and being very kind she spoke to them and took a handful of the peas, which she ate by the way.

When she came to the henwife's, she said, "Lift the lid off the pot and you'll see." So Anne lifted the lid but nothing happened.

Then the henwife was rare angry and said to Anne, "Tell your minnie the pot won't boil if the fire's away." So Anne went home and
told the queen.

The third day the queen goes along with the girl herself to the
henwife. Now, this time, when Anne lifted the lid off the pot, off falls
her own pretty head, and on jumps a sheep's head. So the queen was
now quite satisfied, and went back home.

Her own daughter, Kate, however, took a fine linen cloth and
wrapped it round her sister's head and took her by the hand and they
both went out to seek their fortune. They went on, and they went on,
and they went on, till they came to a castle. Kate knocked at the door,
and asked for a night's lodging for herself and a sick sister. They went
in and found it was a king's castle, who had two sons, and one of them
was sickening away to death and no one could find out what ailed him.
And the curious thing was that whoever watched him at night was never
seen any more. So the king had offered a peck of silver to any one who
would stop up with him. Now Katie was a very brave girl, so she offered
to sit up with him.

Till midnight all went well. As twelve o'clock rang, however, the
sick prince rose, dressed himself, and slipped downstairs. Kate followed, but he didn't seem to notice her. The prince went to the stable,
saddled his horse, called his hound, jumped into the saddle, and Kate
leapt lightly up behind him. Away rode the prince and Kate through the
greenwood, Kate, as they pass, plucking nuts from the trees and filling
her apron with them. They rode on and on till they came to a green
hill. The prince here drew bridle and spoke, "Open, open, green hill,
and let the young prince in with his horse and his hound," and Kate
added, "and his lady behind."

Immediately the green hill opened and they passed in. The prince
entered a magnificent hall, brightly lighted up and many beautiful fairies
surrounded the prince and led him off to the dance. Meanwhile, Kate,
without being noticed, hid herself behind the door. There she saw the
prince dancing, and dancing, and dancing, till he could dance no longer
and fell upon a couch. Then the fairies would fan him till he could rise
again and go on dancing.

At last the cock crew, and the prince made all haste to get on
horseback; Kate jumped up behind, and home they rode. When the
morning sun rose they came in and found Kate sitting down by the fire

and cracking her nuts. Kate said the prince had a good night; but she would not sit up another night unless she was to get a peck of gold. The second night passed as the first had done. The prince got up at midnight and rode away to the green hill and the fairy ball, and Kate went with him, gathering nuts as they rode through the forest. This time she did not watch the prince, for she knew he would dance, and dance, and dance. But she saw a fairy baby playing with a wand, and overheard one of the fairies say: "Three strokes of that wand would make Kate's sick sister as bonnie as ever she was." So Kate rolled nuts to the fairy baby and rolled nuts till the baby toddled after the nuts and let fall the wand, and Kate took it up and put it in her apron. And at cock crow they rode home as before, and the moment Kate got home to her room she rushed and touched Anne three times with the wand, and the nasty sheep's head fell off and she was her own pretty self again. The third night Kate consented to watch, only if she should marry the sick prince. All went on as on the first two nights. This time the fairy baby was playing with a birdie; Kate heard one of the fairies say: "Three bites of that birdie would make the sick prince as well as he ever was." Kate rolled all the nuts she had to the fairy baby till the birdie was dropped, and Kate put it in her apron.

At cockcrow they set off again, but instead of cracking her nuts as she used to do, this time Kate plucked the feathers off and cooked the birdie. Soon there arose a very savoury smell. "Oh," said the sick prince, "I wish I had a bite of that birdie," so Kate gave him a bite of the birdie, and he rose up on his elbow. By-and-by he cried out again: "Oh, if I had another bite of that birdie!" so Kate gave him another bite, and he sat up on his bed. Then he said again: "Oh! if I but had a third bite of that birdie!" So Kate gave him a third bite, and he rose hale and strong, dressed himself, and sat down by the fire, and when the folk came in next morning they found Kate and the young prince cracking nuts together. Meanwhile his brother had seen Annie and had fallen in love with her, as everybody did who saw her sweet pretty face. So the sick son married the well sister, and the well son married the sick sister, and they all lived happy and died happy, and never drank out of a dry cappy.

* * *

And here is the version Lang published, collected by D. J. Robertson:

The Story of Kate Crackernuts

Once upon a time there was a king and a queen, as in many lands have been. The king had a dochter, Kate, and the queen had one. The queen was jealous of the king's dochter being bonnier than her own, and cast about to spoil her beauty. So she took counsel of the henwife, who told her to send the lassie to her next morning fasting. The queen did so, but the lassie found means to get a piece before going out. When she came to the henwife's she asked for eggs, as she had been told to do; the henwife desired her to "lift the lid off that pot there" and see. The lassie did so, but naething happened. "Gae hame to your minnie and tell her to keep her press door better steekit," said the henwife. The queen knew from this that the lassie had had something to eat, so watched the next morning and sent her away fasting; but the princess saw some country folk picking peas by the roadside, and being very affable she spoke to them and took a handful of the peas, which she ate by the way.

In consequence, the answer at the henwife's house was the same as on the preceding day.

The third day the queen goes along with the girl to the henwife. Now, when the lid is lifted off the pot, off jumps the princess's ain bonny head and on jumps a sheep's head.

The queen, now quite satisfied, returns home.

Her own daughter, however, took a fine linen cloth and wrapped it round her sister's head and took her by the hand and gaed out to seek their fortin. They gaed and they gaed far, and far'er than I can tell, till they cam to a king's castle. Kate chappit at the door and sought a "night's lodging for hersel' and a sick sister." This is granted on condition that Kate sits up all night to watch the king's sick son, which she is quite willing to do. She is also promised a "pock of siller" "if a's right." Till midnight all goes well. As twelve o'clock rings, however, the sick prince rises, dresses himself, and slips downstairs, followed by Kate unnoticed. The prince went to the stable, saddled his horse, called his hound, jumped into the saddle, Kate leaping lightly up behind him. Away rode the prince and Kate through the greenwood, Kate, as they pass, plucking nuts from the trees and filling her apron with them. They rode on and on till they came to a green hill. The prince here drew bridle and spoke, "Open, open, green hill, an' let the young prince in with his horse and his hound," and, added Kate, "his lady him behind."

Immediately the green hill opened and they passed in. A magnificent hall is entered, brightly lighted up, and many beautiful ladies surround the prince and lead him off to the dance, while Kate, unperceived, seats herself by the door. Here she sees a bairnie playing with a wand, and overhears one of the fairies say, "Three strakes o' that wand would mak Kate's sick sister as bonnie as ever she was." So Kate rowed nuts to the bairnie, and rowed (rolled) nuts till the bairnie let fall the wand, and Kate took it up and put it in her apron.

Then the cock crew, and the prince made all haste to get on horseback, Kate jumping up behind, and home they rode, and Kate sat down by the fire and cracked her nuts, and ate them. When the morning came Kate said the prince had a good night, and she was willing to sit up another night, for which she was to get a "pock o' gowd." The second night passes as the first had done. The third night Kate consented to watch only if she should marry the sick prince. This time the bairnie was playing with a birdie; Kate heard one of the fairies say, "Three bites of that birdie would mak the sick prince as weel as ever he was." Kate rowed nuts to the bairnie till the birdie was dropped, and Kate put it in her apron.

At cockcrow they set off again, but instead of cracking her nuts as she used to do, Kate plucked the feathers off and cooked the birdie. Soon there arose a very savoury smell. "Oh!" said the sick prince, "I wish I had a bite o' that birdie," so Kate gave him a bit o' the birdie, and he rose up on his elbow. By-and-by he cried out again, "Oh, if I had anither bite o' that birdie!" so Kate gave him another bit, and he sat up on his bed. Then he said again, "Oh! if I had a third bite o' that birdie!" So Kate gave him a third bit, and he rose quite well, dressed himself, and sat down by the fire, and when "the folk came i' the mornin' they found Kate and the young prince cracking nuts th'gether." So the sick son married the weel sister, and the weel son married the sick sister, and they all lived happy and dee'd happy, and never drank out o' a dry cappy.

*   *   *

When you compare the two, you can easily see some of the changes Jacobs made in his retelling. From his notes, we know Jacobs thought the version Lang published needed to be rewritten. But what about my version? Why is it so different from the Jacobs version?

I was familiar with this tale and attempted retellings of it for over twenty years before I managed to retell it in a way that both pleased me and held the attention of my listeners. I loved the story's positive portrayal of the relationship between stepsisters. However, for years, I kept wondering why Kate's mother wanted to destroy Annie. The explanation given in both Jacobs's and Lang's versions, that the king's daughter was bonnier than the queen's daughter, seemed inadequate motivation. In my retelling attempts, Kate's mother's actions never felt truly believable.

Yes, I know that one girl's being prettier than the other seems reason enough for the actions of the stepmother in the previous story, "Rawhead and Bloody Bones," a recent addition to my telling repertoire, and I've been asking myself why. What's the difference? Perhaps my mind accepts the jealousy motivation there because in that story the girls do have equal opportunity for success, and they act alone. In "Kate Crackernuts" Annie doesn't have a chance. The story is not structured as an equal opportunity tale. She is powerless to escape her stepmother's evil plans. She's obedient, she's kind, but it's simply not enough. Without Kate's help, Annie is doomed.

Yes, I also know both stories are fairy tales, so none of it really happened, but for me to tell a story well, the characters have to behave in a manner that I can believe throughout the story. I want to be able to talk about them with the same ease with which I could tell about something that happened to me. "She's prettier, so I'll destroy her" never quite satisfied my need for a believable motivation for Kate's mother.

Then real life provided additional insight. In 1991 a Texas mother was found guilty of attempting to hire a hit man to kill the mother of her daughter's cheerleading rival.[3] The mother wanted to improve her daughter's chances of making the cheerleading team by creating such turmoil in the other girl's life that she would be too upset to try out. Hearing about this incident immediately reminded me of the relationship between Kate Crackernuts and her mother. Both mothers wanted to help their daughters, but their actions reveal a lack of confidence in a daughter's ability to succeed in the world. This real-life incident sent me back to the folktale with a deeper understanding of the possible fears and doubts motivating Kate's mother and even more admiration for Kate's intelligence and courage.

In addition, both the Lang and Jacobs versions begin with the narrator talking about the king and queen, and then telling about the queen setting up the spell with the henwife. Beginning the story with the king and queen simply did not work for me. I wanted to meet the girls right away and learn more about them. Once I changed the narrator's focus to Kate and Annie from the very beginning of the tale, their journey became clearer to me, and I found much more pleasure in recounting the tale. Yes, Kate's mother still makes horrible decisions, but the story I am telling is of Kate, a girl who, even though lacking the guidance of a mother who accepts her strengths and helps her nurture them as she grows up, still manages to know herself, trust herself, and succeed.

And no, I'm not saying getting married is the mark of success. I count Kate successful because she charts her own course. She does what is needed to secure her finances, and it is she who sets the terms for marriage in her bargaining with the king. That Kate sets her own marriage terms is not my invention. It was included in Jacobs's and Lang's versions and was one of the details I found appealing from my first contact with the tale.

In working with this story over the years, I created word outlines, time lines, and story maps (stick figure cartoon-like drawings) as part of my story learning process.

Here's a sample from a word outline:

Beginning—Kate's mother and Anne's father married.
    Kate & Anne like each other
    Kate's mother worries that Anne is prettier, more graceful, talented—dancing and needlework? So, she decides to destroy her.
    Kate's mother sends Anne to henwife for eggs.
    1st time—Anne eats bread crust—nothing happens.
    2nd time—Anne sees gardeners, give peas, eats—nothing happens
    3rd time—Kate's mother goes along
    Anne's head replaced with sheep's head
    Mother overjoyed
Here? Middle?

    1. Mother returns with Anne. Kate takes Anne and leaves.
    2. Kate and Anne find palace of sick prince, reward for spending the night watching him

Kate decides to try for reward (basket of silver)

1st night

Kate learns he is enchanted by fairies who make him dance all night—earns silver

2nd night (for basket of gold)

Kate learns 3 taps of wand will cure sister
rolls nuts to take wand from baby
cures sister upon return to palace

Here's a sample from the time line:

Ages 7–9? Kate's father and Anne's mother die.
Ages 11–13? Kate's mother and Anne's father marry.
Ages 13–15? Kate's mother notices differences between her daughter and Anne and becomes concerned, worried, then obsessed enough to plan Anne's destruction.

Story begins here: 1st day of story—Kate's mother contracts with henwife for spell on Anne.

Day 1—sends Anne to henwife but Anne eats crust.

Day 2—sends Anne to henwife but Anne eats peas from gardners.

Day 3—takes Anne to henwife, spell works, Anne's head replaced with sheep's head.

Same day—Kate's mother returns with Anne. Kate wraps Anne's head in cloth and leads Anne away from home.

? _____ (How long?) the two girls journey (Must take long enough to reach area with another king; yet not so long that they look so raggedy from their journey they are not welcomed)

1st night—Kate stays with sick prince; collects nuts as they journey together; learns nature of spell fairies have placed on him; earns silver.

Next morning—Kate is sitting at fireplace cracking nuts, given silver, makes deal for 2nd night for gold.

As you can see from these excerpts, the word outline and time line, while similar, are not exactly the same. When I create a word outline, I focus on the sequence of events in the story. When I create a time line, I focus more on the passage of time within the story, not just the order of events. Both are learning tools, created while I am working to learn the story to help me see how events might flow.

I also made a story map for "Kate Crackernuts" using cartoon-like stick figure drawings. When I create story maps, I continually ask myself: What is the next picture I need to create for my audience? I'm also creating the map as I'm striving to understand the story, so it keeps changing and changing as my understanding of the story changes. My "Kate Crackernuts" story map is pretty much indecipherable by anyone but me. And that's okay, because I'm the one I created it for!

Okay, I imagine you have the idea. I draw pictures, not great art,

Story Map

Panel 1: Four stick figures, labeled KM (for Kate's Mother), AF (for Annie's father), K (for Kate), and A (for Anne). A line connects Kate's mother and Annie's Father. Another line connects Kate and Annie.

Panel 2: Kate surrounded by trees with circles representing nuts underneath them. Off to the side is a palace with an arrow pointing away from it (to emphasize that this character spends her time outside).

Panel 3: Annie surrounded by musical notes and a needle and thread. Off to the side is a palace with an arrow pointing toward it (to show this character spends her time inside).

Panel 4: A frowning Kate's Mother stands on the left. From her head, a cartoon thought bubble with musical notes and a needle and thread inside. Facing her, a smiling Kate holds a nut in her hand.

but stick figures, as I'm thinking my way through the story. The map for this story continues for thirty-seven panels, with some containing words (Panel 32 says "repeat panels 21–25") to note repeated events. As I work, I notice when I need to return to the text because I can't recall what comes next. I consult the text only as much as necessary to keep myself moving through the story. I do not consult the text for every step as I create my story maps because I'm working to discover how I picture the story, not trying to create a rough duplication of images I could glean from the text. It is the process of drawing the map that contributes to my learning by making me think through the story visually instead of with words.

I also ask and answer questions as part of my work, such as:

- Kate's mother notices Kate and Annie are different, but what does she see and what does she hear that leads her to become so obsessed she is willing to destroy Annie?
- What is Kate's mother so afraid of?
- Why don't the fairies know Annie is cured and wand is missing if they know Annie is at the palace?
- Why don't they catch on and stop Kate—or do they know she is listening?
- Or do they just not check the palace every day?
- Or, is Kate listening to different fairies who are talking about different things, and the fairies themselves have not communicated new information to all before Kate secures the yellow birdie?

And I make notes of my observations, such as:

- Fasting is important to put spell on Annie, but eating is important to break spell on Prince.
- The henwife says "The pot won't boil if the fire is away" to mean the spell is your idea so you need to be here—you are the fire. On this day the henwife doesn't even ask if Annie has eaten, she just gives the message?

I don't usually save the work I create while working on learning a story. I just happen to still have the work from "Kate Crackernuts" because at about the time I was finished using my outline, time line, and map, I was hired to teach a full-day workshop on learning to retell folktales. The workshop coordinator wanted participants to be able to attend the workshop having already selected a story and completed some of the work of learning it before they arrived. Because I did not want participants to fall into the common misconception of believing learning a story meant memorizing the words, we mailed participants copies of my learning work as examples, and asked them to arrive with outlines, time lines, and maps of their chosen stories. Seeing my examples helped the workshop participants really believe my advice that the only way they could create unacceptable outlines, time lines, or maps for their story would be to simply not create them at all. So, I saved my work and have used it as preparation examples for workshop participants in subsequent folktale retelling workshops.

That I do the sort of work I've described—creating outlines, time lines, story maps, asking questions, making observations, and more—while pondering the story I want to retell does not make me unique among storytellers. This is the type of work many tellers who "learn the story, not the words" do as they come to know a story they wish to retell. This is also the sort of work I first learned about in the storytelling residencies with Laura Simms.[4]

Eventually I reach my goal of becoming so familiar with the characters and the story of what happened to them that I can more fully imagine this story from their lives. When you compare my version with the Jacobs version, it is pretty clear I've imagined more details of the girls' lives than the Jacobs text provided. Because I wanted to focus on Kate and Annie's story, I provide more detail so my audience can more fully picture how these two stepsisters, while very different from each other, show love and respect for one another. And, as mentioned earlier, my interest in Kate's mother's motivation led me to more descriptions of what she saw and felt as she watched Kate and Annie grow up.

I've also made smaller deliberate changes. I changed the peck basket to a pound. Maybe you've bought something by the peck recently, but I haven't. When I considered using simply "basket," I kept imagining Kate negotiating the size of the basket before agreeing to her task, and there I was—back to "peck." I dropped the hound because I simply could not picture Kate and the dog at the home of the fairies without also seeing the dog's actions revealing her presence. As for the yellow birdie? Why yellow? I haven't a clue, although I'm fairly sure I harbor no animosity toward Tweety!

In addition to thinking and imagining beyond the text of a story, it's not unusual for me to also think about events in characters' lives that I know I'll never include in my telling of the tale: How did Kate's mother explain the missing girls to Annie's father? Did she tell the truth or lie? How did Annie's father react to these events? Did the girls invite the parents to their wedding? Could Kate and Annie ever forgive Kate's mother? Is any reconciliation ever possible after such events?

I owe a big thank you for my ending of the story to Candy Kopperud, the library services coordinator at Palmer Public Library in Palmer, Alaska. Until Candy heard the story, I had ended it with a reference to the weddings and a happily ever after. After she heard the story, Candy told me she had been sure I was going to mention dancing at the weddings and how Kate's prince did not like dancing, but did not know why. Oh my! I knew an improved ending when I heard one, and with Candy's permission I've incorporated her idea into the ending ever since.[5]

I don't know what happened to the would-be Texas cheerleader, but her mother was granted probation in 1997. The young woman was thirteen when her mother was convicted and seventeen when her mother was granted probation.[6] By now, she is an adult. Like Kate Crackernuts, I hope she managed to know and trust herself and chart her own successful path.

The King and His Advisor

There once lived a king. The king had an advisor. Everywhere the king went, his advisor went. Whenever anything happened, the advisor would say, "Your Majesty, everything happens for the good." The king thought this meant his advisor was incredibly wise.

One day, the king and his advisor were walking in the palace gardens. The king spied an especially beautiful rose. He reached out to pick it, and a thorn cut his finger. His finger began to bleed and bleed.

The king cried, "Look at this. Who could imagine such a cut from a thorn on a rosebush?"

The advisor looked, "Your majesty," he said, "everything happens for the good."

"What? I cut my finger. I am in pain and all you can say is everything happens for the good. Now that I think about it, I see that is all you ever say. I thought you were wise, but perhaps this is the only thing you know how to say. I order you thrown into the palace dungeon. What do you say about that?"

"Your majesty," said the advisor, "everything happens for the good." The advisor was thrown into the palace dungeon.

A day or so later, the king went hunting. When he was far away from his own lands, he was attacked and seized by people whose ways were quite different from his own. One of the customs of his captors was that of killing prisoners in sacrifice to their gods. When the people saw the king, they said, "Look at him! His clothing is magnificent! Surely he will be a perfect sacrifice for our gods." They began planning the sacrifice.

When all was ready, a final inspection was made of the king's body, for it was essential that anyone sacrificed to the gods be perfect—no marks, no scars, no blemishes of any kind.

When the inspectors found the cut on the king's finger, they said, "He isn't perfect! We could never sacrifice him to our gods. Our gods would be displeased." They took the king back to where they had captured him and set him free.

The king hurried to his own lands. He went straight to his palace, then straight to the palace dungeon. He told his advisor the whole story, ". . . and so, my dear advisor, I now understand why, when I cut my finger, you said, 'everything happens for the good,' but I still don't understand why when I said I was going to throw you into this horrible place, you still said, 'everything happens for the good.'"

The advisor smiled. "Your majesty," he said, "that's easy to explain. You see, I go everywhere with you. Had I been with you, I too would have been captured. Your majesty, my body has no marks, no scars, no blemishes of any kind. Me, they would have killed! So, you see your majesty, everything happens for the good!"

COMMENTARY

Sometimes a wonderful story is dropped in a teller's lap, or in this case, arrives in the mailbox. In 1986, I told stories at Thompson Middle School in Southfield, Michigan. Shortly thereafter, I received a letter from Umang Badhwar, a thirteen-year-old student. In her letter, Umang thanked me for my storytelling, saying, "I really liked the way you drew a picture in my mind by just using words." Then she added, "Well, see I know this one story called, 'The King and his Advisor,' and here's how it goes:

The King and his Advisor

Once upon a time there was a king. He was known to be the strongest king in the world. Now, this king had a priest as his advisor. Well one day the king was in his garden admiring his beautiful flowers, when he pricked himself on a rosebush.

"Look!" shouted the king, "I just pricked myself on the bush!"

"Everything that happens, happens for the good," answered the advisor. Everytime something bad would happen, this would be his answer.

"Shut-up!" shouted the king and demanded that the priest or the advisor be locked up in the chamber. "Do you have anything to say before I lock you up?" questioned the king.

"Everything happens for the good," answered the advisor.

The next day the king went hunting alone deep into the jungle. The king saw a tiger and began to follow it. As he was doing so, a native tribe captured the king and took him back to camp. The native people would burn people in respect for their god, but they burned people with no cuts or scars on their body. As soon as the native people saw the cut on the king's finger, they let him go.

As soon as the king got home he demanded that his advisor be let free. Then the king asked the advisor, "The native people did not kill me because of my cut, but why was it good that you got locked up?"

"Because my great lord, if I would have gone with you, they would have killed me instead!" replied the advisor.

*   *   *

Umang ended her letter with the following: "Hope you liked it! My grandfather told me this from India." She hoped I liked it? I loved it! I wrote back to Umang for permission from her and her family to retell the story. In her reply, she wrote: "I would be very happy if you told my story as a part of your collection." And "My grandfather shared this story with me over the summer. He said that it was passed on to him from his father. My grandfather is from India, and so am I. I came to the USA about eight years ago."[1] After that exchange, I added the story to my repertoire, but I did not stay in touch with Umang. In the midst of working on this book, I found her again!

Not long after I visited her school in Southfield, Michigan, Umang's family moved to Bloomfield, Michigan, where she graduated from high school. In college she studied English and psychology. She also lived a year in Chicago and then nine years in New York City. In 2008, she returned to Bloomfield to finish her master's degree in clinical psychology. She is currently in the last phase of the program and is also studying psychoanalysis at the Michigan Psychoanalytic Institute. Someday she hopes to have her own practice. I was delighted to learn of her accomplishments, and I asked her if she remembered sending me the story and if she tells it. Yes! And Yes! The story is one Umang tells to her brother's children.

Compare Umang's version with my retelling, and you can see that while I've stayed true to the basic plot, I have retold the story in my own words, gradually making changes along the way as I filtered the story through my imagination. Looking at both versions, I can see I added more dialogue, changed "priest" to a consistent "advisor," sent the advisor to a "dungeon" instead of a "chamber," changed the single god in Umang's story to the multiple "gods," and had the advisor provide more of an explanation at the end. Other than the consistent change to "advisor" and the explanation at the end, I made none of my changes consciously. I simply told and retold the tale as I remembered it, keeping what seemed to work with each retelling.

Years after adding this story to my repertoire, I found a collection of tales from India, *Folk Tales of Orissa* by Shanti Mohanty, which included a variant of the story.[2] In Mohanty's version the basic plot is the same. Differences between the Mohanty and Badhwar versions include: The advisor is referred to as the king's minister. The king cuts off his finger while attempting to cut a mango. The king has his minister pushed into an old well. The king follows a stag into a forest and is attacked by Savaras.[3] The god to receive the sacrifice is female, while gender is not specified in the Badhwar version.

In *Folk Tales of Orissa*, Mohanty writes, "It is not surprising to note that more or less similar stories are prevalent even in distant states of India."[4] Umang heard the story from her maternal grandfather, whose surname is Sansi. The Sansi family is not from Orissa, but is originally from Multan, Pakistan. Umang wrote, "After the partition of India and Pakistan, Hindus were exiled from Multan, that's how my grandparents settled in New Delhi."[5]

So, what makes a folktale a folktale from a specific place or people? Umang Badhwar became a U.S. citizen in 1990. She tells this story to her brother's children, and perhaps someday they will tell it to their children. Umang heard the story told in Hindi when her grandfather from New Delhi, India, was visiting Michigan. She sent me her English translation of the tale.[6] The family member she heard it from was born in what is now Pakistan. So, is this story a folktale from India? A folktale from Pakistan? At some point does it become an example of American folklore? Is it already an example of U.S. folklore? Who decides how the tale would be classified?

In this book, the Kentucky folktales were all collected in Kentucky. So, if I had encountered Umang in a Kentucky school instead of in a Michigan school, would that make her tale a Kentucky folktale? Is it because she knows her grandfather grew up in India and the story is part of her cultural heritage that makes this story an Indian folktale? What if a Kentuckian retelling a folktale knows the family ancestors are from France, England, or Germany? Are the tales passed down through the generations Kentucky folktales or are they French, English, and German tales?

Could "The King and His Advisor" be classified as an example of Michigan folklore? After all, it was passed along in Michigan, so it could be said to have been collected in Michigan. Yes, it was sent to me in writing, but Umang heard it orally. Many of the Kentucky tales in this book were collected orally by students in classes who then transcribed, or recalled, the tales and presented them in writing to their teachers in college and university classes. From there, the tales have found their way into various archival collections. Some of them include information about where the teller heard the story, but many do not. And all of these tales, unless noted as being collected outside of Kentucky, are considered Kentucky tales.

I don't have any firm answers to offer for the questions I'm posing. I suspect the determining lines are somewhat blurry. What I do know is that when I tell this story to my audiences, I am passing along a version of a story I received from the young teenager of a family who had moved to the United States from India. The tale captured my attention because of the surprising twist at the end, so I tell it today because I enjoy the plot.

Umang enjoys the plot, too, but her connections to the story run deeper and are multifaceted in comparison to mine. When she tells the story, she is passing along family history—after all, this is a story told to her by her grandfather, who heard it from his father. Hearing stories from family members is an experience she treasures from her own childhood. By telling the story to her brother's children, she also creates for them a childhood experience similar to her own.

The story also reflects Umang's religion and culture: "the teaching of patience is continuous throughout the Hindu religion and Indian culture. The story includes the lesson that you cannot let an uncomfortable situation or something you don't understand spur your actions."[7] In Umang's version as she tells it now, the king yells at his gardener because he doesn't understand why on the one day he comes out to smell his roses, he is pricked by a thorn. He has the gardener banished. When the priest tries to explain that everything happens for a reason, the king has the priest banished. After the hunting trip, when the king returns to the priest, it is as if the priest has understood the king had to have this experience to gain understanding. Umang explained that the priest has endured something uncomfortable without letting the incident affect his self-image. He waits, without hate, for the king to return. The king comes to understand that there is a reason and purpose for all of life's events, both negative and positive. In Umang's version the king also apologizes to the priest, who is beneath him. The story teaches that even a king, a powerful person who others look up to and come to for advice and leadership, has difficulty understanding the message that everything happens for a reason. That he apologizes to the priest also shows that he is humbled by his previous arrogance and anger, and now understands the priest is truly an enlightened man. Through the experience of the story, the king now also is enlightened.[8]

"The lesson in this story may also be reflective of 'the times' considering the history of India. My grandparents had to leave their home and begin a new life in a new place. Also, my grandfather was a young man during the time of Gandhi, who was a representation of patience at that time."[9]

It would be a great falsehood for me to ever claim I am passing along "The King and His Advisor" with the same understanding Umang has of the story. Even though my family has many generations in Kentucky,[10] I also cannot claim to have the same understanding of the folktales I've retold here as the Kentuckians who told their versions to other Kentuckians who placed them in archives. My family told stories, but did not pass along folktales. My love of folktales grew from reading and rereading the printed collections I borrowed from my elementary school library.

But what if my family had retold folktales? Would that make my understanding of such stories identical to that of other Kentuckians who grew up with the same folktales? Not likely. Marcia Lane observes, "Even if the teller and the listeners are of the same cultural group (so they start with the same understanding of implied meanings), the difference in personal experience guarantees that each listener will form particular—and sometimes radically dissimilar—images from the teller's words."[11]

What I do have in common with Umang Badhwar and with the Kentuckians who told their stories to students, folklorists, and other scholars who subsequently placed them in archival collections is that I know a story, and I'm willing to share it.

RABBIT AND THE ALLIGATORS

A long time ago, a long, long, *long* time ago, way back, when rabbits had long, pretty tails like foxes, there lived a rabbit. One day Rabbit had been gone from home since early, early in the morning. All day long Rabbit had been working, working, and working. By the end of the day, Rabbit was tired, so very tired. He headed for home. Hop hop, rest. Hop hop, rest. Hop hop, rest. Ooooh, Rabbit was tired. By the time Rabbit reached the edge of the swamp near his house, he was so tired he couldn't even take one more hop.

Rabbit stood there looking out over the swamp. He could see his house. It stood on a little rise of dry land straight across the swamp. Rabbit thought, "I am too tired to hop all the way around this swamp to reach my house. I don't know why this old swamp has to be between me and my house anyway. But I do know one thing: I cannot go hopping around this swamp today. I am way too tired. I could swim across. But those old alligators living in this swamp think anything swimming in the swamp is supposed to be their dinner. No, if I try to swim across, those alligators would just eat me up. What I need is a plan—a plan for moving myself from here straight across this swamp."

Rabbit started thinking. He twitched his long ears, and he thought. He pulled on that long, pretty tail of his, and he thought. He twitched, and he thought. He pulled, and he thought. Pretty soon ideas started flying around in his head. Rabbit twitched his ears, and he thought. He pulled his long pretty tail, and he thought. After awhile, with all that twitching and thinking and pulling and thinking, those ideas started arranging themselves into a plan—a fine plan for moving himself from where he was straight across the swamp to his house.

Now, to work his plan Rabbit needed an alligator. Rabbit watched the swamp until he saw a big, old alligator swimming nearby, and then Rabbit began working his plan. He began singing a song—a song he was making up right on the spot:

Oh, there are many, many, many, many rabbits in this world,
and oh so very few alligators.
Rabbits, rabbits, rabbits, rabbits everywhere.
As for alligators, they just can't compare
with the many, many, many, many rabbits in this world,
and oh so very few alligators.

That big old alligator heard Rabbit's song and swam over to listen.
Rabbit pretended he didn't see him, and kept right on singing:

There are many, many, many, many rabbits in this world,
and oh so very few alligators.
Rabbits, rabbits, rabbits, everywhere under the sun.
As for alligators, you can hardly find a one
for the many, many, many, many rabbits in this world,
and oh so very few alligators.

Alligator swam closer, "Rabbit, hey Rabbit! What is that song
you're singing?"

Rabbit lied, "Oh, Alligator, I didn't see you out there! That song?
Why, that's just a song all us rabbits know. We learn it when we're just
little bitty baby rabbits. Our mamas teach it to us so we learn how many
rabbits there are in the world and how few of you alligators there are.
I can sing it for you, Alligator.

There are many, many, many, many rabbits in this world
and oh so very few alligators.
Rabbits, rabbits, rabbits, rabbits everywhere—

"Rabbit," Alligator interrupted, "Stop the singing, Rabbit. I already
heard the song. What do you mean there are more rabbits in this world
than there are alligators? Rabbit, do you actually believe that song is
true?"

"Well, Alligator, I never really thought about whether or not the
song is true. All rabbits sing it—we learn it when we're just babies."
Rabbit pretended to consider Alligator's question, and then he spoke.
"I guess we do think it's true. Don't you think it's true?"

"No, Rabbit, I believe that song is nothing but a lie. I live out here in the swamp, and I see alligators all the time. I hardly ever see a rabbit." Alligator was upset. "Rabbit, that song your mama taught you is just one big lie, and you rabbits ought not be singing a big lie like that."

"A lie? Do you really think so?" Rabbit pretended to be shocked. "Why, Alligator, when I was just a little bitty baby rabbit, I not only learned that song, I learned a rabbit is always supposed to tell the truth." Rabbit crossed his heart, "Cross my heart. Hope to die. Never tell a lie." And he solemnly nodded his head, "Honest."

"Now Rabbit, I am glad you were taught to be honest, but that song. . . ." Alligator seemed a bit less upset. "Well, I guess Mama Rabbits just don't know any better, 'cause that song is one big lie."

"Oh, Alligator, I know there's not a Mama Rabbit is this world who wants to teach her baby a lying song. So, Alligator, if you want me to I'll go tell the other rabbits that song is a lie, and they're not to sing it anymore."

"Rabbit, you'd do that? You'd tell the other rabbits not to sing that song?"

"Oh, I would Alligator." Rabbit hesitated, "Of course, I would have to prove to the rabbits the song is a lie. But if you'd like for me to I'd be willing to count the alligators, and if it turns out there really are more alligators than rabbits, I'll go tell all the other rabbits we are not allowed to sing that song anymore."

Alligator was excited. He called all the other alligators, and they all came swimming up. Alligator told them all about the song he'd heard Rabbit singing. Got the alligators real upset. Then Alligator calmed 'em all down by telling 'em about Rabbit's offer to count the alligators. Now, all the alligators were excited. They all crowded around, eager to be counted.

"All right, Rabbit," called Alligator, "we are all here. You can begin the count now."

"Now Alligator, I really am willing to count you alligators, and I am willing to report the results to the rabbits, but we got to be sure this count is done fair. Right now, you alligators are swimming this way and that, just milling around. Why, I'm likely to count one of you over here, and you're likely to swim under and come up over there, and I'd be counting you twice. Now that wouldn't be right. No, if I'm going to count and report results to the rabbits, you alligators have got to line up, holding hands, side by side by side, all your heads pointing toward one end of the swamp and all your tails pointing toward the other. Then, you've got to hold still."

Well, the alligators really wanted to be counted, so the first alligator put two feet on the shore near Rabbit. His head pointed toward one end of the swamp. His tail pointed toward the other. With his other two feet, he "held hands" with the next alligator. And so it went. Alligator after alligator after alligator lined up side by side by side until those alligators stretched all the way across that swamp.

Then Alligator called, "All right, Rabbit, we're ready. You can begin the count now."

Rabbit shouted, "Do you alligators all promise to be real good and hold real still so I can hop out on your backs and conduct this counting?"

"Oh, we'll be good," all the alligators shouted. "We'll hold still."

So Rabbit hopped from alligator to alligator, counting:

"One, two, buckle my shoe.

"Three, four, shut the door.

"Five, six, pick up sticks.

"Seven, eight, lay them straight.

"Nine, ten, a big fat hen.

"Eleven, eleven?

"All good alligators going straight to heaven."

Now, those alligators had heard about heaven, and they really wanted to go. They were real good. They held hands, and they stayed still. Rabbit hopped and counted, "Twelve, thirteen, fourteen, fifteen. . . ."

By the time Rabbit reached the far side of the swamp, he was so pleased with himself for tricking those alligators, he started laughing. In fact, Rabbit was so busy laughing he forgot to call out a number when he landed on the last alligator's back.

"Rabbit," the last alligator called out, "Rabbit, I don't believe I heard you call a number when you landed on my back. Rabbit! Why are you laughing, Rabbit?"

"Oh Alligator," Rabbit laughed, "I don't know how many rabbits there are in this world, and I don't care how many alligators there are. I didn't learn that song when I was a baby. I just stood over on the other side of the swamp and made that song up." Rabbit laughed and laughed. "I just wanted to see if I could trick you alligators into being a bridge for me to cross the swamp to my house. My plan worked too. Oh, you alligators just lined up and you all held still. You were real good alligators too! Now I'm almost home." Rabbit held his side and laughed and laughed. He just doubled over laughing.

Now that last alligator didn't much like the idea of Rabbit tricking the alligators, so he came charging out of the swamp, his jaws wide open. Rabbit looked up just in time and made one hop. WHOMP! Alligator snapped his jaws shut.

Rabbit's one hop was big, but not quite big enough. Remember that long, pretty tail I told you about? Alligator got Rabbit's long, pretty tail. And from that day to this, all rabbits have been going around in this world carrying nothing but that little stub of a tail they wear today.

COMMENTARY

Motif K579.2.2* Hare Crosses to Mainland by Counting Crocodiles. Tail Bitten Off or Fur Pulled in Revenge.[1]

In 1985, I was added to the artist roster of the Grand Rapids Council of Performing Arts for Children in Grand Rapids, Michigan. On one of my first classroom visits, with the Arts Council director observing my work, a teacher turned to her second graders and introduced me with, "Children, this is Mary Hamilton. She is a storyteller. Because Easter is coming soon, she is going to tell you rabbit stories for the next hour."

With that introduction I learned my program was one hour instead of forty-five minutes. Even more importantly, I learned I would be telling rabbit stories. Of course, I also learned the importance of controlling my own introduction, but I was completely unaware of that lesson in the panic of the moment. Wanting to make a good impression on the Arts Council director, the children, and their teacher, I didn't dare openly contradict the introduction. So, I told rabbit stories.

I told the children a Brer Rabbit tale I remembered from reading folktales during my childhood. From there, I moved on to other animal stories in my sparse repertoire—stories with Rabbit for a main character that day, even if Rabbit had never been part of the story before.

I looked at my watch. I still had fifteen minutes to go. I also had a vague recollection of a story that included a rabbit and a crocodile or alligator bridge trick which resulted in rabbit losing his tail.[2] I started in telling, my mind whirring like Brer Rabbit's in a tight, but survivable, fix. By the time Rabbit reached the swamp, I decided to let him think a while to develop his plan. After all, the story as I was remembering it could be told in well under five minutes. All Rabbit needed to do was brag about rabbits outnumbering alligators. I had more time to fill than that.

Then, what I think of as the Brer Rabbit spirit of storytelling survival took over, and I knew Rabbit would be trickier than simply bragging. In that moment, Rabbit's song was born, and Rabbit has attracted the attention of Alligator through song in every telling I've done of this story since.

When I tell the story today, I intentionally sing Rabbit's song rather poorly, with a ragged, uneven, somewhat hesitant rhythm. After all, what song, while being made up, sounds as if it has been sung many times? So, for example, Rabbit drags out the sound of "everywhere," holding the note on "-where" to allow himself time to think of a rhyme for his next line. Words and portions of words gain two and three syllables, while other phrases are sung hurriedly, just to make the rhyme scheme work out for the song. As a song, it's something of a mess. As a funny and believable tricky tactic for fooling Alligator, it works.

When the alligators line up, my oral description of their arrangement usually includes few words beyond "side by side by side." My gestures provide the information which lets the audience know how the alligators are lining up their bodies to create the line that becomes the swamp-crossing bridge. For very young audiences, I may literally walk straight through the audience as Rabbit counts alligators, to truly "make visual" Rabbit's trick. I've found preschoolers and kindergartners picture Rabbit's trick better the more visually the crossing of the swamp is presented. Most first, second, and third graders catch on to Rabbit's trick while he works his plan. I vary details and move as needed to be sure my audience catches on before the alligators.

Even during that very first telling, listeners joined in counting. And yes, Rabbit counted many more alligators in that first telling than he does today. After all, I still had time to fill! For the first few years I told the story, I was simply counting, not using the counting rhyme. Most audiences began counting along with me by the fourth or fifth alligator. One day, I used the "One, two, buckle my shoe" counting rhyme[3] and the audience joined in as soon as they heard the familiar rhyme. I had learned this rhyme up through "Nine, ten, a big fat hen" during some no longer remembered part of my childhood. The rhyme of eleven and heaven in the story is my invention, developed over time and tellings to many different audiences. While I don't recall exactly when the counting rhyme became part of the story, it was after I recorded the tale in 1988.[4]

While I remain grateful that I have never since listened to an introduction of my work that scared me as much as that one did back in 1985, I am delighted the unexpected intro eventually led to such a fun to tell tale.

FAMILY TALES
AND
PERSONAL NARRATIVES

In this section you'll find both oral traditional narratives and personal experience narratives. Montell explains the difference: "The personal experience narrative is an *eyewitness* or *firsthand* account; the narrator says, in essence, 'I was there, I saw the action, and this is the way it happened.' . . . Oral traditional narratives, on the other hand, are *secondhand* ('I wasn't there, but my grandmother was, and she described it like this') or *thirdhand* reminiscences."[1]

I first heard most of the family tales here from my father, so my retellings are second-, third-, maybe even fourthhand accounts. I don't tell them the way they are told in the family because I usually tell to strangers. After all, family members already know the people, and they've been to most of the places, so much can remain unsaid. Fact is, if you asked my relatives, "Who is the Hamilton family storyteller?" they will name my father, not me.

You'll find a couple of tales I remember from specific events in my life, and you'll also find the story of an event from my life that I have no memory of. Instead the event was remembered for me and told to me by my parents.

In *The Kentucky Encyclopedia*, Laura Harper Lee describes family stories as "narratives people make up in response to real-life experiences."[2] Hmm, make up? While I understand what she means, in my family we call these true stories.[3]

A PLACE TO START

When my Uncle Sammy was a boy he was a real good eater. Every day, my grandma would send Sammy off to school with two sandwiches, and he would always come home with an empty lunch box.[1]

Now when Sammy began first grade, sandwiches were made from double loaf bread—each slice was twice as wide as the slices of bread we have today. When my grandma made Sammy's sandwiches, she would take a slice of that double loaf bread, put the filling on, and then fold the bread over for sandwich one. She would then take a second slice of double loaf bread, put the filling on, and fold it over—sandwich two.

It was during Sammy's first year of school that single loaf bread, like what we have today, became more popular than double loaf bread. The first day my grandma made Sammy's sandwiches with single loaf bread, she took a slice of bread, put the filling on, and then put a second slice on top for sandwich one. Another slice of bread, filling, a second slice of bread—sandwich two.

When Sammy came home from school that afternoon, my grandma opened his lunch box and she found two sandwiches. He hadn't eaten as much as a single bite out of either one. My grandma looked at him, "Sammy, do you feel okay? Are you sick? Weren't you hungry? You didn't eat your sandwiches."

Sammy looked at his mama, and tears ran down his cheeks, "Oh, Mama, I'm hungry. I'm just as hungry as I can be, but I couldn't eat either one of those sandwiches. They've got something wrong with them. Neither one of them has a place to start."

COMMENTARY

First you need to know that my Uncle Sammy grew up to become an engineer for a nationwide company. Yep, he grew up to be a troubleshooter!

In the telling of this story, I use my hands as substitutes for the slices of bread, showing how the different sandwiches were constructed. I know using a gesture will call attention to specific parts of a story, and in this one I want to be sure my listeners picture the different sizes of bread used to create the different sandwiches. Without that information solidly pictured, the ending will not make any sense. For years, I thought all my listeners pictured Sammy unable to eat the second set of sandwiches because he could not force himself to bite through the crust, but comments from a recent audience let me know that some listeners see the situation as Sammy viewing the first type of sandwich like a hot dog bun so he could start on an end while holding the section with no crust. Hmm, once again, I'm reminded that when a story is told each listener imagines it anew and creates his or her own version of the tale. Whether my listeners see him as unable to bite through crust or unable to find an end to use as a starting place, the story still works.

When I was growing up I never heard this story. Why? It never came up. Then, several of us were visiting my parents. My sister was making sandwiches for the nieces and nephews. When she set a sandwich down in front of one niece (I no longer remember which one, or I would tell you!), the child looked stricken. My father noticed, and commented, "She's like Sammy." My sister immediately picked up the sandwich, cut off the crust, and returned the sandwich to the now happy child. I stood there flabbergasted, completely unable to make the connection between his comment and her actions.

So, I asked, "How does 'she's like Sammy' mean cut off the crust?"

Now my father and sister were puzzled, "You never heard that story?"

And that's how the story ended up being told to me.

Family stories! They exist, but in my family (and I suspect in many families) the stories are not told every time folks get together. Instead, they come up in the context of specific situations that bring them to mind. Even then they are not told full out, but only referred to because the family thinks everybody already knows. Fortunately, curiosity and confusion led me to ask, and voila! A story!

Jeff Rides the Rides

The year my little brother Jeff turned eight was a real important year for him. On his eighth birthday, my daddy looked at him and said, "Jeff, now that you are eight years old, when Meade County Fair time comes, you can go over to the midway and ride all the rides all by yourself. You won't have to have any older brothers and sisters tagging along with you to make sure you behave."

Oh, Jeff was excited. From his birthday in April all the way to fair time in August, he'd look at us and say, "I get to ride all the rides—all by myself. You don't get to watch me. You can't boss me around. You can't follow me. You can't tell me what to do. I get to ride all the rides, all the rides, all by myself, all by myself . . . "

By the time August and fair time rolled around we were all sick and tired of listening to Jeff go on and on about how he was going to ride all the rides.

Finally, the Meade County Fair got set up on the fairgrounds in Brandenburg, the county seat. We all crowded into our car and Daddy drove the fifteen miles from our farm down to the fairgrounds. Everybody jumped out, and Daddy said, "Now, listen up. Tonight is English horse show night. That means there's going to be organ music playing. When the organ music stops, I expect all of you all to come on back to the car because it will be time to go home."

We all said, "All right, Daddy." Then we ran off in all directions to find our friends and enjoy the fair.

When the organ music stopped, everybody came on back to the car—including my little brother Jeff.

On the way home, Daddy asked, "Well, Jeff, did you ride all the rides?"

Jeff said, "Oh, I tried to, Daddy. I rode 'em all except one."

"Jeff, I thought I gave you enough money to ride all the rides. Why didn't you ride that one?"

"Oh, you gave me plenty of money. I rode some of 'em two and three times. I couldn't ride that one because I couldn't figure out where to buy a ticket."

"Jeff, what do you mean you couldn't figure out where to buy a ticket? What was that ride?"

"Well, I'm not real sure I figured out the name of it right because it didn't have a big sign over the top of it like all the other rides did. But I can tell you what it looked like. It was tall—taller than you are, Daddy. And it was white, and there were several of them lined up side by side, and each one of them had a door on the front. From the outside the ride didn't look like it did too much. A person would walk up, open the door, step inside, and close the door. After a while they'd open the door again and step out. So from the outside it really didn't look very exciting, but every time I was anywhere near it there were always great long lines of people looking like they could hardly wait their turn to ride that ride. And after the ride—when they opened the door and walked away, they always looked like they'd had a pretty good time; so I believe it was one of the better rides there."

Now, none of us were laughing out loud—after all, this was the youngest child talking, so we didn't dare laugh—but we were quivering all over from the effort to hold our laughter in.

My Daddy shook his head and said, "Jeff, are you sure there were no words, no words at all associated with that ride?"

"Oh, Daddy, I knew rides had names, so I looked it over real careful and I found some words, I believe that ride was called the Port-a-Car."

It seems the Port-a-Can company was hired to supply the portable toilets at the Meade County Fair that year and an important part of the "n" in their logo was missing. My little brother Jeff really would have ridden the portable toilets, if he just could have figured out where to buy himself a ticket.

COMMENTARY

This story falls into the realm of family folklore. Everyone in our family knows the story because it usually gets told when folks new to the family are meeting Jeff. Because I usually tell stories to strangers, the story has needed some shaping to make it work for my audiences. For example, in the family there is no need to explain who Jeff is. Usually, there is also no need to provide much information about the Meade County Fair because the listeners already know about it. Calling it "the fair" or just saying something like "the county fair" will suffice.[1] So strangers need some background information that family members can easily do without.

In addition, given the actual event, a told version for strangers needed some shaping. The year Jeff told Daddy he could not figure out where to buy a ticket for the Port-a-Car, I did not attend the fair with my family. I'm almost twelve years older than Jeff. I had stayed in Lexington, attending summer classes at the University of Kentucky, and did not go home for the fair that year. I learned about Jeff's experience in a phone call with my father. When I asked my dad how the fair had gone, his reply was, "Now Mary, wouldn't you think Jeff was old enough to be let loose on the midway by himself?" Of course, I had no idea what had happened, but I knew something had gone wrong. In proper conversational fashion, I replied, "What happened?" Then Daddy told me that Jeff reported he'd ridden every ride except the Port-a-Car. When I protested there was no such ride, Daddy responded, "Think about it Mary, the Port-a-Car?" Eventually it dawned on me that Jeff was referring to the portable toilets. When I guessed that, Daddy gave me the details of telling Jeff he could go by himself, then wondering about his decision when he heard Jeff's report of his adventures.

I hadn't even considered telling this family incident to strangers. Then, sometime prior to 1987, I was telling stories to middle-school-aged students in Wyoming, Michigan, a suburb of Grand Rapids. The students asked, "Do you know any true stories?" I remembered the incident with my brother and told it to them. They enjoyed it! After that I sought my brother's permission to tell the story. He gladly gave it with his encouragement.

Now, the telling varies, especially in the section where I'm describing the portable toilets and the behavior of the people waiting in line. It is during this section that audience members reveal through laughter and facial expressions that they have figured out what Jeff is talking about, even though Jeff is still in the dark. Because audiences have more fun when they are ahead of Jeff, I vary description details. Sometimes I'll have Jeff say that some were white and others were a sort of blue green. Sometimes I'll use body language or stance to show how the people looked when "they could hardly wait their turn." Once

I can tell recognition is dawning, I move on to the comments about our suppressed laughing in response to Jeff's telling.

When my brother Jeff was a high school music teacher, he used this story to help his students grasp the concept of improvisation. He began the lesson by playing a recorded version of the story,[2] stopping at the point in the story when my father tells us all to return to the car at the end of the night and we all head off. He then asked his students to brainstorm ideas for the rest of the story. His students always came up with many different ideas. Each idea was discussed and evaluated based on its plausibility. Every time he used this exercise, his students identified multiple equally plausible story endings, but no one ever proposed the actual ending. Then Jeff played the rest of the recording. He explained to the students that the only reason he knew what had actually happened was because he was the "Jeff" in the story. He and his students agreed that their endings also created perfectly viable stories.

It was a relatively small task for him to connect plausible story progressions to plausible musical progressions. Then his students could let go of their reluctance to improvise musically for fear of not getting it right, and embrace the idea that many possible "rights" could actually exist in any musical improvisation, just as they had existed in their story improvisation. That the actual tale was based on a real happening was also freeing for his students because they could see that their improvisations would have been satisfying for listeners, even though they bore little resemblance to the real life event. I'm delighted that my telling of a tale on him proved so useful to my brother, and I applaud his creative use of storytelling in his classroom.[3]

JUMP ROPE KINGDOM

First grade babies
Second grade tots
Third grade angels
Fourth grade snots
Fifth grade peaches
Sixth grade plums
And all the rest are dirty bums.

I heard that rhyme on my first day of school, which at Flaherty
Elementary in Meade County, Kentucky, was the first day of first
grade. I'm not sure who started the rhyme. Could have been the
snots. They were proud of themselves. Might have been the peaches.
Might have been the plums. I don't believe it was the dirty bums
because, if memory serves me correctly, the dirty bums were much
too old for recess.

I heard that rhyme on the playground, day after day, recess after
recess. Even when the bell rang, and our teachers left the school building to meet us and we left the playground to meet our teachers, I could
still hear the rhyme, now a whispered taunt:

First grade babies
Second grade tots
Third grade—

I was in first grade, but I was not a baby. I was the oldest child in
my family, and the only one old enough to walk all the way out our long,
winding gravel driveway, stand by the highway, catch the big yellow
school bus, and ride it to school. I wasn't a baby. I was a big girl. But
somehow I knew if I said, "Teacher, teacher, do you hear . . . ?" there
would be laughter, and I wouldn't think it was funny. The big kids were

the ones who chanted the rhyme, and at my school the big kids were the rulers of the playground.

The big boys ruled the kingdom of marbles. Marbles, a game played in rings drawn in the dust beneath the shade of trees. I can't tell you what happened in the kingdom of marbles, because when I was a girl marbles was a boys-only world.

The big girls ruled a kingdom too—the jump rope kingdom. They decided who was going to turn the rope, who was going to jump, what chants would be chanted—they *ruled* the jump rope kingdom.

When I began first grade, I knew how to jump rope. I did! My mama would tie a rope to a porch post, and then she would string the rope across the porch. My mama would pick up the end of the rope. I'd stand beside the rope and watch her carefully. She would turn the rope, and I would jump. I knew how to jump rope when I began first grade.

But in the jump rope kingdom ruled by the big girls, no one stood beside the rope and waited for the rope to turn. Oh no, the big girls ran in while the rope was turning! They ran in as they chanted the words of the jump rope rhymes:

Not last night but the night before
Twenty-four robbers came a-knocking at my door.
As I ran out [*the big girl would run out*]
They ran in [*and she would jump back in, called "going in the back door"*]
And hit me on the head with a rolling pin
And this is what they said for me to do:
Fancy Dancer, do the twist [*the big girl would twist and jump at the same time*]
Fancy Dancer, give a high kick [*she'd kick and jump on one foot*]
Fancy Dancer, turn all around [*she turned in a circle while she jumped*]
Fancy Dancer, get out of town [*the big girl would run out; the next would run in, and the chant would begin all over again*]

The rope never stopped. If a rope-turner grew tired, a second big girl would walk over, stand beside her, take hold of the rope, and the two of them would turn the rope together. Then the one who was tired would step away—the rope never stopped.

I was not prepared. So I sat on the sidewalk and I watched—recess after recess, day after day. I learned the rhymes, took them home, and taught them to my little sister. But I did not, because I believed I could not, jump rope with the big girls.

One day, one of the big girls, Anna Jo Hinton, walked over, looked down at me, and said, "Don't you want to jump rope?"

"Oh, I do. I do, but . . . "

"But you don't know how, do you?"

"I know how to jump. I know the rhymes and everything. I just don't know how to run in."

Anna Jo looked back at the other big girls. "Hey, she knows how to jump. She just doesn't know how to run in. I believe I can teach her."

Some of the other big girls laughed, but Anna Jo offered me her hand. "You hold my hand. When I say run, you run. When I say jump, you jump."

I held her hand. "Run!" she said. I ran.

"Jump!" she said. I jumped.

Missed—I missed, and the rope stopped. Some of the big girls laughed—at me. But Anna Jo said, "Hey, she almost got it. Turn the rope again."

And again, "Run!" I ran. "Jump!" I jumped. I wish I could tell you I got it on my second try, but it wasn't an easy thing for me to learn.

Over and over Anna Jo made the other big girls turn the rope, until . . .

"Run!" I ran.

"Jump!" I jumped.

And I was jumping rope!

Anna Jo looked at me, "You'd better hold my hand again. I need to teach you how to get out of here." And I stopped the rope several more times learning how to run out.

Anna Jo Hinton was a queen in the jump rope kingdom. A queen who could lead the other big girls with wisdom enough, and courage enough, to offer her hand to one they laughed at and called a first grade baby and bring that first grade baby all the way inside the jump rope kingdom.

COMMENTARY

"Jump Rope Kingdom" is a true story from my life. It is built on the briefest of memories. One day I was thinking about how easy it is to recall specific details of negative events, and I began to wonder what story I would tell if I told of a specific remembered act of kindness. The memory of Anna Jo Hinton teaching me how to run into the jump rope immediately came to mind. Of course, "I remember that when I was in first grade, an older girl named Anna Jo Hinton taught me how to run into the jump rope" does not a story make. So, I had work to do.

I began by asking myself why. Why did I remember this incident? Why did it matter to me at the time? Why do I think it would matter to today's audiences? And the answers came flooding in.

I remembered because Anna Jo's kindness was so unexpected. I was a mere first grader. She must have been a fourth or fifth grader. I not only admired the big girls for their rope jumping skill, I also feared them because some of them were mean to little kids. I remembered the intense longing I felt—wanting to join in, knowing I lacked needed skills, and being too afraid of being laughed at or chased away to approach any of the more skillful girls for help.

Once I understood why the incident had mattered so much that I could still recall it over fifty years later, my task was to figure out how to make the incident live for my audience. By the time I worked on this story from my life, I had told stories long enough to know that the listening experience is stronger for the audience if they put images together and reach their own conclusions. Show, not tell, is one common way of expressing this idea. Instead of telling my audience the big kids were sometimes mean to the little kids, I needed to provide an example. I could remember some of the boys in my first grade class coming back from recess struggling to hold back tears because the older boys had engaged them in a game of marbles, playing for keeps, which meant at the end of the game you kept every marble you won during the game. Given the older boys' greater skills, it was not unusual for a younger boy to literally lose all his marbles. But I needed an example that would apply to girls, or to girls and boys. And then I recalled the first grade babies taunt. At my school it was never a jump rope rhyme, although it had the proper rhythm to work as one; instead it was a means of taunting the younger students. And at that time at Flaherty Elementary School, the first graders were indeed the youngest students. No public school kindergartens or preschools existed in my rural Kentucky community.

In the in-person tellings of the story, there is no need to specify that the older students softened the chant to a mere whispered taunt when they were near the teachers. Instead, I can use one hand to represent the teachers coming from the school building, and use my other hand to represent the students coming from the playground. As my hands move closer together, I can chant the rhyme at a lower and lower volume, bringing it from a loud taunt to a whisper with the sound of my voice. By then the audience knows this chant does not meet with approval from the teachers, and they soon understand my six-year-old self's objection to it too.

Instead of telling my audience the big girls' rope jumping skills awed me, I needed to paint a word picture of the big girls skillfully jumping rope. The logical solution? Use a jump rope rhyme. I was surprised at how many I actually remembered. Some proved too difficult to explain, even though jumping skill was required. Others incorporated popular cartoon characters, and so had the potential for copyright issues I wanted to avoid. Finally, I remembered the one I used. I only made one change. In my memory, the words are "Spanish dancer," not "Fancy dancer," but the more I pondered the rhyme, the more I could see that there was no reason to state a specific origin for the dancer in the rhyme for the rhyme to serve the story. After all, the point of using the rhyme was to demonstrate the fancy jumping skills of the big girls, not provide an example of remembered childhood oral lore. "Fancy" had the same two-syllable beat as "Spanish," so I made the change.

Like all orally told stories, this story has evolved over time. I've had the occasion to write it down before—three times, in fact. First, in my newsletter, *Telling Stories . . . Creating Worlds*, in 1996. Second, when I prepared a written version so the sound engineer would have an easier time communicating with me when I decided to record it in 2001.[1] And third, in 2006, when I typed it up for Ellen Munds, executive director of Storytelling Arts of Indiana, so it could be included in *The Scenic Route: Stories from the Heartland*, an anthology of "stories from a dozen storytellers who have graced our stages and who share our midwestern heritage,"[2] published by the Indiana Historical Society to commemorate the twentieth anniversary of Storytelling Arts of Indiana. I can now look back at the earliest written version and see that the jump rope rhyme and the metaphor of Anna Jo as a queen in the jump rope kingdom are later additions in comparison with the use of the first grade babies rhyme. Both changes were included by the time I recorded the tale, after many, many retellings.

Although I developed this story as a memory of an incident of kindness, the story developed its own life as a commemoration of Anna Jo Hinton after I included it in my newsletter in 1996. At the time I published the story, I did not know what had become of Anna Jo. She was an older girl in school, and this incident is all I remembered of encounters with her. It turns out the newsletter including the story was distributed not long after her death. One of Anna Jo's coworkers, Elizabeth Foote Cross, saw my newsletter, read the story, and called. According to Elizabeth the young Anna Jo's behavior in the story matched that of the adult Anna Jo, who had been a wonderful colleague.

When I visit schools to tell stories, I rarely see children jumping rope on the playground. Oh, sometimes I'll see them jumping rope in physical education classes, but each child is working alone, turning and jumping his or her own rope. Once in a while I'll see a second child run in and jump with the rope-turning jumper, but jumping rope is simply not the communal activity it once was. I'm not sure when this change happened, but even when I first started telling this story, in the early 1990s, I noticed, and I wondered if school children would be able to relate to the story. I received an answer one day at Medway Elementary in Medway, Ohio.[3] After listening to "Jump Rope Kingdom" and other stories, upper elementary students were walking not far from me as they left the school library. I overheard two girls having a conversation that went something like this:

"I know the boys have the basketball kingdom, but what kingdom do we have?"

"I'm not sure; maybe gymnastics, or cheerleading?"

"I think the boys let the younger boys in, but do we let the little girls in . . . ?" and on they walked. I never heard the end of their conversation, but I cherish the moment for the reassurance it gave me that the story could indeed matter to school children, even if they no longer jumped rope.

Adults relate to the story too. I've seen more than one adult's mouth moving when I'm chanting the rhymes because women in my age range, who grew up in certain parts of Kentucky, learned the same two rhymes.[4] Of course, knowledge of the specific rhymes is not a necessity for the story to connect with audience members. After I told the story at the Cherokee Rose Storytelling Festival, audience member and storyteller Tersi Bendiburg[5] told me that hearing the rhymes had taken her back to her childhood in Cuba. Once transported back by the rhymes, many memories from that time in her life had come rising up. No, Tersi had not chanted the same rhymes during her childhood, but she had chanted rhymes—rhymes she hadn't thought about in years. Moreover, the memories that arose were not limited to memories of times she had chanted the rhymes. Instead, as she listened to my story, she was reminded of her own stories.

Reminding listeners of their own stories—that's what the telling of personal narratives in performance settings can do. Something about the story has to resonate beyond whatever has driven the teller to tell it, and yes, the teller needs to do the work of structuring the narrative and recounting the events so the audience hears a tale artfully told. Personal narratives told just to satisfy the teller's need to get the story out are appropriately told to a therapist, with the teller paying to be heard, not to an audience whose members are paying to listen.

Mary Helen's Fiancé

After my great-aunts Mary Helen and Eloise graduated from Mount Saint Joseph Junior College near Owensboro, Kentucky, both secured jobs with the U.S. Department of Agriculture, working in one of its Kentucky offices. During World War II the federal government decentralized its operations by moving many offices out of Washington, D.C., and the headquarters of the Department of Agriculture moved to Cincinnati, Ohio. By the time the war began winding down and government agencies returned to Washington, my great-aunts worked in the Cincinnati headquarters, so when their jobs moved to Washington, they moved too.

After the war Eloise moved to New York with her husband, Ray Martinson, a returning soldier she had married before his three-year overseas assignment. Mary Helen stayed on in our nation's capital.

One day Mary Helen called home and announced she was getting married. Naturally, her mother, my great-grandmother, began asking questions about her intended. Mary Helen explained his name was Charles Ferrara. He was Italian, a U.S. Army veteran, and a native of the Washington, D.C., area.

My great-grandmother listened to all Mary Helen said as best she could, given that her phone service was a party line shared with several other families. Chances were also excellent that she was not the only one hearing the conversation, because when the phone rang all the houses on the party line heard the ringing. Each house had its own ring—maybe two longs and one short, or two shorts and one long—with the idea that you would only pick up if you heard your ring, but in reality many folks picked up and listened to every phone call. So, that combination of multiple people listening in and poor phone lines to begin with made conversing by phone a challenge. Nevertheless, my great-grandmother persisted in learning all she could about the man her daughter was going to marry.

"What does he do for a living?" my great-grandmother asked.

"He's an electrical engineer," she heard Mary Helen reply. Now, my great-grandmother, like most folks in her rural community, had no idea what an electrical engineer did, but it sounded impressive. After she and Mary Helen completed their call, my great-grandmother began calling her friends, telling them about the electrical engineer Mary Helen was going to marry. Even her friends who shared her party line agreed with her assessment of the phone call.

So, you can imagine my great-grandmother's surprise when Mary Helen came home with her husband who owned his own business—a store selling liquor and beer!

COMMENTARY

This is a family story—one that I had never heard until we had a Hamilton family reunion in 2009 at which the descendants of the great-grandmother in the story, including my great-aunt Mary Helen, gathered. One of my father's first cousins, Charlie Hamilton, told the tale. If you doubt such confusion is possible, try saying aloud "he's an electrical engineer" and then "he sells liquor and beer" and imagine hearing either phrase over a crackly phone line. Yep! You could confuse them too.

When I heard this tale, I realized there was a multi-generational thread in the family stories I had heard over the years—mistakes! We tell the stories that evoke laughter at our mistakes! "Jeff Rides the Rides" is another example of the same type of story. So is "A Place to Start," about my Uncle Sammy's sandwiches. Both of these were stories I had first heard from my father. I was aware that he told stories that had humorous mistakes as a common theme, but hearing the story of Mary Helen's phone call at the reunion was the first time I realized that theme had begun before his generation.

For years I thought my daddy just took some sort of unnerving delight in retelling tales of funny errors made by his children and his brother, but then I was interviewed by Pamela Petro for her book *Sitting Up with the Dead: A Storied Journey Through the American South*.[1] When Petro first contacted me to arrange the interview, she told me she wanted to talk with me about how I had grown up to become a storyteller. I insisted that if she wanted to understand, she needed to meet me at my parents' Meade County farm, not at my home in Frankfort. During that meeting my father, mother, and I told her several stories. My father also commented that he knew that sometimes his kids got aggravated over his choice of stories to tell, but he figured if he could give us the gift of being able to laugh at ourselves, that would be a good gift to have. I was astonished. Until I heard him say that, I had no idea my father had ever thought about why he recounted the stories he chose. Although Petro did not include my father's comment about his choice of story topics in her book, I remain grateful to her, for I might never have known my father's storytelling intentions otherwise.[2]

Looking back, I'm a bit surprised I hadn't noticed before the reunion that the thread of mistake stories extended well beyond my father and into other branches of the family. Several years earlier, Mike Jones, an uncle by marriage, from Elizabethtown, Hardin County, Kentucky, arrived at a family gathering along with his son Matt. As soon as they arrived, Mike announced, "Well, I've got one to tell you on Matt."

Now Matt was a young teenager at the time, so he moaned in protest, "Daaaad!"

But Mike replied, "Matt, we're at the Hamilton's. We've got to tell it." Immediately Matt relented. Here's the story Mike told:

Matt and his younger brother Chad had each attended a week-long basketball camp, but because they were different ages they attended different weeks. At the basketball camp statistics were kept on every player in a variety of categories—field goal percentage, number of assists, free throw percentage, number of steals, and so forth. At the end of the week, the camper with the highest stats in each category won a basketball.

On his last day of basketball camp, Chad came home and Matt asked, "Did you win a basketball?"

"No, I came in second in everything."

"But Chad, if you came in second in everything, it seems like you should have won a basketball, because last week when I went to camp, nobody could win more than one basketball."

"But I didn't win," Chad repeated, "I came in second in everything."

This made no sense to Matt, and he began insisting Chad could not possibly have come in second in everything and not won a basketball. Their father, Mike, overheard the conversation, so to help Chad out, he explained:

"Okay Matt, let's say John Doe had the best field goal percentage, and Chad was second. John Doe wins the basketball. Then let's say Jimmy Doe had the most assists, and Chad was second. Jimmy Doe wins the basketball. Then let's say Jerry Doe had the best free throw percentage, and Chad was second. Jerry Doe wins the basketball. And then—"

Matt interrupted, "Okay, Dad, I get why Chad didn't win a basketball, but who are these Doe kids anyway?"

* * *

At the time I thought: "Wow, we have a strong storytelling tradition in this family if a teenager will give up that easily." Now I see that it was not just the telling of a story but also the type of story that was part of the tradition. At the time I thought humor was the thread, but now I see humorous mistakes as the thread. And thanks to the Hamilton family reunion, I can see that this story thread was woven into the Hamilton family fabric long before my father became a family storyteller.

Okay, in fairness, I should also tell you at least one tale on myself:

A few years ago I told stories for a gathering at Indiana University in Bloomington, Indiana. I was living in Louisville at the time, so I decided to return home after the evening performance. When folks learned I was driving back to Louisville in the dark, several people warned, "Be careful. That road has lots of curves, and be sure you watch out for deer."

I promised I would and set off. There I was, just driving along in the darkness, listening to the radio, when I thought: "Hmm, those people sure do have their deer statue close to the road. Why, it's so close it could be a mailbox. And look, there's a second one right behind it."

Fortunately, that second deer statue moved, and my mind registered—"Deer! Brake!"—just in time.

That's one of my favorite anecdotes to tell on myself. Of course, I told it many times before I realized it, too, fit within the Hamilton tradition of telling and retelling humorous tales of our mistakes.[3]

In March 2011, I was talking on the phone with my sister, Pat, when the conversation turned to family stories. She told me her favorite story to tell on herself was about the time the two of us were up in the silo pitching down silage for the cows while belting out songs from *The Sound of Music*. According to Pat, Daddy yelled at us to quit singing because we were scaring the cows—they were walking toward the barn to be fed, but upon hearing our singing they were running away! I was amazed. This was her favorite family story, and I had no memory of the incident. Sure, we did climb up into the silo, and we did have the chore of using a pitchfork to throw down silage for the cows. Acoustics inside the silo were great, so I have no doubt we sang while in there. To this day I know the lyrics of most of the songs in *The Sound of Music*, so I must have listened to and sung them repeatedly. But the specific incident of scaring the cows? I don't recall it at all. Just because people grow up in the same family, it would be a mistake to assume they all share the same family stories.

So, these family stories are all true stories, right? Well, yes and no. When I began retelling the story about my great-aunt Mary Helen's phone call home, I told my audiences she worked in Washington, D.C., because so many men were away fighting in World War II. I had always heard that Aunt Mary Helen and Aunt Eloise wound up in Washington because of the war. Over the years, I had also heard and read about women being hired to do men's jobs during the war, so I assumed this was why Mary Helen and her sister Eloise, both high school graduates, moved from Kentucky to Washington, and I included that information as part of the story. It set the time period and included a bit of history for my listeners.

When another cousin, Dale Hamilton, told me Mary Helen and Eloise were college graduates, I decided I needed to do some fact-checking with Aunt Mary Helen. Oh, I knew she and Eloise had gone to Mount Saint Joseph, but I thought they went there for high school, not college.[4] After all, my grandfather, their older brother, had graduated from eighth grade and not attended high school, so I thought graduating from high school was the added accomplishment by the daughters of the family. Through fact-checking with my great aunt, I not only learned about their going to college, but also learned that while World War II was indeed a factor in the move to D.C., they hadn't moved because of a need for women to fill jobs formerly held by men. They had held their jobs before the war began. When the war wound down, the jobs they held then moved to Washington, so they moved with their jobs. I was wrong on several bits of information and changed the story accordingly.

However, I did not change everything. During the fact-checking Aunt Mary Helen also told me she is sure she never said, "sells liquor and beer." Instead she told her mother he owned a "liquor store," which her mother heard as "electric store." In fact, Mary Helen first heard the reference to an electrical engineer when she heard the story retold at the family reunion! After learning that Aunt Mary Helen's memory of the incident differed from how it had been told at the reunion, my father told me he remembers Mama Ham[5] saying that Mary Helen was marrying a man who owns an electric store, and "she even added, 'he sells all kinds of electrical appliances.'"[6] My father went on to say that electricity was relatively new to our rural area at that time, so the idea of anyone selling a variety of electrical appliances was quite a novelty.

Obviously, I've chosen to keep "he's an electrical engineer." I think I would need to incorporate lots of additional detail to explain my great-grandmother's excitement over an electric store, even though her contemporaries shared her feelings. In addition, I also suspect most of my audience members, like me, have no detailed idea what an electrical engineer does, but we've heard of such a profession, and it still sounds impressive, so my great-grandmother's excitement in the story is a feeling we understand. Even more importantly to me as a storyteller, I liked the sound of "he's an electrical engineer" and "he sells liquor and beer" when I heard my cousin tell it that way at the family reunion, and I like the sound of it now. Even after my fact-checking, I decided to keep that phrasing. I also began to wonder if Charlie had consciously changed the story because he liked the phrasing too. A phone conversation with him revealed he was telling the story just the way he recalled his father, Lamar Hamilton, telling it.[7] Ah, the wonders of oral transmission!

This Is the Story . . .

Many of us have heard stories about ourselves set in that time before the earliest memories we are certain we recall. Here is a story I heard from earliest childhood, retold as I remember my mother and father telling it:

You were born on August 3rd. When we brought you home from the hospital, it was so hot we dressed you in a diaper and an undershirt and put you in your baby bed. We had just drifted off to sleep when you began to cry. Well, you were our baby, so we tried to help you. You weren't hungry; you didn't need your diaper changed, but you cried. We just held you, and then you drifted back to sleep. We went back to bed and were just about asleep when you began crying again. This went on all night.

You'd cry. One of us would get up, determine you were not hungry and did not need your diaper changed. We would hold you. You would drift off to sleep. We'd put you back in your bed. We'd return to our bed. Just as we began to sleep, you'd cry again.

We eventually decided you wanted to be held because you always went back to sleep if we held you. But every time we set you down and we tried to sleep, you'd cry.

We thought: "What's wrong with this baby? We can't be holding this baby all the time? She's not even a week old; how can she already be so spoiled she wants to be held all the time?" We didn't know what was wrong, but we couldn't imagine how we had ended up with such a spoiled baby.

This crying, holding, and no sleep for us went on for your first three nights home. Then Mama Lillian[1] came to visit. We told her our problem. She asked, "How have you been dressing this baby for bed?"

And we told her, "In a diaper and an undershirt."

"Why, this little baby's cold," she said. "It's August, so it may be hot to you, but it is still colder than this baby is used to. This little girl is just cold." She dressed you in a long flannel nightgown with flaps that pulled down over your hands. That night you slept all through the night, and you slept every night after that.

Why, you slept through the night sooner than any of our later babies. You were such a good baby.

COMMENTARY

So, what is this story about?

This is the story of how my grandmother shared her knowledge born of experience to help my parents and me. It shows how important good grandparents can be.

This is the story of how my parents, though smart people, were not smart enough to figure out that the inside of a human body is much warmer than a hot, humid, upstairs, no air-conditioning August night in Kentucky.

This is the story of why, to this very day, I am easily chilled.

This is the story that shows how fortunate I was to have parents who loved me and struggled to meet my needs even when they could not name the need they met—instead of having parents who, thinking only of themselves, could have silenced me for good.

This is the story that shows how I, as their first child, along with my grandmother, helped teach my parents how to be parents. This is a job done by every oldest child, willingly or not.

This is the story of how I learned not to bother people by asking for what I wanted so I would not be considered spoiled.

This is the story of how, even before time I can remember, I knew I must have my needs met. It tells how I succeeded even though I could not clearly communicate what my needs were.

This is the story that shows, when it truly matters, I am persistent and so are my parents. Perhaps persistence can be inherited.

This is the story with no fixed meaning. It changes and changes. Perhaps the meanings of all of our stories, those we tell and those we are told, can become this fluid when we allow ourselves to listen to them anew.

PERMISSIONS AND ACKNOWLEDGMENTS

Adaptation of "Stormwalker," from Roberta Simpson Brown, *The Walking Trees and Other Scary Stories* (Little Rock, Ark.: August House, 1991). Used by permission of Marian Reiner on behalf of the publishers.

"The Wedding Ring," in Berniece T. Hiser, *Quare Do's in Appalachia: East Kentucky Legends and Memorats* (Pikeville, Ky.: Pikeville College Press, 1978), 164–168. Heard and compiled by Berniece T. Hiser, copyright 1978 by Berniece T. Hiser. Reprinted by permission of Susan Hiser and Shirley Hiser Fugate.

"The Gingerbread Boy," by Mary Hamilton, was first published in *The August House Book of Scary Stories: Spooky Tales for Telling Out Loud*, edited by Liz Parkhurst (Atlanta: August House, 2009), 22–26.

"2010 Gingerbread Boy," by Linda Gorham, is used with her permission.

"The Blue Light," archival text by Mrs. Dicey Hurley or Mrs. E. McClanahan. "The Bushel of Corn," by J. B. Calton. Excerpts from an untitled text collected by Euphemia Epperson from Ted Middleton. All from the Leonard Roberts Collection, Southern Appalachian Archives, Berea College.

"How She Paid Her Debt," or "Flannel Mouth," by Nora Morgan Lewis. From the Nora Morgan Lewis Collection, Southern Appalachian Archives, Berea College.

"The Open Grave" is adapted from William Lynwood Montell, *Ghosts Along the Cumberland: Deathlore in the Kentucky Foothills* (Knoxville: Univ. of Tennessee Press, 1975), 187–190. It is used with permission of the publisher.

"The Farmer's Smart Daughter" is adapted from "The Farmer's Daughter," in Marie Campbell, *Tales from the Cloud Walking Country* (Bloomington: Indiana Univ. Press, 1958), 198–200. Adaptation undertaken courtesy of Indiana University Press.

"Kate Crackernuts" is reprinted from Joseph Jacobs, *English Fairy*

Tales, 3rd ed. (New York: G. P. Putnam's Sons and David Nutt, 1898), 198–202.

"The Story of Kate Crackernuts" is reprinted from Andrew Lang, "English and Scottish Fairy Tales," *Folk-Lore* 1, no. 3 (September 1890): 289–312.

"The King and His Advisor," adapted by Mary Hamilton, with the permission of Umang Badhwar and her family. Text of May 1986 correspondence from Umang Badhwar to the author reprinted by permission of Umang Badhwar.

"Jump Rope Kingdom," by Mary Hamilton, first published in *The Scenic Route: Stories from the Heartland*, ed. Ellen Munds and Beth Millett (Indianapolis: Indiana Historical Society Press, 2007), 1–3.

NOTES

Introduction

1. By "kitchen table storyteller" I'm talking about telling stories around a kitchen table or in some other informal setting. In addition, the listeners generally have not gathered for the purpose of hearing stories, but the storytelling has sprung from the ongoing conversation. The type of storytelling for which I am paid is not kitchen table storytelling, but "platform storytelling." My storytelling has usually been arranged by a presenter (for example: a festival artistic director, a librarian, a teacher) who has hired me to tell stories at a specific place to listeners the presenter has gathered for the purpose of hearing stories. Just as kitchen table storytelling does not always happen with a teller sitting at a kitchen table, platform storytelling does not always happen with a teller standing on a platform. These terms "kitchen table storytelling" and "platform storytelling" are also used by others to talk about different types of storytelling situations with different degrees of formality; however, not all users describe the terms the same way I have.

2. National Endowment for the Arts website: "The folk and traditional arts, which include music, crafts, dance, storytelling, and others, are those that are learned as part of the cultural life of a community whose members share a common ethnic heritage, language, religion, occupation, or geographic region. These traditions are shaped by the aesthetics and values of a shared culture and are passed from generation to generation, most often within family and community through observation, conversation, and practice." By contrast, most of the stories I tell are not stories that have been passed down in my family over the generations, nor did I grow up hearing these stories from others around me. In addition, most of my storytelling training has come from other professional storytellers through workshops they've offered and through their presentations at various storytelling conferences. While we may share a common occupation, professional storytellers do not traditionally work side by side, transmitting storytelling knowledge and skills as an integral part of our typical workdays.

3. The *Captain Kangaroo* television show ran on CBS from 1955 to 1984. The books I recall Captain Kangaroo (portrayed by Robert Keeshan) reading were all published before Captain Kangaroo began—Virginia Lee Burton's

The Little House in 1942 and her *Mike Mulligan and His Steam Shovel* in 1939; Esphyr Slobodkina's *Caps for Sale* in 1938.

4. Yes, Mary June—I used both names in school. In my predominately Catholic community, many girls were named Mary after the Blessed Virgin Mary, so we all either used middle names or double names at school.

5. Many teachers today share the belief that it is important for students to learn to speak before groups and have opportunities to develop listening and audience skills; however, most teaching today is driven by assessment. By that I mean that what can be, and is, assessed becomes what is taught. It takes time to allow every child in a classroom to speak in front of peers, and assessing speaking ability does not lend itself to standardized testing. While speaking and listening skills are indeed often included in curriculums, school and individual teacher success is measured primarily through standardized assessments. Therefore, when time is short and assessment stakes are high, what is taught must match what will be assessed by state and national standardized tests.

6. Barbara Freeman and Connie Regan-Blake each began telling stories in the early 1970s. For twenty years, from 1975 to 1995, they traveled the world as The Folktellers, a storytelling duo. Since 1995 both Barbara and Connie have established solo storytelling careers. Learn more about Barbara at barbarastoryteller@gmail.com, Connie at www.storywindow.com. I had heard of them before the conference because they had been featured on the cover of a *School Library Journal* issue while I was in library school, but I had not sought out an opportunity to hear them tell prior to the conference.

7. For more information about the impact of my studies with Laura Simms, see note 4 in "Little Ripen Pear" and the commentary after "Kate Crackernuts." Learn more about Laura Simms at www.laurasimms.com.

Stormwalker

1. When telling this story for Kentucky audiences, I usually interject a bit of directional information, "and if you wanted to go there from here, you would just. . . ." Kentucky has 120 counties, so we Kentuckians tend to talk in terms of counties, especially when talking about rural areas.

2. No, I do not have a photographic memory, but I do have my appointment calendars from previous years, where on December 19, 1990, I wrote "go to Lonnie & Roberta's to tell 'Stormwalker' around 5:00 or 5:30 p.m."

3. In 1991, August House published *The Walking Trees and Other Scary Stories* by Roberta Simpson Brown. Roberta titled her story "Storm Walker"—two words; however, when I heard the story, I heard the single word, "Stormwalker." *The Walking Trees* was Roberta's first book. Learn more about Roberta Simpson Brown, and about the ten books she has written, at www.robertasimpsonbrown.com.

4. Storytelling World Awards, presented yearly since 1995, are juried awards presented to Winner and Honor recipients in seven categories. Another CD of mine, *Sisters All . . . and One Troll* was awarded a 2007 Winner Storytelling World Award in Category 6: Storytelling Recordings. Learn more about Storytelling World Awards at www.storytellingworld.com.

5. Kentucky Crafted: The Market is produced by the Kentucky Craft Marketing Program, a division of the Kentucky Arts Council. The Market includes days for buyers from retail stores throughout the country, followed by two open to the public days. Traditional, folk, and contemporary craft exhibitors are juried in the Kentucky Craft Marketing Program. Two-dimensional artists are juried through the Kentucky Arts Council. Performing artists are selected from the juried Kentucky Arts Council's Performing Arts on Tour Directory, and their recordings, along with books from Kentucky Arts Council Fellowship Artists and from Kentucky publishers, are also available. In addition, The Market offers specialty food products with the Kentucky Proud Program of the Kentucky Department of Agriculture. Learn more about Kentucky Crafted: The Market at www.kycraft.ky.gov.

Promises to Keep

1. In 1867, for about $120,000, William S. Culbertson built his three-story, twenty-five-room home. With its hand-painted ceilings, carved rosewood staircase, and marble fireplaces, his home reflected his affluence. After his death in 1892, the mansion and its contents were sold. A series of owners painted over the ornate ceilings and boarded up rooms. Since 1985 this annual event, rated a "Top 10 Halloween Haunted House" by *USA Today* in 1991, generates funds to restore the mansion to its Victorian glory. Culbertson Mansion State Historic Site is a part of the Indiana State Museum and Historic Sites Division of the Department of Natural Resources.

2. Henson, *Tragedy at Devil's Hollow*, 107–108.

3. Hiser, *Quare Do's in Appalachia*, 164–168.

4. Henson, *Tragedy at Devil's Hollow*, 107.

5. Ibid., 108.

6. Hiser, *Quare Do's in Appalachia*, 164–168. Hiser also wrote: "My sister Grace E. Jones told me the story of 'The Wedding Ring' which took place in Breathitt County about 1862, the old lady was Mrs. Polly Daingey McIntosh, telling the tale in 1918, in Owsley County."

7. Murray (n.d.) confirms what I had been casually told by the curator.

8. Johnson and Buel, *Battles and Leaders of the Civil War*, 1:537–538, 3:29–30.

9. *Report of the Adjunct General of the State of Indiana*, 4:550–551, 6:302–304. This report includes the residences of soldiers and the muster dates of the specific companies.

10. Hiser used Polly Daingey (also spelled Daingy) McIntosh and John McIntosh (*Quare Do's in Appalachia*, 164, 165). Henson used Josephine Tyler and George Thomas (*Tragedy at Devil's Hollow*, 107).

11. Johnson and Buel, *Battles and Leaders of the Civil War*, 1:538, 3:29.

12. Ibid., 1:458.

13. Dyer, *A Compendium of the War of Rebellion*, 3:1147.

The Gingerbread Boy

1. If you are thinking, chopping cotton? In Kentucky? I can tell you that surprised me too, but I do know that cotton has been grown in southwestern Kentucky, so it is possible to be sent to "chop out the cotton" in Kentucky. The mention of "chopping cotton" was in the version of the story from Billie Jean Fields (see additional information in the commentary), and I elected to keep it in my retelling.

2. This is the first of many, many references you will see to Leonard Roberts in this book. Leonard Roberts was a Kentucky scholar, teacher, folklorist, and storyteller to whom all Kentuckians interested in storytelling owe a great debt. Upon his death, his family donated his work to Berea College (in Berea, Kentucky), where today the Leonard Roberts Collection is part of the Southern Appalachian Archives, housed in the Hutchins Library. The Leonard Roberts Collection is one of the most important archives of sound recordings and manuscripts of traditional storytelling in the entire United States. For Roberts's field recordings, I've provided complete call numbers. (Each begins with LR OR.) Call numbers are not assigned to individual manuscripts within the collection. To learn more about Leonard Roberts and his work, including a complete bibliography, please see the Leonard Roberts memorial issue of *Appalachian Heritage* 15 (spring 1987): 4–65. Carl Lindahl, a scholar and folklorist, is currently writing a book tentatively titled *One Time: The Kentucky Mountain Folktale World of Leonard Roberts*.

3. Leonard Roberts Collection, Berea College, manuscript, "The Family," from Billie Jean Fields of Martin County, Kentucky, 1970. Sound recordings LR OR 024, Track 3, "Candy Doll," from Mary Day, and LR OR 024, Track 4, "Candy Doll," from Margie Day, both recorded at Polls Creek, Leslie County, Kentucky, on October 15, 1952.

4. Roberts, "The Candy Doll," *I Bought Me a Dog*, n.p.

5. Ibid., n.p.

6. Leonard Roberts Collection, Berea College, LR OR 024, Track 4, "Candy Doll."

7. Leonard Roberts Collection, Berea College, LR OR 024, Track 3, "Candy Doll."

8. Leonard Roberts Collection, Berea College, manuscript, "The Family."

9. Parkhurst, *The August House Book of Scary Stories*, 22–26.

10. Gorham, email correspondence with the author, September 2, 2010.

11. Ibid., April 19, 2011.

12. Lord, *The Singer of Tales*, 36. In his book, *The Singer of Tales*, Lord includes several comments about the nature of oral tradition and the relationship between oral tradition and fixed text. He writes: ". . . if the printed text is read to an already accomplished oral poet, its effect is the same as if the poet were listening to another singer. The song books spoil the oral character of the tradition only when the singer believes that they are *the* way in which the song *should* be presented. The song books may spread a song to regions where the song has not hitherto been sung; in this respect they are like a migrant singer. But they can spoil a tradition only when the singers themselves have already been spoiled by the concept of a fixed text" (79). Later in the book he says, "Those singers who accept the idea of a fixed text are lost to oral traditional process. This means death to oral tradition and the rise of a generation of 'singers' who are reproducers rather than re-creators" (137). He concludes: "The change has been from stability of essential story, which is the goal of oral tradition, to stability of text, of the exact words of the story" (138).

13. Gorham, email correspondence with the author, April 19, 2011.

14. Ibid.

15. Since 2003, Linda has met monthly with her coaching group, fellow storytellers Donna Dettman and Sue Black. They usually meet for five to six hours. At the beginning of each session, they allow time for relaxing and catching up. Then, when they begin working, they are focused. First they discuss everyone's priorities. A schedule is set that usually allows each teller an equal amount of time. Occasionally, when needed, they allot extra time to those who may have upcoming projects that need extra attention.

Topics they have tackled over the years include: creating, coaching, developing, refining, and presenting stories; editing written work for publication; crafting keynote speeches and workshop presentations; planning, editing, and designing CDs; and developing marketing materials and websites. The coaching sessions also serve as a time to relax and share the trials and tribulations of storytelling as a profession. The group always breaks for lunch and sometimes, in celebration of their hard work, they share a glass of wine at the end of the day.

Linda, Donna, and Sue stress that getting the right mix of skills and personalities in a coaching group is important. Participants must feel comfortable and safe, and there must be a shared respect for each person's work.

16. Gorham, email correspondence with the author, April 19, 2011.

17. Ibid., September 3, 2010.

18. Ibid., April 19, 2011.

19. Learn more about Linda Gorham and her work at www.LindaGorham .com.

Little Ripen Pear

1. Sierra writes, ". . . . in 1910, Finnish folklorist Antti Aarne published a catalog of tale types that today remains the standard system for folktales of European and East Indian origin. Each tale type is basically a plot type, and is assigned both a number and a standard title, for example, Tale type 510A *Cinderella*. American folklorist Stith Thompson revised Aarne's work and translated it into English as *The Types of the Folktale*" (34).

Hans-Jörg Uther created a more recent revision of Aarne's and Thompson's work, thus ATU stands for Aarne, Thompson, Uther. When I have been able to find a tale type, I note it for you at the beginning of the story commentary. Many folktale collections will contain an appendix listing the stories included by tale type. To learn which tale types are included in this book, see the index.

Why, as a storyteller, do I care about tale types? Many indexes of folktales, Ashliman's *A Guide to Folktales in the English Language* for example, are arranged by tale type. Once I know the tale type of a story I'm interested in learning more about, I can use such indexes to locate variants of the story from a wide variety of sources and cultures. Reading multiple variants often provides me with more insight to a story than I can glean from any single version.

2. Leonard Roberts Collection, Berea College. For details on all ten versions, see table 1, "Little Ripen Pear" Comparison Chart. It includes the storytellers' names and the call numbers for the field recordings or the notation "manuscript" for each version.

3. From 1983 to 1987, while living in Grand Rapids, Michigan, I studied voice with Gordon Van Ry. My goal was not so much to learn to sing as it was to improve my vocal stamina. I chose to work with Mr. Van Ry because he had worked not just with singers, but also with lawyers and others who wanted to improve their speaking voices and with folks in need of vocal rehabilitation. From Mr. Van Ry I learned the importance of vocal warm ups and proper breath support for speaking and singing, which has served me well over my storytelling career. Yes, working with him improved my singing, but the singing was a means to an end, not the goal of our work together.

4. Trust me, if I knew exactly who to credit with this idea, I would. My memory says I was first introduced to it by Laura Simms, a storyteller who has been an important storytelling teacher for me. However, I have heard this idea stated nearly this same way in almost every storytelling workshop I've ever attended.

I do know it was Laura Simms who introduced me to a wide variety of ways of learning a story, as opposed to a focus on word memorization. Laura also introduced me to Howard Gardner's work with multiple intelligences when I first studied with her at her 1983 storytelling residency. Working with Laura changed how I go about learning stories and influenced how I help

others learn to tell stories now. At Laura's yearly storytelling residencies, each participant focuses on a single story throughout the week-long residency. I studied with her from 1983 to 1986, in 1988, and again in 2007, when I devoted the week to grappling with "Little Ripen Pear."
Learn more about Laura Simms at www.laurasimms.com.

5. Boyd, *On the Origin of Stories*, 209. Boyd contends the draw storytelling has for humans stems not just from a love of narrative, but from evolutionary adaptations: ". . . we have evolved to engage in art and in storytelling because of the survival advantages they offer our species. Art prepares minds for open-ended learning and creativity; fiction specifically improves our social cognition and our thinking beyond the here and now."

Birch and Heckler express a similar idea: "The evolution of the opposable thumb on the human hand allowed us to grasp, to wield, to manipulate devices both delicately and powerfully. Perhaps stories are a mental opposable thumb, allowing humans to grasp something in their minds—to turn it around, to view it from many angles, to reshape it, and to hurl it even into the farthest reaches of the unconscious" (11).

Flannel Mouth

1. Nora M. Lewis Collection, Southern Appalachian Archives, Berea College, Berea, Kentucky, Tale 31c, "Flannel Mouth."

2. I have been unable to verify which relative told me this. A number of years passed between that conversation and my decision to write this book. In the interim, the relatives I could recall by name from our brief conversation had either died or suffered disease-related memory loss.

3. Jack D. Lewis, M.D., correspondence with the author, August 2003.

4. Nora Morgan Lewis Collection, Southern Appalachian Archives, Berea College, Tale 31c, "Flannel Mouth." Lewis first wrote out the title as "How She Paid Her Debt," then marked it out and replaced it with "Flannel Mouth."

The Blue Light

1. Leonard Roberts Collection, Berea College, manuscript, "The Blue Light." Handwritten notes clearly establish that the story before this one, "The Unwilling House," comes from Mrs. Dicie Hurley of Majestic, Kentucky, and the story after this one, "Blue Beard," comes from Mrs. E. McClanahan of Freeburn, Kentucky. "The Blue Light" begins on the same page as "The Unwilling House" and ends on the same page as "Blue Beard." Mrs. Hurley's name is written at the top of "The Unwilling House" and Mrs. McClanahan's name is written at the top of "Blue Beard." Because this tale is

such a close variant of "Blue Beard," I'm inclined to believe Roberts collected it from Mrs. Dicie Hurley, not Mrs. McClanahan, but I cannot be sure.

2. Leonard Roberts Collection, Berea College. On sound recording LR OR O24, Track 2, recorded by Roberts at Polls Creek, Leslie County, Kentucky, on October 15, 1952, Chrisley Day states the story title as "The Three Girls and an Old Man." On the transcript of Day's telling, the title is given as "The Bad Old Man."

3. WOW (Working on Our Work) Storytelling Weekends were small group storytelling coaching retreat-style events I co-facilitated with Cynthia Changaris from 2001–2011 at her Storyteller's Riverhouse Bed and Breakfast in Bethlehem, Indiana. At each of the thirty-four WOW Weekends four to ten storytellers from as far away as Florida and the Dakotas gathered as peers to coach each other. During WOW Weekends participants worked on developing stories for telling, storytelling workshops, marketing materials, or other matters related to the art of storytelling, with each participant guaranteed a one-hour turn to put the intelligence of the full group to work in service to whatever that storyteller wanted the group's help with.

Cynthia and I participated in the weekend as equal participants, not head coaches. While we did act as facilitators by helping participants use a formal response process, we also each took our own one-hour turns to receive help with our work. We used a five-step response process based on the story coaching techniques developed by storyteller Doug Lipman (see *The Storytelling Coach*) and the critical response process developed by dancer Liz Lerman (see "Towards a Process for Critical Response"). Learn more about Doug Lipman at www.storydynamics.com. Learn more about Liz Lerman and the book she wrote with John Borstel about the Critical Response Process at http://danceexchange.org/projects/critical-response-process/.

What set WOW Weekends apart from other storytelling coaching sessions was that we ignored conventional wisdom that all tellers participating in a mutual coaching session needed to already know each other and be at about the same level of telling experience and expertise. Instead we brought strangers together, including relatively new storytellers and storytellers with years of professional experience. Their common bond was a love of storytelling and a desire to give and receive help to strengthen their work. Shared meals and lodging generated the comfort level needed. We treated participants and their work confidentially, and asked all participants to do the same. While new storytellers sometimes worried they had nothing to contribute, they soon understood that the more experienced tellers wanted to create works with audience appeal. When new tellers recounted their experiences as listeners to works in progress, they provided valuable information.

While I can't reveal names or specific projects worked on, I can state that work in progress at WOW Weekends wound up in at least three published books and on at least two award-winning CDs. No, we did not keep statistics to track what happened to the participants and their work—those are just results I happen to know about. In addition to working on "The Blue Light" at a WOW Weekend, I also worked on other stories in this book, "Flannel Mouth," "The Gingerbread Boy," and "Kate Crackernuts," when I was first developing my retellings. At our final WOW Weekend in February 2011, participants read and commented on drafts from this book during my one-hour turn.

4. Leonard Roberts Collection, Berea College, manuscript, "The Blue Light."

The Open Grave

1. Montell, *Ghosts Along the Cumberland*, 187–190. Lynwood Montell taught at Western Kentucky University from 1969 to 1999 and is the author over twenty books of Kentucky folklore. You can learn more about his work at http://www.wku.edu/Dept/Academic/AHSS/cms/lynwood-montell.

2. Benjamin, email correspondence with the author, January 27, 2010.

Tall Tales and Outright Lies

1. Livo and Rietz, *Storytelling*, 251.

2. Sierra, *Storytellers' Research Guide*, 4.

3. Leonard Roberts Collection, Berea College, untitled manuscript. In 1959, Mrs. Madelyn McKamy from Greenup County, Kentucky, reported that the way to put a finishing touch on a tall tale was to say, "Now, everybody that believes this, stand on your right eyebrow."

Daniel Boone on the Hunt

1. Leonard Roberts Collection, Berea College, untitled manuscript. Jean Singleton of Knott County, Kentucky, reported a version in 1961. In that version Will is hunting and a wounded bear attacks with mouth wide open. Evelyn Gooding of Pineville, Bell County, Kentucky, collected a version from Mayme Dean (also of Pineville) during the 1955–1956 school year. Curtis Sams of Bell County, Kentucky, collected a version from seventy-six-year-old S. D. Sams of Girdler, Knox County, Kentucky, in 1957. Zora S. Lovitt from Williamsburg in Whitley County, Kentucky, attributed a first-person version collected in 1957 to eighty-five-year-old Frank Kedd, also of Whitley County, who Lovitt reports was known as "The Great Prevaricator." None of the reported versions features Daniel Boone, and in all versions the encounter takes place on the ground, not in a tree.

Farmer Brown's Crop

1. Leonard Roberts Collection, Berea College, manuscript, "The Bushel of Corn," collected by J. D. Calton, n.d.

Hunting Alone

1. Leonard Roberts Collection, Berea College, manuscript, "Half Pint," collected by Walton T. Saylor from Charlie Day, 1956.

2. Leonard Roberts Collection, Berea College, manuscript, "Tall Tale," collected by Lena Ratliff from Boon Hall, 1960.

3. This was the Florida Storytelling Association StoryCamp 2004 at Eckert College, in St. Petersburg, Florida. Learn more about the organization and its events at www.flstory.org.

Otis Ayers Had a Dog—Two Stories

1. Thompson, telephone interview with the author, February 17, 2010.

2. Clarke and Clarke, *The Harvest and the Reapers*, 98.

3. Leonard Roberts Collection, Berea College, untitled manuscript, from Cleadia Hall, 1956.

4. Thompson, telephone interview with the author, February 17, 2010.

Some Dog

1. Reading? Yes, that's what you are doing; however, when I tell the story, of course, I say "hearing." Should you happen to read this story aloud, "hearing" would be a better word choice for your audience, too. All in all, I've tried to make very few changes between these written versions and what I say when I'm telling. Sometimes more words or different words strike me as taking better care of my audience—in this case, you, a reader.

2. Leonard Roberts Collection, Berea College, untitled manuscript, collected by Euphemia Epperson, 1957. The turtle story is part of a longer untitled tall tale collected by Epperson in Harlan County, Kentucky. A handwritten note on the Epperson manuscript reads: "This was reported to me by one of the evening loafers." In Epperson's retelling she uses Ted Middleton, an attendant at the Baxter Service Station, as the narrator whose telling is prompted by three small boys walking by with a turtle they had caught. When one loafer comments, "That's the biggest turtle I ever saw," Middleton responds with his tall tale. To read a published version of this story, see: "The Tale of the Big Turkle," in Roberts, *Old Greasybeard*, 36–41, 180 (notes).

Leonard Roberts Collection, Berea College, untitled manuscript, collected by Charles Patton, 1959. A second giant turtle story in the Leonard Roberts Collection tells of a sheep-stealing turtle. The narrator kills it with a hog rifle and stores forty bushels of seed corn in the shell. In 1959, Charles Patton of Floyd County, Kentucky, reported collecting this story and two more tall tales from "my uncle who had heard them from an old Sloan man from Caney Creek when he was a boy. The old man would come through Knott and Floyd County selling herbs" (Patton untitled manuscript).

3. While I have no doubt that I read a reference to this smart dog story in a book, I have been unsuccessful in locating that publication. However, I can verify the tale is in Kentucky folklore because three Kentucky-collected versions are in the Leonard Roberts Collection at Berea College: Charles A. Blair of Letcher County, Kentucky, reported the version "Tall Tales: A Real Hunting Dog" in 1961. William Ace of Leslie County, Kentucky, collected a version (untitled manuscript) in 1957 from Henery Gibson. Elizabeth L. Dye of Knox County, Kentucky, collected the version "A Good Hunting Dog" from Johnie Miracle in 1955.

4. Leonard Roberts Collection, Berea College, Epperson manuscript.

5. Ibid.

6. Ibid.

7. Ibid.

8. Tale Talk, a monthly gathering of storytellers in the Louisville area, has met monthly for over twenty years now. Participants are welcome to tell old favorites, new work, or be supportive listeners for others' tellings.

9. Folklorists have identified the split dog story as tale type 1889L, one of many tales known collectively as Munchausen tales. For more information on the mix of folk and literary heritage of Munchausen tales, see Ashliman, *A Guide to Folktales in the English Language*, 300.

10. Leonard Roberts Collection, Berea College, untitled manuscript. In 1960, Dorothy Major from Greenup County, Kentucky, collected a version from Marquita Dunaway, age eighteen, also from South Shore, Greenup County (untitled manuscript).

In the Appalachian Sound Archives, see LR OR 012, Track 15, Dewey Adams recorded by Leonard Roberts in Perry County, Kentucky. For a published version of Adams's telling, see: Roberts, "The Split Dog," *South From Hell-fer-Sartin*, 145, 262 (notes).

11. The Meade County Fair takes place every summer. It probably evolved from the Meade County school fairs my parents (Robert F. Hamilton Jr. and Martha Jane Hager Hamilton, both born in 1930) remember attending during their childhoods. Those events featured students from each school marching in parade and being judged for their parade presentation. There were academic competitions, livestock competitions, bicycle races, a small carnival ride area, and more. My parents recall the Meade County school fairs taking place on the grounds of what was once Brandenburg High

School, near the corner of Bland and West Broadway in Brandenburg, Kentucky.

During my childhood (I was born in 1952), we attended the fair every summer. I looked forward to catching up with friends I hadn't seen since the end of the school year. In my memory the Meade County Fair always took place in Brandenburg, Kentucky, the same location as today (the northeast corner of the intersection of Highways 1692 and 1051; for locals that's Fairgrounds Road and Brandenburg By-pass). I don't recall how long the fair ran when I was young, but today the Meade County Fair is an eight-day event with over 45,000 paid admissions. (This in a county with a population of 28,602 in the 2010 census.) The 2010 fair featured a parade (no unaccompanied pets allowed), entertainment shows including a Community Gospel Sing, and competitions galore—beauty pageants, a talent contest, baby shows, livestock shows, tractor pulls, demolition derbies (even a lawn mower demolition derby), a Rook tournament, 4-H and FFA events, a *Guitar Hero* contest, a 5K race and other athletic events, a cornhole tournament, and exhibits where judges awarded prizes for fruits and vegetables, field crops and forages, plants and flowers, fine arts, cooking, canning, sewing, knitting, quilting, and much, much more. Learn more, including upcoming Meade County Fair dates, at www.meadecountyfair.com.

12. I'm not talking about raising and lowering of the theatrical fourth wall. Instead I'm referring to something more akin to meta-narration and narration. The theatrical fourth wall is already down in the telling of a story.

More Kentucky Folktales

1. Lindahl, *American Folktales from the Collections of the Library of Congress*, 1:lii.

The Enormous Bear

1. Spellings vary. I've seen "Sody Sallyraytus" (Chase, *Grandfather Tales*, 75–80), "Sody Saleratus" (Tashjian, *Juba This and Juba That*, 55–59), and "Sody Sallyrytus" (MacDonald, *Twenty Tellable Tales*, 79–89). I've spelled it like I pronounce it.

2. Roberts, *Old Greasybeard*, 44–47.

3. Roberts, *South From Hell-fer-Sartin*, 155–156.

4. Ibid., 157–158.

5. Roberts, *Sang Branch Settlers*, 256–257.

6. Leonard Roberts Collection, Berea College. For details on all eight versions, see table 2, "The Enormous Bear" Comparison Chart. It includes the storytellers' names and the call numbers for Roberts's field recordings. To

learn more about Appalachian Sound Archives Fellowship, see http://www
.berea.edu/hutchinslibrary/specialcollections/amfp/amfp.asp.

7. To learn more about Barbara Freeman and Connie Regan-Blake, see
note 6 in the Introduction.

8. Ed Stivender has told stories professionally since 1977. Learn more
about Ed by contacting Storyclan@aol.com.

9. Chase, *Grandfather Tales*, 75–80.

10. Ibid., vii. "In this book I have taken a free hand in the re-telling. I have
put each tale together from different versions, and from my own experience in
telling them. I have told the tales to all kinds of listeners, old and young; and
only then, after many tellings, written them down."

11. Chase, *Grandfather Tales*, 235. Chase notes the tale was collected from
"Kena Adams of Wise County, Virginia."

12. Chase, *Grandfather Tales*, vii.

13. Davis, *Telling Your Own Stories*, 76–83.

The Farmer's Smart Daughter

1. Campbell, *Tales from the Cloud Walking Country*, 198–200.

2. Ibid., 261.

3. Ashliman, *A Guide to Folktales in the English Language*, 175.

4. Campbell, *Tales from the Cloud Walking Country*, 199.

5. Ibid., 200.

The Fortune Teller

1. Black, interview with the author, January 2009 and January 2011.

The Princess Who Could Not Cry

1. Leonard Roberts Collection, Berea College, LR OR 003, Track 3, "The
Princess That Could Not Cry," collected from Agnes Valentine, 1949.

2. DeSpain, *Thirty-Three Multicultural Tales to Tell*, 47–49, 122 (notes).

Rawhead and Bloody Bones

1. Ashliman lists over fifty different variants.

Ruth Stotter's book, *The Golden Axe*, includes the full text of thirty-three
variants, summaries of seventeen more, plus summaries of another six in her
notes on the other tales.

In my own artist-in-residence work for the Kentucky Arts Council, I have
found the underlying pattern in tale type 480 is so strong that, once exposed

to several variants, even young elementary school students are capable of creating original stories using the folktale plot type as a base.

2. Leonard Roberts Collection, Berea College. Stand-alone versions collected by Roberts include: LR OR 002, Track 6, "Rawhead and Bloody Bones," recorded from Jane Muncy, age eleven, from Leslie County, who heard stories from her grandmother, recorded in October 1949; LR OR 016, Track 7, "Rawhead and Bloody Bones," recorded from Patricia McCoy, age eighteen, from Leslie County, who heard it from her grandmother, recorded in May 1950; LR OR 028, Track 3, "To the End of the World," recorded from Dave Couch in 1952 near Putney, Harlan County, Kentucky.

The segments where the girls encounter the rawhead and bloody bones at the well are included in multiple versions of a longer story, LR OR 056, Track 15, "Rushy Coat," recorded from Rachel Williams by Leonard Roberts, and in additional manuscripts collected by students of Leonard Roberts. One version, "Russia Coat," was collected from Margaret Mosley by Elizabeth Lee Dye, in Knox County, Kentucky, in 1955. Four versions were collected by Gerald Syme of Knox County, Kentucky, in 1958: (1) "Rusha Coat," collected by Gerald Syme (his source is not given); (2) "Rusha Coat," told by Margaret Mosley and written down by Geneva Mosley; (3) "Rushy Coat," collected by Gerald Syme from Mary Hannah Marcum; and (4) "Rusha Coat," "told to Georgia Williams by her mother Mrs. George Williams" (note at beginning of the story) and/or "told by Rachel Williams most of this recorded from Mrs. Miracle, Trosper, [Knox County] KY" (note at end of story).

3. Nora Morgan Lewis Collection, Berea College, Tale 32e, "Rawhead and Bloody Bones." Nora Morgan Lewis was an aunt of Jane Muncy, from whom Leonard Roberts recorded a version of the tale, cited above. Jane Muncy reported hearing many stories from her grandmother, Nora Morgan Lewis's mother. Notes at the end of the Lewis manuscript state, "It is a story passed down from many generations and told to the children, especially at family gatherings and events such as July 4th or Christmas."

To learn more about the storytelling traditions in the family of Jane Muncy and Nora Morgan Lewis, see works by folklorist Carl Lindahl listed in the bibliography. Lindahl's book in progress about the life and work of Leonard Roberts, tentatively titled *One Time: The Kentucky Mountain Folktale World of Leonard Roberts*, will also contain information about Nora Morgan Lewis and Jane Muncy.

4. The rawhead and bloody bones characters from the well are sometimes called bloody heads, sometimes bloody skeletons, but the visual image is consistently of a raw, bloodied head and bones, except in the Couch version, where this role is played by little foxes laying in the road. Many people also use "rawhead and bloody bones" as synonymous with the "boogyman" that will get you if you don't behave. Before encountering the phrase in this story, that was the only way I'd heard it used. However, the rawhead and bloody bones

in this story struck me as powerful but—as voiced by the various recorded storytellers—not especially terrifying or even threatening.

5. Leonard Roberts Collection, Berea College, LR OR 016, Track 7, "Rawhead and Bloody Bones," recorded from Patricia McCoy, age eighteen, from Hyden, Leslie County, Kentucky.

Kate Crackernuts

1. Jacobs, *English Fairy Tales*, 258 (source note), 198–202 ("Kate Crackernuts").

2. Lang, "English and Scottish Fairy Tales," 289–312 ("The Story of Kate Crackernuts," 299–301).

3. *Dallas Morning News*, "Jury Convicts Mom of Hiring Hit Man in Cheerleader Case," September 4, 1991; Kennedy, "Cheerleader's Mother Guilty in Murder Plot," *Los Angeles Times*, September 4, 1991; Koidin, "'Cheerleader Mom' Freed After Serving Six Months," *Texas News*, March 1, 1997.

4. See the note 4 in "Little Ripen Pear" for information on Laura Simms.

5. Candy Kopperud heard "Kate Crackernuts" at a two-day storytelling course she coordinated and co-taught with me at Palmer Public Library in 2001. Participants had received copies of my outline, time line, and map in advance as examples for their own workshop preparations. At the end of the course, they wanted to hear the story told.

6. The mother was not jailed the entire time. Koidin reported that the mother "served six months of a 10-year sentence" and "initially was sentenced to 15 years in prison in 1991. That conviction was overturned when it was discovered a juror was on probation." Smith reports, "On September 9, 1996, a month before her second trial was to begin, she pleaded no contest and was sentenced to 10 years imprisonment."

The King and His Advisor

1. Umang Badhwar, correspondence with the author. The story arrived as one note in a packet of thank you notes from the Thompson students given to me by her teacher, Mrs. Frona Foner. A subsequent letter from Umang Badhwar to me is postmarked May 19, 1986.

2. Mohanty, "What God Allows Is for Man's Good," *Folk Tales of Orissa*, 84–86. *Folk Tales of Orissa* is the fourth volume in a twenty-volume series of folk tale collections from various places and people of India, published by Sterling Publishers.

3. Mohanty footnotes Savaras as "An aboriginal tribe of Orissa. The Savaras are great hunters" (85).

4. Mohanty, *Folk Tales of Orissa*, 13.

5. Email correspondence with Umang Badhwar, November 20, 2011.

6. The version of the story I received in the mail from Umang and reprint in this book, was her translation of the story from her first language, Hindi, into her second language, English. She not only translated the story when she was thirteen, but she also retold it simply so I would be able to grasp the basic plot.

7. Phone call with Umang Badhwar, November 27, 2011.

8. Umang Badhwar explained her understanding of the story in a phone call with me on November 27, 2011. She also observed that whenever she tells the story to her brother's children, she always begins with wording like, "Once upon a time there was a king in India," and then she describes the grandeur of his palace so her listeners will know he is truly a powerful and wealthy king.

9. Email correspondence with Umang Badhwar, November 20, 2011.

10. According to family genealogy records, my first ancestor to die in Kentucky was George Edelen, born in Maryland in 1760 and died in Kentucky in 1809. The first to be born in Kentucky was Nelson Claycomb, born 1811 to parents born in Virginia. The last to be born outside the United States was either Daniel Foushee, born in France in 1775, or his son William Foushee, a great-great-great-great-great grandparent, who was born 1795 in an unknown place and died in Kentucky in 1860. In addition to strong Kentucky ties, I also have strong ancestral ties within Meade County and neighboring Breckinridge County. I must go back to my great-great grandparents to find an ancestor who was not born in one of those two counties.

11. Lane, *Picturing the Rose*, 9.

Rabbit and the Alligators

1. MacDonald, *The Storyteller's Sourcebook*, 285.

2. One print variant of the tale I suspect I had read and barely recalled that long ago day was "The Counting of the Crocodiles," in Courlander, *The Tiger's Whisker*, 87–89. This version is a Japanese folktale. Courlander refers to other Asian variants in his notes.

Another was "Why Rabbit Has a Short Tail," in Leach, *How the People Sang the Mountains Up*, 69. In her notes Leach cites A. H. Fauset, *Negro Tales From the South*, published in 1925, and discusses other variants.

I suspect these are the variants I had read because these sources were part of the folktale collection in the children's department of the Grand Rapids Public Library.

3. "One, two buckle my shoe" is in #385 in Opie and Opie, *The Oxford Dictionary of Nursery Rhymes*, 333. They cite many sources from the 1800s and state the rhyme was in use as early as 1780 in Wrentham, Massachusetts. Versions described include counting going up to twenty and thirty.

4. My first audiocassette, *The Winter Wife and Other Stories*, recorded in 1988, included both "Rabbit and the Alligators" and "Jeff Rides the Rides," told in the Family Tales and Personal Narratives section of this book. I later released "Rabbit and the Alligators" on my CD *Alligators, Bees, and Surprise, Oh My! Folktales Revived!* a compilation of several previously recorded tales from my early audiocassettes. The CD won a 2010 Honor Title Storytelling World Award in the Storytelling Recordings category.

Family Tales and Personal Narratives

1. Montell, *Don't Go Up Kettle Creek*, 8.
2. Lee, "Folk Narrative," 337.
3. I understand that the story is not the same as the experience. While the experience is actually lived, the story of the experience is created or made up. Even though transforming an experience into a story may involve embellishment or reshaping, the resulting story is still essentially true. In my family, when we say, "You made that up," in response to something we've just heard, we mean the person is not telling the truth, but is instead attempting deception.

A Place to Start

1. Uncle Sammy went to Flaherty Elementary, in Meade County, Kentucky.

Jeff Rides the Rides

1. To learn more about the Meade County Fair, see note 11 from "Some Dog" or visit www.meadecountyfair.com. Also, the fair does not take place in August, but in July. In the telling, Jeff's annoying us from April to August simply sounds better than his annoying us from April to July.
2. I recorded this story on my first audiocassette, *The Winter Wife and Other Stories*, in 1988. I recorded it a second time for my *Some Dog and Other Kentucky Wonders* CD in 2001. It ran five seconds shorter the second time around, and no, I haven't attempted to figure out what changed!
3. This is not the only story Jeff used in his vocal music classroom. Early in each school year Jeff also told his students about the time he, our other brothers, and our father were in the tobacco barn, stripping tobacco, and Daddy asked them how they would manage to run the farm if he died. Jeff replied that he would climb the silo so he could see what other nearby farmers were doing, and the next day he would do that. Of course, climbing a silo has nothing to do with singing, so his students thought they were just being entertained instead of working when he told that story in chorus class.

However, in a chorus it is very important to listen to those singing around you. After a student missed a chorus class, all Jeff needed to say was "climb the silo" and the returning student knew to listen to other singers in the same vocal section to learn missed material.

Jump Rope Kingdom

1. The story appeared on my CD *Some Dog and Other Kentucky Wonders*.

2. Munds and Millett, *The Scenic Route*, preface. Learn more about Storytelling Arts of Indiana at www.storytellingarts.org. Some of you may question whether Kentucky can be considered a midwestern state. In the *A Kentucky Journey* exhibit at the Thomas D. Clark Center for Kentucky History, there is a display which talks of Kentucky's role as a border state during the Civil War. It concludes with, "The debate over Kentucky's regional identity continues today. Some geographers classify Louisville and Covington as midwestern cities. Others identify the state as southern on the basis of cultural characteristics. Kentuckians surveyed in 1988 identified themselves as southerners, but respondents in states to the south did not include the commonwealth in this region."

3. Medway Elementary is in the Tecumseh Local School District in New Carlisle, Ohio. I told stories at the district schools in 1993, 1994, and 1996. I'm not sure which year I told the story. Many thanks to the current library aides at Medway and Donnelsville Elementary Schools, Jo Ruiz and Helen Mullins, for using my fifteen-year-old memory of a school library configuration to help me identify the specific school in which I overheard this conversation.

4. When time and circumstance permit, I'll often talk after programs with audience members I've seen chanting along to learn where they heard the rhymes. The jump rope rhyme is known well beyond Kentucky, but the first grade babies rhyme has so far been familiar mostly to women who attended Catholic elementary schools in the Owensboro, Louisville, and Bardstown areas of Kentucky. While I did not attend a Catholic school, I did attend a public school in an overwhelmingly Catholic community and Ursuline nuns were among the teachers at my school. Now, I'm not saying the Ursuline Sisters taught the first grade babies rhyme to children; I'm only saying the common threads I've found most prevalent among the women from my audiences who grew up with that rhyme are Kentucky and Catholicism. My observations are far, very far, from a scientific study!

5. The Cherokee Rose Storytelling Festival took place in Carrollton, Georgia. I told there in October 1990 and again in September 1996. I'm not sure which year I met Tersi Bendiburg. Tersi has told stories all her life, and professionally since 1993. You can learn about Tersi's Cuban background, her storytelling experiences, and her programs at her website: www.tersibendiburg.com.

Mary Helen's Fiancé

1. Petro recounts her time spent talking with me and my parents (302–317). She titled that chapter "The Farmer's Smart Daughter" and she intersperses my telling of that tale, also in this book, with her experiences on my parents' Hidden Spring Farm.

2. In her *Storytellers' Research Guide*, Judy Sierra comments, "I believe that people share information with me during a formal interview that they wouldn't share during a simple conversation. The situation evokes a sense of history that leads people to remember long-forgotten events, and to have new insights" (68). So, perhaps this insight was new to my father during that interview, or perhaps he had long been aware of his intent but never saw the need to mention it before.

3. Zeitlen characterizes these types of family stories as stories of innocents. He compares them to traditional tales and jokes about fools and says they are often told about children, noting, "A child's solution to a problem often seems comical to us, yet forgivable and charming because it makes perfect sense from the young person's point of view" (52). He adds, "Sometimes these stories are told to teach a lesson, to tease a child or an absent-minded adult into changing his behavior, and thus resemble moral or cautionary stories. But perhaps more often, the celebrated mistake is so much the product of a child's stage of life, or an adult's established way of thinking, that the tales are just playful and forgiving. We don't laugh at these innocents derisively, but gently. . . . We all do them [the actions told of in the stories], succeeding most of the time, but failure is inevitable" (52–53).

4. Mount Saint Joseph Academy for girls was founded at Maple Mount, near Owensboro, in Daviess County, Kentucky, on August 14, 1874, by the Ursuline Sisters. Postgraduate courses to prepare young women to take the state teachers' exam began in 1894, and the Mount Saint Joseph Junior College was established in September 1925. By 1929 Mount Saint Joseph Junior College was a member of the American Association of Junior Colleges and the Southern Association of Secondary Schools and Colleges. My great aunts would have attended during the mid- to late 1930s. In 1950 the location of the college was transferred to Owensboro, and the name was changed to Brescia College, now Brescia University.

5. Mama Ham was my great-grandmother, Lena Frances Ritchie Hamilton. My father's parents, Robert Francis Hamilton Sr. and Alice Elizabeth Bunger Hamilton, raised their family on a farm between both their parents' farms, near Big Spring in Meade County, Kentucky, so my father had the opportunity to hear family news directly from his grandparents.

6. This came from an April 22, 2011, phone call with my parents, Martha Jane Hager Hamilton and Robert Francis Hamilton Jr., after they read a draft of this chapter.

7. This detail came from a May 23, 2011, phone call with my cousin, Charlie Hamilton. Both Charlie and Dale Hamilton are sons of Lamar Hamilton, an older brother of Mary Helen Hamilton Ferrara. Lamar's family lived in Jefferson County, Kentucky.

This Is the Story . . .

1. My mother's mother, Lillian Clara Medley Hager, lived in Meade County, Kentucky. Because I had four grandparents, four great-grandparents, and two great-great-grandmothers when I was born, none of them were known to me by the more common grandma, grandpa, or other grandparent titles. As a result, I grew up knowing the given names of most of my grandparents.

BIBLIOGRAPHY

Adams, James Taylor. *Grandpap Told Me Tales: Memories of an Appalachian Childhood.* Edited by Fletcher Dean. Big Stone Gap, Va.: Fletcher Dean, 1993.

A Kentucky Journey. Thomas D. Clark Center for Kentucky History. Kentucky Historical Society, Frankfort, Ky., May 14, 2011.

Alvey, R. Gerald. *Kentucky Folklore.* Lexington: Univ. Press of Kentucky, 1989.

Ashliman, D. L. *A Guide to Folktales in the English Language: Based on the Aarne-Thompson Classification System.* New York: Greenwood Press, 1987.

Badhwar, Umang. Correspondence with the author, n.d., 1986, and May 19, 1986. Email correspondence with the author, November 20, 2011. Phone interview with the author, November 27, 2011.

Benjamin, John. Email correspondence with the author. January 27, 2010.

"Biography for Robert Keeshan." http://www.imdb.com/name/nm0444828/bio. Accessed June 1, 2011.

Birch, Carol L., and Melissa A. Heckler, eds. *Who Says? Essays on Pivotal Issues in Contemporary Storytelling.* Little Rock, Ark.: August House, 1996.

Black, Patrick. Interview by Mary Hamilton. Talton K. Stone Middle School, Elizabethtown, Kentucky. January 2009 and January 2011.

Boyd, Brian. *On the Origin of Stories: Evolution, Cognition, and Fiction.* Cambridge: Belknap Press of Harvard University Press, 2009.

Brown, Roberta Simpson. *The Walking Trees and Other Scary Stories.* Little Rock, Ark.: August House, 1991.

Campbell, Marie. *Tales from the Cloud Walking Country.* Bloomington: Indiana Univ. Press, 1958.

"Captain Kangaroo." http://www.answers.com/topic/captain-kangaroo. Accessed June 1, 2011.

Chase, Richard. *Grandfather Tales.* Boston: Houghton Mifflin, 1948.

Clarke, Kenneth, and Mary Clarke. *The Harvest and the Reapers: Oral Traditions of Kentucky.* Lexington: Univ. Press of Kentucky, 1974.

Courlander, Harold. *The Tiger's Whisker, and Other Tales and Legends from Asia and the Pacific.* New York: Harcourt, Brace, and World, 1959.

Dallas Morning News. "Jury Convicts Mom of Hiring Hit Man in Cheerleader Case." September 4, 1991. http://articles.sun-sentinel.com/1991-09-

04/news/9102030597_1_verna-heath-amber-heath-wanda-holloway. Accessed May 10, 2011.

Davis, Donald. *Telling Your Own Stories.* Little Rock, Ark.: August House, 1993.

DeSpain, Pleasant. *Thirty-Three Multicultural Tales to Tell.* Little Rock, Ark.: August House, 1993.

Dyer, Frederick H. *A Compendium of the War of the Rebellion,* vol. 3, *Regimental Histories.* New York: Thomas Yoseloff, 1956.

Ferrara, Mary Helen. Correspondence and in-person conversation with the author. Silver Spring, Maryland. March 22, 2011.

Gorham, Linda. Email correspondence with the author. September 2–3, 2010. Email correspondence with the author. April 19, 2011.

Hamilton, Bobby, and Martha Hamilton. Telephone conversation with the author. April 22, 2011.

Hamilton, Charlie. Telephone conversation with the author. May 23, 2011.

Henson, Michael Paul. *Tragedy at Devil's Hollow and Other Kentucky Ghost Stories.* Bowling Green, Ky.: Cockrel Corporation, 1984.

Hiser, Berniece T. *Quare Do's in Appalachia: East Kentucky Legends and Memorats.* Pikeville, Ky.: Pikeville College Press, 1978.

Jacobs, Joseph. *English Fairy Tales,* 3rd ed. New York: G. P. Putnam's Sons and David Nutt, 1898; reprint, New York: Dover, 1967.

Johnson, Robert Underwood, and Clarence Clough Buel, of the Editorial Staff of "The Century Magazine.", eds. *Battles and Leaders of the Civil War: Being for the Most Part Contributions by Union and Confederate Officers. Based upon "The Century War Series,"* vol. 1, *From Sumter to Shiloh.* New York: Thomas Yoseloff, 1956.

———, eds. *Battles and Leaders of the Civil War: Being for the Most Part Contributions by Union and Confederate Officers. Based upon "The Century War Series,"* vol. 3, *Retreat from Gettysburg.* New York: Thomas Yoseloff, 1956.

Kennedy, J. Michael. "Cheerleader's Mother Guilty in Murder Plot: Verdict: Prosecutors Said She Schemed to Demoralize Her Daughter's Rival. The Defense Saw a Post-Divorce Frame-Up." September 4, 1991. http://articles.latimes.com/1991-09-04/news/mn-1560_1_terry-harper. Accessed May 10, 2011.

Koidin, Michelle. "'Cheerleader Mom' Freed After Serving Six Months." March 1, 1997. http://www.texnews.com/texas97/mom030197.html. Accessed May 10, 2011.

Lane, Marcia. *Picturing the Rose: A Way of Looking at Fairy Tales.* New York: H. W. Wilson, 1994.

Lang, Andrew. "English and Scottish Fairy Tales." *Folk-Lore: A Quarterly Review of Myth, Tradition, Institution, and Custom [Incorporating The Archeological Review and The Folk-Lore Journal]* 1, no. 3 (September 1890): 289–312.

Leach, Maria. *How the People Sang the Mountains Up: How and Why Stories.* New York: Viking, 1967.

Lee, Laura Harper. "Folk Narrative." In *The Kentucky Encyclopedia,* edited by John E. Kleber, 336–338. Lexington: Univ. Press of Kentucky, 1992.

"Leonard Roberts—Memorial Issue." *Appalachian Heritage* 15, no. 2 (spring 1987): 4–65.

Leonard Roberts Collection. Southern Appalachian Archives, Berea College, Berea, Kentucky.

Lerman, Liz. "Towards a Process for Critical Response." *Alternate ROOTS Newsletter* (fall/winter 1992): 4–5.

———. "Understanding and Using the Critical Response Process." *Alternate ROOTS Newsletter* (winter/spring 1996): 8–9.

Lindahl, Carl, ed. *American Folktales from the Collections of the Library of Congress.* 2 vols. New York: M. E. Sharpe, in cooperation with the Library of Congress, 2004.

———. "Faces in the Fire, Images of Terror in Oral Märchen and in the Wake of September 11." *Western Folklore* (Western States Folklore Society) 68, no. 2/3 (spring/summer 2009): 209–234.

———. "Leonard Roberts, the Farmer-Lewis-Muncy Family, and the Magic Circle of the Mountain Märchen (American Folkore Society Fellows Invited Plenary Address, October 2008)." *Journal of American Folklore* (Board of Trustees of the University of Illinois) 123, no. 489 (2010): 251–275.

———, ed. *Perspectives on the Jack Tales and Other North American Märchen.* Special Publications of the Folklore Institute No. 6. Bloomington: Folklore Institute/Indiana Univ. Press, 2001. 7–98.

Lipman, Doug. *The Storytelling Coach: How to Listen, Praise, and Bring Out People's Best.* Little Rock, Ark.: August House, 1995.

Livo, Norma J., and Sandra A. Rietz. *Storytelling: Process and Practice.* Littleton, Colo.: Libraries Unlimited, 1986.

Lord, Albert B. *The Singer of Tales.* New York: Atheneum, 1970.

"Lynwood Montell." Folk Studies and Anthropology Department, Potter College of Arts and Letters, Western Kentucky University. February 26, 2011. http://www.wku.edu/Dept/Academic/AHSS/cms/index.php? page=lynwood-montell. Accessed November 14, 2011.

MacDonald, Margaret Read. *The Storyteller's Sourcebook: A Subject, Title, and Motif Index to Folklore Collections for Children.* Detroit: Neal-Shuman Publishers, 1982.

———. *Twenty Tellable Tales: Audience Participation Tales for the Beginning Storyteller.* New York: H. W. Wilson, 1986.

MacDonald, Margaret Read, and Brian W. Sturm. *The Storyteller's Sourcebook: A Subject, Title, and Motif Index to Folklore Collections for Children, 1983–1999.* Detroit: Gale Group, 2001.

Meade County Fair. www.meadecountyfair.com.

Miller, Pat Hamilton. Telephone conversation with the author. March 27, 2011.

Mohanty, Shanti. *Folk Tales of Orissa*. New Delhi: Sterling Publishers, 1970.

Montell, William Lynwood. *Don't Go Up Kettle Creek*. Knoxville: Univ. of Tennessee Press, 1983.

————. *Ghosts Along the Cumberland: Deathlore in the Kentucky Foothills*. Knoxville: Univ. of Tennessee Press, 1975.

Munds, Ellen, and Beth Millett, eds. *The Scenic Route: Stories From the Heartland*. Indianapolis: Indiana Historical Society Press, 2007.

Murray, R. "Shiloh Medical Report (1862)." *eHistory @ The Ohio State University*. http://ehistory.osu.edu/osu/sources/documentview .cfm?ID=10. Accessed April 17, 2011.

National Endowment for the Arts. "Lifetime Honors: NEA National Heritage Fellowship." http://www.nea.gov/honors/heritage/nomination.html. Accessed November 15, 2008.

Nora Morgan Lewis Collection. Southern Appalachian Archives, Berea College, Berea, Kentucky.

Opie, Iona, and Peter Opie. *The Oxford Dictionary of Nursery Rhymes*. Oxford: Oxford Univ. Press, 1980.

Parkhurst, Liz, ed. *The August House Book of Scary Stories: Spooky Tales for Telling Out Loud*. Atlanta: August House, 2009.

Petro, Pamela. *Sitting Up with the Dead: A Storied Journey Through the American South*. London: Flamingo, 2001.

Report of the Adjunct General of the State of Indiana: Containing Rosters of Enlisted Men of Indiana Regiments Numbered from the Sixth to the Twenty-Ninth Inclusive. Vol. 4, *1861–1865*. Indianapolis: Samuel M. Douglas, State Printer, 1866.

Report of the Adjunct General of the State of Indiana: Containing Rosters of Enlisted Men of Indiana Regiments Numbered from the Sixtieth to the One Hundred and Tenth Inclusive. Vol. 6, *1861–1865*. Indianapolis: Samuel M. Douglas, State Printer, 1866.

Roberts, Leonard. *I Bought Me a Dog and Other Folktales From the Southern Mountains*. Edited by Chad Drake. Berea, Ky.: Council of the Southern Mountains, 1954.

————. *Old Greasybeard: Tales From the Cumberland Gap*. Detroit: Folklore Associates, 1969.

————. *Sang Branch Settlers: Folksongs and Tales of a Kentucky Mountain Family*. Austin, Tex.: American Folklore Society, 1974.

————. *South From Hell-fer-Sartin: Kentucky Mountain Folk Tales*. Lexington: Univ. of Kentucky Press, 1955.

Sierra, Judy. *Storytellers' Research Guide: Folktales, Myths, and Legends*. Eugene, Ore.: Folkprint, 1996.

Smith, Tom. "Wanda Holloway Trial: 1991—Plea Agreement Ends Second Trial." Net Industries, copyright holder. http://law.jrank.org/pages/3484/Wanda-Holloway-Trial-1991-Plea-Agreement-Ends-Second-Trial.html. Accessed May 14, 2011.

Stotter, Ruth, reteller. *The Golden Axe and Other Folktales of Compassion and Greed: Versions From Around the World of the Classic Story "The Kind and Unkind Girl," Known as Tale Type 480.* Tiburon, Calif.: Stotter Press, 1998.

Tashjian, Virginia. *Juba This and Juba That: Story Hour Stretches for Large or Small Groups.* Boston: Little, Brown, 1969.

Thompson, Butch. Telephone interview with the author. February 17, 2010.

"Ursuline Sisters of Mount Saint Joseph History." http://www.ursulinesmsj.org/history/. Accessed May 24, 2011.

Ursuline Sisters of Mount Saint Joseph. "The History of Brescia University." http://www.ursulinesmsj.org/history/brescia_university.php. Accessed May 24, 2011.

U.S. Census Bureau. State and County Quick Facts. http://quickfacts.census.gov/qfd/states/21/21163.html. Accessed November 17, 2011.

Uther, Hans-Jörg. *The Types of International Folktales: A Classification and Bibliography, Based on the System of Antti Aarne and Stith Thompson.* 3 vols. Helsinki: Suomalainen Tiedeakatemia, Academia Scientiarum Fennica, 2004.

Zeitlin, Steven J., Amy J. Kotkin, and Holly Cutting Baker. *A Celebration of American Family Folklore: Tales and Traditions From the Smithsonian Collection.* New York: Pantheon, 1982.

INDEX